GULF LYNX

THE LYNX SERIES

FIONA QUINN

GULF

Lynx

Fiona Quinn

THE WORLD OF INIQUUS

Ubicumque, Quoties. Quidquid

Iniquus - /i'ni/kwus/ our strength is unequalled, our tactics unfair – we stretch the law to its breaking point. We do whatever is necessary to bring the enemy down.

THE LYNX SERIES

Weakest Lynx

Missing Lynx

Chain Lynx

Cuff Lynx

Gulf Lynx

Hyper Lynx

MARRIAGE LYNX

STRIKE FORCE

In Too DEEP

JACK Be Quick

InstiGATOR

Uncommon Enemies

Wasp

Relic

Deadlock

Thorn

FBI Joint Task Force

Open Secret

Cold Red

Even Odds

Kate Hamilton Mysteries

Mine

Yours

Ours

Cerberus Tactical K9 Team Alpha

Survival Instinct

Protective Instinct

Defender's Instinct

Delta Force Echo

Danger Signs

Danger Zone

Danger Close

This list was created in 2021. For an up-to-date list, please visit FionaQuinnBooks.com

If you prefer to read the Iniquus World in chronological order you will find a full list at the end of this book.

To the fierceness, capability, and tenacity of women.

"Credit belongs to the [wo]man who is actually in the arena, whose face is marred by dust & sweat & blood; who strives valiantly; who errs, who comes short again and again because there is no effort without error and shortcoming; but who does actually strive to do the deeds."

— TEDDY ROOSEVELT

1

OKAY, THIS WAS UNCOMFORTABLE.

I arrived breathless after being summoned to the Commander's Wing at Iniquus, STAT. General Elliot's secretary, Leanne, held the conference door wide, offering up a better-you-than-me smile.

A cloud of turbulent energy filled the spacious room and billowed out like the black viscous smoke of an oil fire.

A woman—tall and thin, with long brown hair, dressed in a sleek well-tailored pants suit—leaned her face into the wall. One arm curled to protect her head as she sobbed forcefully into the crook of her elbow.

Leanne squeezed my shoulder. "I'll get some tissues." She turned her focus to me. "And you'll probably want some coffee. Extra strong."

I made my way farther into the plush room with its thick carpeting underfoot and the rich glow of the mahogany table that could seat twenty. Two of our three Iniquus owners, Mr. Spencer and Col. Grant, stood by the bank of windows on the far side. Both pressed their cell phones to their ears. It looked to me like they were calling in favors or asking for off the record information. The tilt of their heads, the tight posture of their stances told me they were coming up empty.

Not knowing what else to do, I pulled out a chair and sat down.

No one seemed to notice.

Lacing my fingers, I rested my hands on my lap, focusing my attention on the owners. Their conversations were comprised of grunts and "all rights" with nothing substantive that would give me a clue as to what was going on. Why was this woman here? Why was she so upset? And why was I summoned instead of our team leader, Striker?

Some people called Iniquus a group of mercenaries. And in most ways, they were right. Yes, our security teams and force missions were for-hire. But in the public's mind, bad connotations viscously dripped from the word *mercenary*. News clips and articles talked about rogue and lawless groups that went off into the world and did as they pleased, their guns brandished and triggers pulled at will.

That didn't describe Iniquus *at all*.

Iniquus prided itself on being the knights in shining armor. For being the saving grace, the miracle when all hope was lost. Our teams carried hostages to safety. They hacked through jungles, jumped from helicopters, swam through oceans toward pirated ships to protect innocent lives.

Day in and day out, success came because our field operators were culled from those leaving the special forces, trained by Uncle Sam to be the best in the world. Their mission to protect America and her interests hadn't changed for them. All that had changed for these SEALs and Delta operators, Marine Raiders, and Green Berets was who signed their paycheck.

And I was none of those things. I was on the Strike Force

team as a creative thinker. An out-of-the-box envelope stretcher.

I didn't do case intake because I wasn't a field operator. My contract specifically stipulated that I was *not* field trained and therefore not deployable on missions outside of a very slim scope. I could go out and do spy work—basic stuff.

I most certainly wasn't supposed to shoot anyone or blow anything up.

I wasn't saying that was how it always worked out. I was just saying that it was never my *intention* when I opened a file on any given mission that it should end with a bang.

Attached to Strike Force, my job mostly kept me here at headquarters, where the operators would hand me bits and pieces of crime puzzles, and I was tasked with figuring things out.

I'd like to figure *this* situation out.

Still, I sat.

Still, the woman cried.

Still, the commanders yacked, nodded, and huffed.

I wondered if this was how this kind of thing always went. I'd ask Striker later.

Leanne came back with a tray that she set on the credenza. She moved a box of tissues to the far end, closest to the woman. Then, moved a small trash bin to the floor for the woman's convenience. After setting a bottle of water and a glass near her, Leanne said, "Mrs. Foley, if this would be of comfort." Without waiting for a response, Leanne moved to pour three coffees. I watched her add cream and sweetener to one. That one, she set down in front of me. She placed the other cups and saucers, black, where I assumed the owners would sit once they got off their phones.

Leanne reached a platter with artisanal mini-muffins and strawberries to the center of the table with a stack of bread plates and napkins, took her tray, and left.

Mrs. Foley, that name was my first bite of information.

My only information.

Yup. Here I was, waggling my foot, sending my gaze to the Iniquus owners on my left, back to the woman on my right, back to my hands in my lap.

Uncomfortable.

"Lynx," Mr. Spencer said as he tapped his phone to end his conversation and headed over to the table. "Good that you're here. We're waiting for one more—"

The door swung open, and Damian Prescott moved into the room. As a special agent with the FBI, Prescott led a joint task force that had to do with international criminal organizations that wanted to set up shop here in the United States.

I had brushed past him on several Iniquus cases.

Through those encounters, I knew that Prescott was bright and dedicated, but I hadn't seen enough of his personality to form a solid opinion of him outside of his role with the FBI.

As he moved into the conference room, I stood and turned to face him with a smile and an extended hand.

Prescott reached for a shake. "Good, Lynx, you're here." He reached for Mr. Spencer's hand and nodded to Col. Grant, still standing at the bank of windows, working his phone. Prescott ended by resting stormy eyes on Mrs. Foley.

From his look and stance, Prescott knew her. And he knew exactly what this was about.

Mrs. Foley was taking advantage of the tissues, blowing her nose loudly, swiping at her eyes. Her mascara blackened her orbs, giving her face structure a skeletal cast.

"We *just* buried Kaylie on Wednesday." Her nostrils flared as she glared at Prescott. "And now—*now*—you tell me she's alive?"

2

THAT WAS QUITE THE OPENER.

Everyone in the room stilled.

"Did you realize her funeral was this past Wednesday?" She took an over-long, aggressive step toward Prescott. "My family put Kaylie to rest, in our minds." She pressed her lips together and swallowed audibly. "The judge issued a declaration of death. We went out and bought a beautiful plot of land." She turned her attention to Mr. Spencer. "Kaylie's tombstone is under an oak tree. That oak is over two hundred years old. Its trunk massive and craggy. Kaylie would have *so* loved that tree. The limbs so wide." Mrs. Foley reached her arms out as if to give us an idea of the expanse. "Generously embracing our memories." It sounded like she was quoting something she'd heard at the funeral. Something readily accessible when her own thoughts were so visibly tied up with stress.

She sniffed and scrubbed a tissue under her nostrils. "Kaylie left funeral instructions with her will. She wanted to be buried in a basket and a tree planted on top. That way, her decaying body could nourish its roots. She wanted, in death, to be a force for good. Of course, that's not possible when you don't have a body…" Mrs. Foley looked at the floor and whispered, "We thought she was eaten by wild animals." Her focus moved to Prescott. "You *told* us she'd died, and her body was *eaten* by animals. The 'most-likely' that you added, we thought—we believed—was legal speak, something the FBI made you tack on."

Mrs. Foley spread her legs to give her wavering frame some stability, tearing and kneading the damp tissue in her hand.

"Have you any idea about the nightmares I've survived over the years, Damian, not knowing how long Kaylie was alive as the animals clawed her skin open and ate her intestines?" She sent honed daggers Prescott's way.

She'd called him by his first name…

"*Those* are the pictures I've lived through night after night as I sleep. Most nights, though, I lay there, wide-eyed in the dark, wondering what it felt like to have sharp teeth puncture my skin, sink into my muscles, scraping at my bone. I wonder how it would feel to have my flesh tear as a beast shook me in its jaws, knowing the pain was going to get worse, and the torture would only stop when I died. Can you see what I see in my mind, *Damian*? How Kaylie must have screamed? How she must have called out to God to end it and let her die?"

Mrs. Foley turned her focus to me for a moment.

She rejected me as a piece of the puzzle that didn't belong in this box and settled her gaze back on Mr. Spencer. "I've watched days, weeks, months of nature videos, studying how the animals kill their prey, hoping against hope that they pierced Kaylie's artery, and she bled out quickly instead of lying there awake and aware as a predator devoured her thigh muscles." Her body juddered. She gasped and clamped her lips tightly together, staring at the table for a long moment.

No wonder there was horror in her eyes—what a grotesque nightmare.

If Mrs. Foley was watching nature videos, these must be exotic animals on foreign soil.

Images of lions stalking their prey filled my imagination.

I sat silently. The men stood stoic.

Mrs. Foley broke her trance with a flutter of her lashes. Without lifting her gaze, she muttered, "We bought a coffin. With no body, we put her things inside. Pictures. Art. Diaries." She frowned so forcefully that her mouth hardly moved as she spoke, making her words garbled. She took a staggering step forward.

Prescott reached out, ready to steady her if need be.

But she caught herself, then tripoded her hands on the table to give herself stability. "It was a lovely funeral service." She told her warbled reflection, peering up from the polished wood. "Her friends came, and the faculty from her department. The family. Almost two hundred people filled the pews as we praised my sister's short life." Mrs. Foley lifted her head toward the recessed lighting and blinked against the brightness, her thoughts visibly sliding sideways. "I held my mother up, *physically* held her up, as she threw the first handful of soil onto Kaylie's coffin." She turned to Prescott. "Mom doesn't weigh much anymore."

Prescott bore her ire with a level of grace I wouldn't have ascribed to him from our past dealings. I was trying to work out this unusual dynamic between them and wondered if Mrs. Foley and Prescott had dated in the past. The family references seemed oddly placed for a law enforcement relationship.

"You remember how plump and jolly mom used to be."

His teeth tightened down. The muscles at the side of his jaw bulged rhythmically.

"Mom stopped eating and stopped laughing. It took almost no effort at all to hold her up when her knees went out from under her."

Mrs. Foley turned to shoot barbs at Mr. Spencer. "I will *not* tell anyone, not a *single* soul, that this is happening. Can you imagine the pain, the horror of finding out your family gave up hope and buried you, when in reality you were *alive* out there, needing help?" She struck her pointer finger onto the tabletop. "Unless and until Kaylie is back on U.S. soil, there will be no communication that would torture my parents further."

"Melody." Prescott pulled out a chair two down from mine at the corner of the table and brushed a hand toward the seat. "Let's sit down and talk about this." He waited for her to comply, then rounded to the other side to sit cattycorner. "We don't know that she's alive. First, you know Mr. Spencer and Col. Grant, but let me introduce you to Lynx." He lifted an open palmed hand my way. "She's been added to Kaylie's team."

All right, then. I was on Team Kaylie.

Everyone believed Kaylie was dead.

Someone now thinks that's not true.

Melody Foley focused glassy eyes my way and nodded, turning quickly back to Prescott.

Tears dripped off her chin as she clutched a fist to her chest. "I'm trying to wrestle down hope." She sucked in a ragged breath. "But I have found that hope defies gravity. It's lighter than air. And so painful. I *hate* hope." She lifted her head and stared around the table. The censure she was sending out didn't include me. "And I *hate* even more that after I finally popped my delusions and buried my sister, so I could find some peace that you suddenly say there's a possibility that Kaylie can come back to us." She clutched and pulled at the fabric over her chest as if she was physically trying to release her distress. "And I will *not* bring this pain to my family."

"I understand this is very difficult, Melody." Prescott modulated his voice to be calm and even. "It's not my intention to hurt you or your family. I know you've been through a lot over these past years. But we do need to check in with you to see if you'd had any further contact with anyone involved in the case."

She twitched her head, no.

"And I need to show you the photo. Images of Kaylie, from around the time of the incident, were entered into the NSA data system," Prescott said. "That system flagged a picture of a woman in Syria. The computer algorithms have focused on a single image that has a sixty-seven percent probability for being your sister."

I couldn't see Melody Foley's face, but her whole body jolted.

"In Syria?" She yanked her head back, tucking her chin. "Syria?" Her inflection scaled up then dropped to a whisper. "It's been years, and I suppose that if she were alive, she could be anywhere. But she was in Nigeria. The other people's body parts were found scattered across the northern border near Niger. How would Kaylie be the one who survived? Why would anyone take her to Syria of all places?"

"We don't know," Prescott said. "The computer system offers us a probability." He slid an eight-by-ten photograph from a manila envelope and laid it on the table in front of Mrs. Foley.

She reached out hesitant fingers, and raked the photo closer.

I held my breath as she stared down at the image.

From my angle, I could see muted earthen colors, and that was all.

Mrs. Foley lifted the photograph, tipping her head to the side this way then that, far and then near. She blinked her eyes at the face, then pulled the photograph to her chest, hugging it to her. "I want it to be Kaylie so badly that if this were a bearded man, I'd probably say yes, it's her." She petted her hand over the back of the photo like she was soothing a young child. "My imagination…I can't tell." She stood and stumbled to the space beside the credenza—her crying spot—and pressed herself back against the wall.

Her sobs rose up, forming a cloud over our heads.

A storm of grief and pain.

We sat in silence as we waited for Melody Foley to return to the conversation.

I dropped my head, thinking.

I didn't mind being thrown off the deep end to see if I could stay afloat, but a briefing would have been helpful to my understanding this scene. A missing Kaylie, dead "others," a family in mourning. Nigeria. The northern border near Niger. Syria. The event had to have taken place over seven years ago, or a judge wouldn't have been involved in declaring the missing person as deceased.

I sought back, trying to remember what it was that Damian Prescott had done for the FBI that long ago. I believed he had worked on an FBI team overseas.

In Africa? Possibly.

The cases that had put me in the same room with Prescott before mostly had connections with former USSR countries.

Africa and the FBI…

The only time the FBI got involved with helping US citizens overseas was in cases of hostage-taking, kidnapping, and terrorist acts.

And yes, now that I thought about it, Damian Prescott did have that kind of background. If I remembered correctly, he had been a Green Beret for the US Army. When he didn't re-up, he'd joined the FBI, where he'd put his specialized training to work in CIRG, their Critical Incidence Response Group. CIRG was sent in to negotiate and do hostage rescue of American citizens across the globe. But Prescott was in his mid-thirties now. He'd probably aged out of that group.

Or not…what did I know?

His new role as special agent in charge of a joint task force might all be part and parcel with CIRG.

I'd bet Prescott got the image from NSA because he had led the case, or he was the highest-ranking person left from the case after so many years.

One piece confused me. I'd never heard of a missing Kaylie before. Or even a scientist that had gone missing from her research trip. Eaten? That would have made the news.

There was that terrible event last year. A young woman, twenty-two years old, was on safari in South Africa. Lowering her window to take pictures, a female lion attacked her through the small opening. The guides fought off the lion. Medical help arrived immediately—minutes. But that woman succumbed to her wounds while the rescue workers tried to save her.

My skin tightened with goose flesh. *Can you imagine?*

Mrs. Foley's horror-energy swirled around me. The images she painted danced vividly. My imagination was solidly on that story of the young woman and the lion's jaw—the teeth sinking deep into flesh and bone.

The blood and screams.

Melody Foley had said there were other bodies. Wouldn't *that* have made the news?

Not necessarily.

Three years ago, a serial killer, Travis Wilson, had me in his crosshairs. I survived while other women did not. I could have been a better help in getting Wilson caught sooner had there been even a single file available for the police to find. But no, the powers that be had decided it was safer to seal the files and hide the data. That's why I didn't know the crazy guy stalking me was a killer.

The reason the files were hidden on Wilson was to prevent copycats from hurting other women and muddying the evidence. And as it turned out, there were political and self-serving reasons thrown into that mix.

If an American woman was taken hostage in a foreign country, there must be a reason for it not being played out in the media. It could be something shitty, like someone's political agenda, or it could be lifesaving to keep it under wraps. Perhaps that story would have increased the dangers of others in the area or put her neck under her captor's sword.

Prescott dragged a second manila envelope from his briefcase. He stretched that photograph toward me.

The second photo pictured a serious young woman. Her curly honey brown hair was pulled into a messy bun at the nape of her neck. She wore a pair of khaki shorts and an over-sized T-shirt, crouching down in the dirt next to a small boy. She looked like an athlete, someone who enjoyed the outdoors. She looked intelligent; there was depth in her blue-green eyes, Concern, yes. But the picture was happy. Whatever this child was doing tugged at her in a maternal way. This child wasn't a stranger who walked into the photo.

I turned the photo over and read the printed sticker: Kaylie Elizabeth Street, Ph.D.

I turned it back and looked into the woman's eyes. *Kaylie, are you alive?*

3

A KNOCK SOUNDED AT THE DOOR, AND LEANNE STEPPED IN.

Inside the top drawer of Leanne's desk in the anteroom was a small screen that allowed her to watch what was going on inside of the conference room. Leanne wore an earbud in one ear so she could keep track of what was happening inside and respond when something was needed while allowing her to field office calls and tend to anyone who came into the anteroom.

If information was passed within the conference room that required a security clearance, then a signal was given, and the feeds were scrambled with the push of a button. We'd know it was okay to continue the confidential exchange when the overhead lights flashed. Once our topics were back on safer grounds, someone would dial Leanne, and she'd be back to monitoring the room.

One of the commanders must have signaled because Leanne walked through the door, right over to Mrs. Foley, and placed a hand around her shoulder.

"This has been a difficult morning, Mrs. Foley," Leanne said, warmly. "I have a room set up for you where you can freshen up and rest." Leanne trapped Mrs. Foley in a little side hug, reaching for the photograph Mrs. Foley clutched to her chest and placed it on the credenza as she turned Mrs. Foley toward the exit.

Mrs. Foley nodded, relief visibly washing over her. She didn't acknowledge anyone or say good-bye as she walked back out.

As soon as the door shut, Mr. Spencer and Col. Grant stood.

"Lynx, glad to have you involved," Mr. Spencer said with a nod. He pulled his phone from his pocket as he left the room.

The nod seemed to say that he knew I'd handle this.

A missing person case that started over seven years ago in Nigeria with a possible move to Syria? A single NSA picture with a slightly better than even probability that this was even the right woman to solve a case? Yeah, I thought I was good at my job, but unless they had other crumbs on the trail, maybe he should tamper down any optimism.

"Prescott will get you up to speed," Col. Grant said, and with a nod to Prescott, then me, he followed Mr. Spencer out.

The door shut, leaving Prescott and me facing each other.

I sent him a flat lipped smile.

"I asked for you." He stood, moving over to the credenza with long strides. He came back with the photograph in hand, reached it out to me, and took a seat to my right.

The image was a closeup of a woman whose face was mostly obscured by her *khimar*—a long cape-like veil worn in parts of the Middle East.

"I don't have a lot to tell you to get you up to speed. We're trying to determine if Dr. Street is alive and in need of rescue. The FBI never closes a case until the crime is solved. But it is believed, as Melody said, that Kaylie Street died with her colleagues under suspicious circumstances."

"You knew Kaylie before the event." I lifted my gaze from the photograph to lock eyes with Prescott.

Prescott patted his hands on his lap and tipped his head back. "Leanne, scramble the room, please."

I thought that Leanne didn't have an earbud in because she was escorting Mrs. Foley to another room. But the lights flashed three times.

"Kaylie and I grew up in the same neighborhood. When CIRG was inserted, I had no idea that Kaylie was in the group that my team was looking for."

"How are you doing in all this? What do you think about this photo?"

"I think Melody hit it on the head." He sniffed a deep breath. "I don't know if I'm seeing things through an unadulterated lens. Wishful thinking can cloud reasoning."

"And what do you wish?"

"Now that's the real question." He reached up and scratched the back of his neck. The exact spot where I'd been tingling ever since I'd imagined the lion's fangs sinking into skin.

"I don't know," he admitted. "Nigeria to Syria that's a bad route with serious possibilities attached. That she was the single person who survived from her group? That's hard to fathom. In my roles with the Army and with CIRG, I've pulled some people out of their situations whom I thought were broken beyond repair. I almost believed that some of them would have been better off not surviving. I'm not sure what to hope for in this circumstance. I'm putting the personal on a shelf and doing my duty. Trying to."

I nodded. He let me peek at the Damian part of him and then shut that door with a solid thud. He was back to Special Agent in Charge Prescott. And I'd been warned; I was not to make this personal for him.

"I got this photo," he tapped it with his middle finger, "and a heads up from NSA last night. The background—seven years ago, Dr. Kaylie Street was an environmental researcher whose focus was on land preservation and rehabilitation to counter desertification and global warming. She was doing her post-doc research as part of an international team at Cornell. The group was in Nigeria as one leg of a year-long research grant, gathering baseline data for a study on the effects of a project called the Great Green Wall. This research started in Tanzania." He stopped and pulled out a map from the same folder he'd pulled Kaylie's photograph, pointing to Tanzania on the east coast. "And she, and her team, progressed along the beltline of the experiment." He drew his finger across the widest part of Africa and stopped in northern Nigeria. "Her team disappeared from here."

"Everyone?"

"The camp cook had been hired from the village two kilometers from their site. She had gone home that night to buy fresh eggs and produce. The cook speaks one of the myriad dialects found in Nigeria. As the researchers were busy around the campfire, talking and looking at equipment, the cook couldn't understand what they were saying. She couldn't tell us what their plans had been. She went back in the morning to cook their breakfast. No one was up and around. When it was mid-morning, she checked the tents. None of the cots were made. None of their backpacks were gone. Their boots were there. Their solar shower bags full. The wind was high, but she discovered some barefooted tracks in the dirt. She said that the scientists always had something on their feet—boots, or if they were showering, bathing suits and flipflops."

"And what did she do with this information about the state of the camp?"

"She walked back to the village and told her tribal leader,

who knew how to drive. He hiked back to the camp with her and looked around, then drove one of the research Jeeps to the nearest town several hours away, to notify the authorities there. Things moved quickly from that point. They contacted the US Embassy. The embassy contacted the university and the FBI. The university put the pedal down. From the time when the insurance company contacted Iniquus, and Iniquus was boots on the ground on location, was twelve hours."

"Twelve hours. I'd imagine that meant that whatever had happened had happened at least twenty-four hours prior. The cook, then the tribal leader, had looked around the site. Animals. Weather. It wouldn't have been a pristine crime scene to investigate and gather clues. What was the original hypothesis?"

"At the time, we thought this might be associated with Boko Haram and was perhaps a terror attack, or possibly a kidnapping for ransom event."

"I'm going to ask more about your conclusions about that, but I'd like to stay on the Iniquus timeline. Body parts were found and identified."

"The conclusion discussion is a quick one. We have no idea what happened. All we have is speculation. Partial remains. And one missing American, Kaylie Street. Iniquus deployed with both live-search, and human remains detection K-9s. The K-9 team tracked the remains. The FBI did the identifications."

"You said it was an international team?"

"Kaylie was the only one on the research team that was an American citizen, though the others lived in the US with green cards or had student visas. The insurance, though, was contracted through the university and covered all of the participants equally."

Insurance contracts were tricky things.

Insurance companies kept kidnapping contracts secret from

the very people they were insuring. Kaylie wouldn't have known if she was covered or not, unless and until she'd been captured, and a demand was made. Or she disappeared, and it looked like there was foul play. The reasoning behind this was simple. If you knew you had a policy that would pay the bad guys a million bucks to get you home safely, you could affect your own kidnapping and cash in. That was *if* you yourself were a bad guy at heart.

On the other hand, if someone knew that you had a million dollars available to pay out when you were captured, wouldn't that make you more of a target than, say, your average Joe-sightseer?

And those contracts didn't just cover kidnapping. Strike Force had been sent out many times to pull a group of students to safety when they happened to be studying abroad in a country that was experiencing a coup or a natural disaster. We had several teams over in Japan after the tsunami, digging in the rubble for Americans, finding them in shelters and up in the mountains, camping under the trees. And Haiti after the earthquake…

Sometimes our operators used shovels for their job, sometimes rifles.

Just the other day, I read about a Swedish-Iraqi student who had returned to Iraq a few days earlier because he was afraid for his wife and his two kids as ISIS had approached their home in the north. He found himself and his family in a life-or-death situation. The student sent a text message to his professor saying that if he wasn't back in the next week, she should remove him from his doctoral program. Obviously, the professor called to see what was up. She found that the family was in terror. All seemed hopeless. ISIS was attacking northern Iraq and massacring and enslaving thousands of Yazidis, this student's religious minority group.

The borders had been closed.

The family couldn't get to the airport.

ISIS was advancing.

While the student was planning how to escape into the mountains with his wife and kids, his professor was trying to figure out how to rescue them. It was when the professor went to their university's security chief that she discovered that their students were covered by the secret insurance. The insurance paid people like us at Iniquus to get the student and his family out. Sometimes getting folks to safety meant negotiation and ransom. And sometimes, like in this student's case, it meant six armed men driving two four-wheel-drive vehicles to the student's house, collecting the family, driving them to an airport, and popping them onto a private plane.

It wasn't Iniquus. It was one of our allied counterparts.

Still, impressive.

But did Prescott think that Iniquus would do something similar? Saddle up the four-wheelers and head into ISIS-held territory on a sixty-seven percent chance that maybe Kaylie had been at a certain GPS coordinate twenty-four plus hours in the past?

"Obviously, the FBI is still working the case," I said. "You're here. What about Iniquus? What role are we playing?"

Prescott leaned back in his chair, his arms crossed over his chest, his brows drew in. "Iniquus Command says they'll follow any lead to find Kaylie, but without actionable information, their hands are tied. I was able to get you assigned to this case. If this is Kaylie…" He tapped the photo again, then shook his head. "Here's the thing I need you to hear. We don't have time to mess around. The clock is ticking." He leaned forward, so we were eye to eye and inches apart. "If this is Kaylie, her continued survival is tenuous at best."

I didn't like him in my space, and he seemed to realize it because he eased back.

"Why the time pressure?" I asked with a tip of my head.

"Syria is volatile. From field reports, women in the area are specifically in great danger. I'd say we have days to find her to keep her alive."

I pulled the photo in front of me and stared down. "You can say that from this picture?"

"This image was captured via satellite on a road moving toward a northern refugee camp yesterday evening. If this group followed on their trajectory, it was about an eight-day walk to the camp. If she gets to that camp, and she's identified as American, I don't hold out a lot of hope for her survival."

"Syria. Don't we have any contacts who can just go and talk with this woman? CIA?"

"Not in this region, no. Right now, she's in a hot zone."

"Iniquus won't put boots on the ground unless we can produce solid information that this is indeed Kaylie."

"Exactly."

Send a team into a hot zone? Yeah, I was going to feel pretty darned sure of any intel I could raise before I put an Iniquus team in danger's way, especially for a fool's errand.

4

Leanne knocked then stuck her head around the door. "Mrs. Foley is going to go home now. I'm just checking in. Do either of you have anything to ask before she goes?"

"Yes, please," I said. "Would you take her to the infirmary and get a blood draw first?"

"I… She's going to ask why."

"Yes, she is." I wrinkled my nose. "You can't lie to her. Just tell her that there are new ways that investigators are using familial DNA."

The door pushed a little wider, and Leanne stepped into the room, closing it softly behind her. "Mrs. Foley's file says that there's a sample of Kaylie's DNA in CODIS."

CODIS was the acronym for *Combined DNA Index System.* It was the FBI's database of DNA files and the software that makes it searchable. Kaylie's DNA would be useless for my needs. "Does Mrs. Foley know that Kaylie's DNA is in that system?"

"I don't know." Leanne shook her head.

"Okay, can you just try to schmooze this? I need a sample of her blood. I'll call the infirmary and tell them you're coming."

"I'll do my best," she said and backed out the door.

I looked at my watch. Time had flown. I thought Prescott and I had been talking for just a minute or two. If the week flew by like this, it meant bad things for the possibility of saving Kaylie. "I have to go as soon as she gets that vial up. I have an appointment."

"You can't tell Mrs. Foley why you want her blood, but can you tell me?"

"It's a long shot."

"Better than no shot," Prescott said.

"Last December, you got pulled into a case with Dr. Zoe Kealoha. Do you remember that case?"

"Hard to forget. A couple of men try to kidnap her from her apartment. She texts me an SOS from under her bed. Your guy in Panther Force, Gage Harrison, kills them with his bare hands. What could that possibly have to do with this?"

"Zoe's research project, BIOMIST."

"Blood markers?"

"Familial blood markers. In the absence of Kaylie's blood, we can use Mrs. Foley's. Unless, of course, you somehow have a sample of her blood that isn't just a DNA code."

"It was never relevant for me to look for one," he said. "As I remember it, Zoe's BIOMIST project was based on her research that blood had certain biomarkers. These biomarkers could indicate close genetic ties like DNA, but it was much quicker and less costly, though it wasn't permissible in court."

"BIOMIST is interesting here because there are two points at which we can try to tell if Kaylie survived. One from Nigeria and two from the Middle East. The photo isn't great. Honestly, all it did was get our noses in the air to sniff. Other than boots on the ground, it's meaningless."

Prescott nodded.

"But stick with me here. We recently solved a case with the help of Zoe's BIOMIST data. Panther Force had a woman with a brain injury and consequent memory loss. We put her blood sample into the BIOMIST system, and it identified two women who had moved through refugee checkpoints from Syria as they relocated. Our operators knocked on the women's doors in Europe and got a confirmation of the unknown subject's identity."

He tapped his index finger against the tabletop like he was trying to scroll quickly down a page and read further into the story. "Kaylie isn't to the refugee camp yet."

"Here's why I think we might possibly luck out. When the United States wanted to collect blood samples from everyone in the Middle East, in order to have a reference database to identify possible terrorists or the remains of individuals, they sent out those medical units to go village to village and tribe to tribe in Iraq doing basic health assessments, right? Each man, woman, and child who went through these assessments had their data—name, age, gender, and basic health picture collected along with their biomarkers. As the war expanded, so did the collection effort. Afghanistan was included, and when the people started to flee across the borders, the medical teams were set up at the asylum and refugee camps. My thought here being if Kaylie has been in the Middle East for a while, it's possible that she moved through the medical check and has her blood markers on file in the BIOMIST system."

"And we'd know she was alive at some point past the Nigerian case." Damian's focus went inward as he processed this line of thought. "We'd have a date and location. But we'd need to access that data, and it's known to few people. I can't just ask for it or even subpoena it. It's top-secret for a reason. If that information became public, the whole program shuts down."

"And if the database has been rendered inaccessible to protect its integrity, it's not useful either. Look, I can't promise anything. But Zoe was willing to help us before. It might be that she'd do it again." I looked at my watch. "I need to scoot soon. My appointment is on that side of town. I'm going to head to our infirmary." I glanced at the picture of Kaylie squatting in the dirt that rested on the table. "I can take the sample with me in a cooler and stop by to pay Zoe a visit." I shifted my focus to the door. "I guess I should have asked if Mrs. Foley and Kaylie are genetically connected. Maybe they were adopted, and this would be a meaningless exercise." I looked back to Prescott. "Are they biological sisters?"

"I'll verify that," he said, adding another note to his list. "For now, let's assume so. If Zoe will allow it, the BIOMIST system is worth a try. But if Kaylie were my hostage, I wouldn't let her get anywhere near an American aid worker."

"Right, I wouldn't either. The only reason why I feel hopeful is that the tribal leaders were often offered presents if everyone participated, an envelope with Viagra, for example. The tribal leader might have had her go through, but perhaps they threatened her somehow to keep her from talking or calling attention to herself. If she was wearing a veil or a burka, it wouldn't be hard to disguise her. Perhaps they let her go through and get her medical checks and, if necessary, any medicines because they wanted her to be healthy… Granted, this is a shot in the dark. Other than someone tapping on that refugee woman's shoulder or our finding her blood markers in the BIOMIST system, I think we've hit a brick wall, and there is no moving forward. Right now, I can't think of a single other way to save her."

5

I SAT IN THE WAITING ROOM OUTSIDE MY PSYCHIATRIST'S OFFICE for my appointment with a vial of Mrs. Foley's blood in a cooled biohazard box in my bag. I let the Kaylie Street case paint across my thoughts.

When I had looked at the image collected by NSA laying next to the last known image of Kaylie in Nigeria, I didn't see much of a resemblance, but that wasn't a reason to give up. People change physically, emotionally, mentally with time.

Just a few years ago, I had what I called my "fluffy bunny" look. It was my go-to disguise—a cute girl who thought that international news was what she read in Cosmo about the Paris fashion houses' new fall color palette. It was a *great* disguise. Looking cute and powerless allowed me to go in places and do things that normally would raise red flags.

But life had thrown me some curveballs in the last few years. I'd seen too many things, been through too many things, to be able to pull on my bunny mask at will. To me, I looked about the same as I always had when I examined my reflection in the mirror, but I knew that the cute girl-next-door role I had played was no longer available to me. I had too much history in my eyes, and in the way, I held my muscles—a heightened startle effect.

That could be the case for Kaylie. Time and experience might have changed her face to where she was only recognized to a 67% chance of accuracy through an AI software algorithm.

She was seven years older than the picture of her in Nigeria, wearing the shorts and squatting beside the child. She'd be in her mid-thirties now. She would have lived through the night when her colleagues did not. She would have been kept, possibly…*probably* against her will in a foreign country without any outside communication.

Boom. I caught myself making a presumption.

Assumptions often led to wrong conclusions, so says my mentor Spyder McGraw.

I'd look through the file and see if Kaylie had a religious or political affiliation.

My phone buzzed with a text from Zoe:

Yeah, come by after you've done your appointment with Dr. Limb. I told security, and they have your visitor tag ready for you. I was going to call you later, anyway. I need to talk to you, too. Running a quick errand. If I'm not back, it won't be but a few minutes.

GREAT. Zoe was expecting me. She was a smart cookie; she'd know I wanted to swing by for an ask. I didn't want to wear out my welcome or get her into any conflict of interest or security issues with DARPA or the CIA. But I'd leave it up to Zoe to tell me if this was problematic. Zoe had no issue whatsoever about being abundantly honest and blunt. These were traits I appreciated. I never had to think about what was going on behind my back. She wouldn't be bitching about me to someone else. She'd just come right out and say her truth. Though, I couldn't imagine Zoe bitching about anyone.

She was a unique woman, and I liked her a lot.

The door opened, and a man passed into the hall and walked toward the elevators. My psychiatrist, Avril Limb, looked down at me and hooked her hand to wave me into her office. "I'm ready for you." She smiled.

I moved into the room, familiar after a year of being her patient. *Client*. She didn't like to refer to those who sought help as patients. She thought it made us sound ill.

I *was* ill. Why not sound that way? I was recovering from a couple of traumatic brain injuries and some life-threatening experiences. To me, the brain was like any other part of the body. If it gets damaged, you treat it. I thought that Avril using the word "client" sanitized things in a way that I didn't particularly appreciate. I wasn't her typical client, though. Her expertise was brain injuries suffered on the battlefield. I got on her roster because she was supposedly the best of the best, so having her as my psychiatrist was a big deal to my fiancé, Striker Rheas.

It was the least I could do, showing up here at Avril's office each week. Striker had been through enough these past few years with me and my crises.

I wasn't an easy person to be in love with.

But since he did love me, and I loved him back, having Avril say "client" wasn't a big deal.

I settled onto the couch and curled up comfortably.

Avril took a seat in her brown leather captain's chair with its high back. She rested her hands in her lap, the way she always did, with her palms open and facing up, showing me through her body posture that she was open and receptive to what I had to say today.

"You look distracted. New case?"

I nodded.

"Let's put that to the side for now and focus on you. What's been on your mind this week?"

It was her usual opener. It put us squarely in line with our relationship. I would talk. She would listen. Possibly, she'd ask me some clarifying questions. She'd repeat things back to me so I could hear my own words with a different inflection.

I wasn't an open-kimono kind of girl. I didn't like to share personal things. I came here because—besides loving Striker and wanting to put him at ease—my job required me to. I needed her stamp of "still not certifiably crazy," so I could continue with my work.

Since I started coming here, I haven't seen a big change in my issues; nightmares still attacked me every night.

That was uncharitable.

I had found some relief moving through the grieving process from our sessions. Well, I found relief in understanding that sometimes grief was complicated. At least Avril could let me know that what I was experiencing, the survivor guilt and the thought intrusions, weren't out of line. Since both were getting worse for me lately, I decided to make that our topic.

"I think my husband went to Hell. And I think he wants me to save him," I started.

Avril weighed my words.

She settled her elbow on the arm of her chair and rested her chin in her fist, her index finger curling over her upper lip. Her brain whirred behind intense brown eyes. "We're approaching the second anniversary of Angel's death," she said, tipping her head the other way and pushing her finger contemplatively into her chin. "It would make sense that you're thinking about Angel and considering what happens after one dies."

My gaze traveled around her office. There were no windows. Just cream walls with Avril's medical and psychiatry diplomas, a couple Rorschach-like art pieces, and a plant that could use more light.

"You have more experience with death than most," she said in her professionally detached tone. "You remember your experience of dying and being brought back to life with consistent and vivid details. I want to talk about your death experience, and then circle that back to your thoughts about Angel and why you feel like you have to save him from Hell."

"All right," I said, lacing my fingers and placing them on my lap.

"Pick a point and go from there."

I took in a breath and let my eyes lose their focus, settling my gaze on the corner where her bookcase angled against the flat industrial gray carpeting. "I was sitting in the pilot seat of the plane when I died. I'd dragged myself there because of the vultures circling over my head outside of the plane. I'd set out three signal fires to try to get help. The smoke filling the air around me billowed in thick acrid clouds. It kept the birds at bay. But eventually, the fires would die. I thought if someone were to find me before I decomposed—if the birds had already pecked out my eyeballs—it might be a pretty traumatic visual. I wanted to save them from that."

"To protect the rescue crew, you got back into the plane. That was a valiant last act." She uncrossed her legs and crossed them the other way, shifting around in her seat.

"I don't know." I pushed my lips to the side as I considered whether my intention had been valiant or not. "That was the surface thought that I remember. I probably had some self-preservation in there somewhere. Not that I'd know or care, after

I was dead, what happened to my body. Bird's chewing on my eyeballs or what have you. But still…"

Avril didn't like to talk about eyeballs, apparently. She was a little green around the gills at the visual I'd painted. "You died. At the moment of your death, what happened next?"

"Yes, well…what I thought would happen didn't. I was out there all by myself. I was in terrible pain—both physical and mental…spiritual—I knew that my death was imminent, and I felt abandoned."

"By…?"

"My parents. By Angel. My parents and my husband having died before me, I would have thought that they would have been there to guide me to the light." I looked Avril in the eye and gave a shrug. "But no one showed up. And there was no light."

"Do you think that's because it wasn't your time to die?" She pulled her brows together. "Permanently die, I mean."

I shrugged again.

"Your team found you and had the equipment that saved you. Did you feel angry with Angel's memory once you came back to consciousness?"

"No." My voice was soft. "I'm not really sure why I thought that anyone would show up. That's not in my day-to-day belief system. It was in my last-gasp belief system."

"What do you believe now that you've experienced your own death?"

My gaze found a resting spot where the ceiling and wall made their crease. I struggled to find a way to put my beliefs into words. "I think that it depends on the person. Though a white light and loved ones welcoming me wasn't my experience. Maybe it was…" I stopped talking.

A long moment passed in silence.

"Go on. I'd like to understand." Avril gave me a smile of encouragement, leaning forward.

"I believe that the pain of this lifetime stays in this body at death." I rubbed my hands down my torso. Under my turtleneck, I was covered in scars from the times I'd been attacked by a killer, Travis Wilson. Two attacks. I'd survived when the other women he targeted had not. It had made me think that there was a reason I needed to stay here on Earth. So far, I hadn't figured out the why. But it must be *something*. "I've lost count of the numbers of times Death and I have brushed past each other. When we finally meet, it will be as old acquaintances."

Avril nodded, not in agreement but to keep me talking.

"During our lives, each of us has a concept for what happens next. A lot of people construct their ideas about what happens once the body dies based on their religious background—Nirvana, Heaven, or maybe if you're agnostic or atheist, then nothingness. My way of processing it is this—after a body is no longer needed, we call that death. The soul is then shuffled into a belief box that is held in a larger system. That system is the truth for everyone, though everyone has their own belief box."

"I'm not following."

"I think that when our souls leave our bodies at death, it's a shock. Our soul kind of gentles us through that process by constructing our personal pictures of what "next" looks like. It's individualized. Everyone can pull up whatever they'd like, whether it's good or bad. If you think you're going to Hell, for example, your afterlife will be hellish until your soul's ready for the next step."

Avril didn't say a word.

"If you believe in a Heaven of Pearly Gates and St. Peter with his list, then that's where you'll go. If you believe that you'll join your ancestors in a circle of wisdom, then that's what happens. This explains why there are a variety of experiences that people tell others when they've had a death event like I've had, and they come back and talk about it."

"And you?"

"What do you mean?"

"Well, you said that in death, even if it didn't line up with your conscious belief system, that you thought there would be a white light and loved ones to guide you and welcome you. I'd like to know about your belief systems when you aren't on the cusp."

"I think I'll go to a floaty place, beautiful and peaceful. There, I'd eventually get acclimated and go to the next level—the larger system that is the truth for all souls, once they've calmed down enough to accept the change from corporeal life to spirit life."

"Any ideas about what that would look like?"

"It's unknowable. But if I were to guess? Oh…maybe a great hall of records where I'd go to hang out with the souls in my learning circle, and we'd plan what we wanted to experience and learn next." I offered up a smile. "I like my theory because it makes everyone's belief in the afterlife true. Everyone is right about what happens once their body is dead. Well, in the first step of the journey."

Avril gave me a nod.

"Like I was saying, I thought I would experience pure love, float weightlessly in beauty. But no. There I was, strapped into the pilot's seat, wondering why my loved ones had abandoned me. No bliss waited for me." I focused on my lap.

"And why do you think that is?"

"My soul didn't detach. I wasn't supposed to die."

"What were you *supposed* to do?"

I looked Avril in the eye. "Stay in my body with its pain and learn some more lessons."

Avril tipped her head to the side. "How much of your time are these thoughts predominant? Thinking about what happens to a soul after it has left the body. Would you say it's the topic that bubbled up for our session today as one end of the spectrum?" She set her hand out to her left. "Or are they pervasive thoughts on the other end of the spectrum?" She set her other hand out to the right.

"I'd say over the last week, thoughts about Angel in Hell have sucked up most of my free brain space."

"Is there a specific reason?" Avril posted her elbows on her pad. She brought her pen to her mouth, held in her fingers like she was chewing on a corn cob. This was the position she took when I started off a topic, and she'd just hunker in and listen.

"Do you believe in Heaven and Hell?" I asked. Shifting around on her leather sofa.

"What I believe has no consequence in this conversation. While you were dating, and after he left for the Middle East, did you and Angel talk about his beliefs of the afterlife? What did Angel think would happen to him when he died?"

"He thought he was going to Hell. Catholic Hell in the bowels of the Earth to burn. He thought it was a possibility, anyway. He believed in the Ten Commandments, and 'Thou shalt not kill.' He killed a lot as an Army Ranger. He would confess his sins and receive absolution from the priest, knowing that he'd be called to kill again. Every time he killed, he apologized to God. I'm not Catholic. These aren't my beliefs."

"How do your beliefs square up with Angel's job that entails killing others?"

"I think about it like the Native American hunters who thank the deer for giving up its life to provide food and sustenance for the tribe. Something like that. It doesn't work out seamlessly. But in my mind, the terrorist had to die so that non-violent people can live. I believe there was some kind of spiritual contract that Angel decided on before he was born. He was assigned to kill those that were meant to be killed. Angel was the weapon and hand of God. It was that person's time and place…" I paused for a long moment, wishing I had a cup of tea to wrap my hands around and feel the radiant warmth, to breathe in the spices, to give myself a moment to sip and not talk. "A belief system is hard to put into words. Those thoughts are formed in a different part of my brain."

"I'm following. You're doing just fine. But it seems your belief system and your experiences aren't lining up in a linear way like you want them to."

"People have tried very hard to kill me. I'm not completely comfortable thinking about who has the right and duty to kill. I really don't know." I turned to the plant like it was another person in the room and reiterated. "I really *don't* know."

"Did Angel believe that? That he was the instrument of God, doing what he was destined to do, but that it put his soul at risk of going to Hell?"

"He believed killing would send his soul to Hell unless he asked forgiveness and was given absolution from a priest."

"And you think that on the day Angel was killed that he had also killed someone?"

"Yes."

"And he had not yet been absolved of his sins."

"Right. His team was on the road, headed back to their post after a successful mission. That's what I was told."

"Following your thought continuum, if Angel died thinking he was going to Hell, then he would go to Hell while his soul acclimated to leaving his body and his terrestrial life behind."

"Yes."

"You believe that Angel went to Hell."

"Yes." I kneaded my hands together. "I think that's what's happened. And now, I think he wants me to save his soul. And I have no idea how to do that."

6

I WAS SLOWING FOR THE RED LIGHT WHEN MY PHONE RANG. I thumbed the button on my steering wheel to answer.

"Lexi! Good." It was Miriam. "I'm so glad to reach you. You've been on my mind all week. How are you?"

If I was on her mind all week, then she already knew. "I don't feel like going through pleasantries. Is it okay with you if I tell you the truth and tell you I'm struggling?"

"It feels like you're having a rough time. You're driving your car. Can you pull over for a moment to be safe, so we can talk?"

"There's a strip mall up ahead, two seconds."

Silence fell.

I knew that Miriam would be using the time to search the ether for information. She did that for a living. Miriam was an Extrasensory Criminal Investigator, working cold cases by clairvoyantly reading events that had happened. When she held something in her hand that was there at the time of an event—touching the walls of a room, fingering a piece of cloth, even a shard of bone—she'd read the vibrations. Almost anything attached to the crime could become a vehicle by which she could gather information that might drive the investigation forward.

Miriam was less successful reading the present in terms of specificity. She couldn't, for example, read my mind and know about the Kaylie Street case or that Angel was haunting my every thought.

She could get a good enough impression that she'd guess.

I pulled into an empty space and shifted into park. "Okay."

"I don't like how you feel to me right now."

"You caught me on my way out of my shrink's office."

"Avril was pulling out uncomfortable threads?" she asked. I could imagine Miriam pushing her long curly blonde hair back over her shoulder as she tucked her chin and closed her eyes to focus on this conversation.

"We were talking about Angel's death."

"Ah, that would explain why his energy is swirling around you so forcefully."

"She thinks I'm having trouble because the anniversary of his death is coming up."

There was a long pause. "Do you agree?"

I powered my chair back so I wasn't staring into the sun's glare. "It explains things as much as anything else."

"Funny how things work out. I was actually calling about Angel. Well, about Abuela Rosa."

"Oh?"

"I have a contract on a cold case. I was scheduled to go down to Puerto Rico, but the week before I was to head out, Hurricane Maria struck. They're just now getting back to me about that case."

"They had other priorities."

"Just terrible, the devastation. The lives lost. I'm heading down tomorrow night and was wondering if you wanted to come with me? I bet Abuela Rosa would be thrilled to see you. And the anniversary of Angel's death is probably hitting her as hard as you, just differently."

I wondered if there were a bone fragment from the Kaylie Street case that I could hand off to Miriam, and she could see if there were pictures that she could bring up from that day. Some piece of the puzzle as to what happened that Kaylie's remains weren't found. Of course, even if Prescott had a stray piece of evidence sitting in a locker somewhere, that wasn't a for-sure thing. Pulling up psychic impressions, after all, wasn't like pulling up a computer program or turning on a TV channel.

Big energy, life-or-death energy was clingy; it left a stronger vibration. That was important, or Miriam would be weeding through every bump and bruise that a bone experienced.

Miriam might pick up on the woman choosing her peach-colored skirt that day, see her clearly examining her image in the mirror, and that was it. No clue as to what happened next.

It was a tricky thing. And Miriam did a great job of not speculating. She said what she got in the way of information and didn't try to fill in the holes or even to narrate the information. Miriam's interpretation might convolute the data and take the investigator farther afield. It was hard not to try to form a picture, a sensation, or add words into a story. I knew that, personally. I had trained to be Miriam's protégée.

After years of training, we had learned that while Miriam had dexterity with the past, I was much more able in the moment. If the person had the shimmer that told me they were in a life-or-death situation, then with a picture, BOOM, I was there, seeing what they were seeing, hearing what they were hearing.

This ability would be a marvelous tool for missing persons,

in theory. In reality, not so much. In order for me to access information in the ether, I had to become so energetically entangled with the victim that I felt what they did.

"Lexi? Did you hear me?"

"Oh, uhm, sorry. My mind wandered."

"I was asking if you can come down to Puerto Rico with me. I leave tomorrow night."

"I so want to!" I scratched my fingers into my hair, shifting the strands from where they tickled my face. "This morning, I was handed a case. I'm kind of *it* when it comes to the team. An FBI agent and I are working a very cold case where the woman involved might have turned up in a surveillance photograph, alive and in danger. If it's her, her days could literally be numbered. I'm on my way to check on a piece of evidence, and then I'll have a better idea if I need to stick close to home. You already called Abuela Rosa?"

"She knows I'm coming. She hinted that she'd really like you to come, too. She said she had something she wanted to do but needed you there. Her energy says she's in bad shape. I'm pretty concerned."

"If I can't come with you tomorrow night, I'll go as soon as I'm freed up. Can you text me your flight and hotel information?"

"Yes, I'll do that now. We'll trust the universe to put us where we need to be when we need to be there."

"Amen to that. I'll call you tonight and let you know. Thank you!"

As soon as I pressed the end button on my steering wheel, a *knowing* swirled my vision. *Knowings* come over the emergency channel on my psychic communications system. I wondered if talking to Miriam or talking about Abuela Rosa had floated this to the top of my consciousness.

This one sang, "*As I was going to St. Ives, I met a man with seven wives.*"

Panting, I pressed the phone button. "Hello?"

It was Zoe. "Letting you know I'm back in my lab."

"I'm about twenty minutes out, depending on traffic."

"It's cool. See you soon." She hung up.

"*As I was going to St. Ives,*" cycled through my brain again. Bigger this time. Bright red oscillating letters. I had no idea why most of the messages came to me from children's rhymes and sometimes children's stories. The only thing I could figure was my subconscious was harkening back to the time before too many facts got in the way of my connection to my higher self. The time when I had the clearest communication with the divine. Or what Miriam called my "pre-schmutz-age."

It was a theory.

There were lots of theories when it came to what was ultimately unknowable.

Maybe this warning had bubbled up from my discussion with Avril, and it had to do with Angel.

The thing about *knowings* was it wasn't until after the fact when I could see what clear messages I was receiving. Once I had heard the warning, "Jack, be nimble, Jack, be quick. Jack, jump." I texted it to Jack when he was standing on the roof of a three-story building. I had no interpretation. I just sent the warning to Jack because of the name similarity. Jack read it and jumped off the roof of the building onto a car below. That jump had cost him leg surgery but saved his life. The building exploded as he leaped. Something in Jack's own psyche must have interpreted the message and made his body act. He said he pulled it up, and the next thing he knew, he was flying through the air.

It didn't usually work that way.

Usually, my psychic warning system was encrypted and needed to be deciphered.

St. Ives.

St. Ives, that was in England, wasn't it? I met a man with seven wives…

This didn't have to be about me.

Sometimes I got information for the men on my team—like I did for Jack—and it helped to keep them safe.

Strike Force *was* headed overseas. But Poland, not England.

I shifted around in my driver's seat uncomfortably. Getting information without context revved my limbic system but left me flailing for answers.

Knowings should *never* be ignored.

They saved lives.

And more often than not, my own.

7

Zoe was heading down to meet me at the security desk at Montrim, where her lab was housed. Her contract was with DARPA, Defense Advanced Research Projects Agency.

Montrim was contracted by the Defense Intelligence Agency to send out medical teams in the Middle East to do health checks on the population, providing immunizations and basic care as a cover, surreptitiously collecting biomarkers for Zoe's BIOMIST database that the DIA shared with the CIA to keep tabs on terrorist networks by tracking family ties.

Zoe had never envisioned or intended for her work in identifying blood biomarkers to be used this way. Originally, she was working to develop a presumptive field test so that innocent people were less likely to be arrested. Here, I meant for it to work the same way. If Zoe's system got a hit, then I would know that Kaylie had survived Nigeria. But if Zoe's system didn't find a match, it wouldn't lead to any conclusions.

It wouldn't mean that Kaylie was dead. It simply meant she wasn't in the system.

If this came up a null set, I'd be right back to where I'd started this morning. Which was nowhere.

If the CIA, the FBI, the NSA, the DIA—no one had heard of this American scientist, it seemed improbable that she survived. But never say never, right? I mean, I'd come through some events where I was surprised to wake up to a new day.

My last chance where I might be able to pull a rabbit from my magic hat was to head over to Sophia Abadi's house after I was done checking the blood sample and see if Sophia had some contact in her Syrian underground network who might have heard a rumor at some point.

Honestly, this was worse than the proverbial needle in a haystack. It was a needle in the haystack if that haystack was being blown about by the winds of war.

Zoe walked out of the elevator. Her long black hair was in a bun at the nape of her neck. It looked like she was using it as a pincushion with the three pencils sticking out of it. She had on yoga leggings and track shoes under her white lab coat. She finished off the look with her oversized geek-girl glasses.

The security guard looked over, then gave me a nod. I headed Zoe's way.

"Hey there."

She smiled in reply then pushed the button to take us back up to her lab.

Up we went without a word. Zoe wasn't big into words. And I didn't mind the silence between us. It felt comfortable.

As the doors opened, I glanced at my watch. "What are you up to this evening? Do you want to grab some dinner when you get off?"

She swiped her badge across the sensor, then pushed the door wide. This was why I couldn't just go up to Zoe's lab by myself. She worked under all the bells and whistles, locks, and alarms that were associated with having a designation of Sensitive Compartmented Information, one of the highest security clearances in the US government.

"I would, but I can't. Gage and I have an appointment with the wedding planner this afternoon." She stopped by her door and pressed her palm onto the plate, waiting for a beep. "For me, a trip to the judge would be fine. But my parents want the big wedding with the swords and the pageantry. I'm not going to plan it," she said, pushing the door open after the signal buzz. "But I'll show up, wear the dress, and cut the cake to make them happy."

"It's a long-distance to plan a wedding from Hawaii."

"Mom flew into town for the week."

I sat on the stool that she indicated with a flick of her finger. And opened my bag to get the blood sample that Leanne coerced out of Melody Foley this morning.

"Gage told me you and Striker are getting married in June. If you need any of the names of the people Mom hires," Zoe said, "let me know."

Why did that wash of dread just douse me?

"Are you and Striker going to have a big wedding?" she asked.

I pulled out the biohazard box. "We haven't gotten past the possible June date. I have family as far away as India that I need to fly in, and I wanted them to get it on their calendars. But I'm with you, simple is happy. My first marriage, it was just me and Angel in front of a judge. That did make me a little sad. I wished at the very least that his great aunt, my Abuela Rosa, could be there. Some friends would have been nice. It just didn't work out that way. The support of loved ones is important."

"If I asked you to be a bridesmaid, would that be something comfortable for you? Uncomfortable?"

"I..."

"I didn't do that well. Let me try again." She smiled. "Gage and I are planning our wedding party. I'd like you to be one of my bridesmaids. But I know I'd cringe if someone were to ask me. I don't want you to feel obliged. But if you didn't mind, I'd like you to be an attendant. Gage is getting his best friend Holden to be his best man, then he's inviting the Panther Force to stand with him. On my side, I have three close friends from childhood. Then I thought—you, Sophia, Arya, and Meg. The bride's party will wear white dresses and leis." She walked over to a side counter next to a small machine, pulled on a pair of Nitrile gloves, and picked up a bottle of test strips.

"I'd be honored to stand with you. Just tell me when and where to show up."

Zoe smiled.

"Seven. That's a big bridal party. I'm surprised you agreed to that," I said.

"I agreed to taste the cake, try on the dress, and show up at the event. I'm not obligated to do any other planning or pre-parties. And Gage said he'd make sure that our honeymoon will be someplace where there are no other people and a good dose of introversion to balance things out."

Her gaze moved to the box in my lap. "I thought you wanted to meet here because you needed access to BIOMIST." Zoe stretched out her hand, accepted the red biohazard box, and popped the lid. She looked down at the vial

I watched silently as Zoe used a pipette to drip blood from the vial onto the strip then pushed the test strip into an analyzer. She sat on a rolling chair and tapped into the computer, pressed ENTER, then spun toward me. "We should know if there are any matches in the system in about a half-hour."

"Thank you so much."

She shrugged. "It adds to my body of research to see how you use this information. Helping to locate the sisters who came through the Syrian points of entry and how they moved through Europe was remarkable. Is this a similar case, or am I allowed to know?"

"It's classified for the time being. But if we get anything from this, I'll ask that you be read into the program. Certainly, you should be able to have at least a redacted version so you can use it to support your work, especially if your work turns out to be a linchpin. And to be honest, I'm crossing my fingers pretty hard. If you get nothing, I'm not sure where to head next with the case."

"We'll know soon enough." She glanced back at the vial of blood that sat in the holder. "Can you tell me if this is the subject?"

"It is not. It's a relative's sample."

"I see. A close relative?"

"The sister."

"Okay, just checking to make sure. You know it has to be a pretty tight biologic group. I'm going to focus back on my work if you want to make yourself comfortable."

Next to me on the table was a tray with some tiny components, a microscope, a magnifying glass, a cloth with various sized tweezer-looking implements. I wanted to play. But who knew? That odd little squiggle of black might be a ten-thousand-dollar micro-robotics component. I moved my stool over by the window to be out of the way of any accidents I might cause.

Leaning over, I pulled my laptop from my bag. Since I was in a secured location, I went ahead and pulled up the file that Prescott had sent me.

The file held the photos and the data points on each of the people who went missing that day. As I clicked on one man's sub-file, I found photos in the wild, plastic tents, demarked pieces of clothing. These were followed by grisly close-ups of remains that were given a string of case numbers. Deceased was stamped at the bottom of the page.

I didn't need to see these. Didn't need them as part of my headspace, at least not right now. I could come back and revisit them if they became relevant later.

I wasn't trying to solve the crime. I was trying to save Kaylie if she were alive.

Right now, the only thing I needed to know was yes or no, was Kaylie dead? And if she was alive, did the NSA computers correctly identify that woman as Kaylie amongst the people moving toward the refugee camp?

I opened Kaylie's file, and the bottom stamp was MISSING, PRESUMED DEAD.

The case notes indicated that there were vehicle tracks at the site.

Tracks, in general, were hard to date. In the movies, the guy crouches in the dust, rubs his chin, then says, "These tracks were made three days ago." But the reality was, without a major weather system that one could say, "these were made before the rain," or "these were made after the rain," there really was no way to date a track in the dust.

The tire tracks could have been made weeks before.

They weren't helpful.

As I read along, that's basically what the report indicated. While they found bullet casings, none of the bodies had wounds associated with a bullet's impact. Or the impact of any weapon, for that matter. It could be that the bleeding parts of their bodies attracted the bugs and animals first, and so they were destroyed first.

Looking at the wide camera angles, if there were shots

ringing out, it didn't look like there was any place that Kaylie could have run to be safe. There were no walls or homes or even trees in these photographs—just wide expanses of scrub and dirt.

I flipped to the folder that documented the state of the research camp, the scientists' point last seen. Well, last seen by a friendly.

All the Jeeps had been accounted for, so the research group must have been driven away by someone else.

The scientists had to have been moved in a vehicle or vehicles because the Niger border was too far to walk in the time between when their disappearance was reported and the time when the Iniquus K-9s tracked the remains.

The body decomposition indicated that they had been dead for more than forty-eight hours when they were collected and put on ice. Forensics determined that the subjects most likely died the night they moved or were moved from their camp.

I drummed my fingers on my keyboard.

The researchers were in the vehicles for a reason—all of them. Including the local help, except for the cook. Had the cook not gone back to her home, it might have been a great deal longer before red flags were raised.

Still, not soon enough to save the group.

Why were they driven toward Niger?

Surely the FBI and Iniquus, the CIA, everyone with a chit in the game, would have looked into Niger. I flipped through the files until I saw that had indeed happened.

Nothing was found.

If the plan had been to kill the researchers, why not just kill them in their camp?

So many questions. And none of the answers really mattered. The how and why of Kaylie being in Syria wasn't dependent on the how and the why that Kaylie disappeared in the first place, I didn't think…

"Lexi," Zoe said. "How long has this woman been missing?"

I pulled myself from my thoughts and focused over on Zoe. "Seven years."

"This is reminding me of the last Syrian case you brought me." She was looking at her computer screen.

I closed my laptop and left it on the stool as I hustled over.

She turned to me. "The last time, we found two women who were associated with your subject."

"This woman wouldn't have any relatives in the Middle East."

"My data would disagree. The computer didn't find the biomarkers for your missing subject. It did find three biomarkers with familial traits." She stretched her face closer to the screen, rolling her lips in with concentration. "I'm assuming from the birthdates that are listed that these are her children."

"Children?" I whispered.

"A girl who would be five now. A boy who would be three now. A girl, eleven months."

My heart was racing. Kaylie had survived Nigeria. She was alive in Syria. She had kids. "Together? You have a location of the data collection?"

"Three different dates when they were treated by the medical teams. Three different GPS locations, all in Iraq. Three different last names."

8

I SAT IN MY CAR, MY PHONE PRESSED TO MY EAR, CALLING Prescott.

She was alive!

Well, she had been alive as of the birth of her youngest daughter. Up until eleven months ago, Kaylie Elizabeth Street still breathed.

The call rang and rang and rang. "Come on, Prescott," I growled into the receiver.

His voice mail answered. "I'm unavailable. Please leave your name, number, and a brief message."

After the beep, I said, "She's alive," and hung up. If he couldn't figure out who the heck I was and how to get in touch with me, then he shouldn't be a special agent in charge at the FBI.

"Now what?" I asked the air. I was buzzing too hard with excitement to just sit still. I opened my contacts, scrolled down the list, and called Sophia Abadi.

After her, "Hello?" I asked, "Hey there, do you happen to be at home? Could I swing by?"

"Sure, I'm here."

"I wanted to ask you about some Arab cultural norms, but I was also hoping you'd help me with images of some GPS coordinates and what you know about the area."

"Both of these are about Syria?"

"Potentially," I said, thinking it was better not to talk about this over a cell phone connection.

"You don't sound like yourself right now. Are you okay? I'm assuming this is about an Iniquus case?"

"A missing woman. Her file was handed to me this morning, and I'm afraid our window for finding her and getting her back safe is a very small one."

"It's after dark in Syria. I won't be able to look at real-time satellite images. But I do have access on my computer to the last seventy-two hours. Will that help? I'm surprised Iniquus doesn't have this available."

"We do. But…I want your unique perspective and regional expertise. Would it be okay if I came right now? I'm about a half-hour away."

"Yeah, sure. That's fine. Brian is picking the boys up from daycare on his way over. We're having dinner together. Can you stay?"

"Probably not. I'd love to. It's just, I'm really focused."

"Your small window. I understand. I'll see you when you get here. And I'll do what I can to help."

I reached out to put my car into gear. The glitter of diamonds in sunlight stalled me.

On my right hand was the ring that Striker had designed for me back when we started dating. It was a redesign of the gold and stones from my engagement and wedding rings that Angel had given to me.

After Angel's death, wearing Angel's vows on my left hand dropped me into awkward conversations. People got confused about Striker's and my relationship. Some of his friends had even been offended that he'd gone off and gotten married without his telling them.

With my blessing, Striker took my rings to a jeweler friend of his. They used the gold to create a setting for the sapphires and diamonds, creating the suggestion of an infinity symbol with the design.

Striker made it easy for me to deal with my Angel grief. Striker recognized that Angel had always been and probably always would be a force in our relationship.

Striker didn't even want me to take down Angel's pictures in my home. It didn't really matter though, even without the pictures up, Angel was always there. Not a day went by when I didn't think about him.

Before his death, Angel and I'd had a hurry up and wait kind of relationship.

We met the night my apartment building burned to the ground. He had been in town on leave from the Army to visit his great-aunt, whom everyone called Abuela Rosa.

I recognized Angel as part of me the very moment our eyes locked, standing in the parking lot that horrible January night.

Valentine's Day, I said yes when he pulled out a ring box and asked me to marry him.

When I said, "Til death do us part," at the courthouse, I had known him for all of three weeks, but it felt like I'd always known him, that we'd been destined to be together.

The morning after we were married, Angel headed off with his Ranger team to fight.

Nine months later, when he came home, it was in a coffin.

I'd had three weeks of time with him.

I spun my Angel ring. I was glad to have it glittering there on my right hand. I'd ceded my left ring finger to Striker and his engagement ring.

"Explain that," I said aloud. Even if I was in love with Striker, even if we planned our future lives together, I still wasn't ready to take off Angel's rings.

He still had a hold of me.

These nightmares that I'd had all week reminded me of the night Angel died. I woke up awash of horror and knew that something devastating had happened.

I was at Iniquus when I was told that the trucks carrying Angel's team had hit an IED and been blown up. Striker was by my side when I got the news. My team had stuck to me like glue, getting me through those first horrible moments, days, weeks.

No, I couldn't ask more of my team or Striker.

I couldn't really ask more of myself.

I thought by now, things would be easier.

But all week long, Angel had been part of every inhale, and every exhale, and I *hated* it.

I hated how I felt.

I hated living this way.

My hand shot out, slamming my gear shift into drive, and took off with a screech of tires.

Perhaps I needed another trip to see Dr. Carlon, my traumatic brain injuries specialist. Since Avril Limb wasn't helping, maybe there was a physical reason for these intrusive sensations and thoughts.

An explanation.

Some means to get relief.

And there it was. The guilt. The pervasive guilt.

"Stop it!" I yelled at myself. "*Focus*. A woman's life is on the line. Three little ones are potentially in harm's way."

I swiped my hand over my face, trying to get rid of the sensation of Angel. But it did nothing to silence his begging. "I'm burning! Help me!"

9

I PARKED AT THE END OF THE CUL DE SAC IN FRONT OF SOPHIA Abadi's house. Brian Ackerman came roaring up in an Iniquus Land Rover and parked beside me.

Ah, and here comes the junkyard dog to nip at my heels and warn me off.

That was unfair. Brian was a good guy. Kind, intelligent, but he was rabid when it came to protecting Sophia and her sons, and with good reason. She had NEAD, a seizure disorder that was associated with PTSD. Brian wouldn't want anything to trigger her. Iniquus business could certainly do just that.

Shifting into park, I pulled my visor down to make sure my face had softened and I didn't look like a wolf on the hunt. I took a moment to slick some gloss on my lips, unbuckled and reached for my bag.

Sophia was standing in her open door, waiting for us.

I met Sophia, and we became friends after an event where I had been the closest person—vicinity-wise—on the highway when Panther Force thought Sophia had been in an accident. They'd been talking to her on the phone while she drove through

Washington D.C., heading toward Headquarters when they heard a bang, and Sophia stopped talking. Panther Force couldn't be sure what had happened.

I was supposed to get eyes-on.

Sophia had blown a tire. She hadn't responded on the phone to Brian and the team because she went into one of her NEAD seizures. We had to break into the car to get to her.

Brian had lifted her from the driver's seat, rolled her into his chest, and carried her back to his vehicle. I knew from the way he moved, the tenderness of his touch, the concern and more… the fear in his eyes, that he loved her deeply.

And I also knew he had been at a loss for how to help her.

I tipped my head to watch as Brian rounded to open his back door and unstrap Sophia's two little ones. He was a natural at the daddy business. The boys' biological father had died right after Chance was born. They needed someone to step in—someone who loved them and made them feel safe.

My involvement on Sophia's Iniquus case had been minuscule. But it had been immensely interesting.

Dr. Sophia Abadi worked for AACP—The Ancient Artifact and Cultural Preservation Society. Sophia was fighting to safeguard Syrian relics from being stolen and sold into private collections by terrorists.

Her colleagues were in harm's way in Syria. They were being kidnapped, tortured, and killed. And Sophia, her knowledge, and her connections meant she too could become a target. Prescott's FBI task force had hired Iniquus to keep their eyes on her.

Seeing Prescott today had made me think not only of the professional expertise of Dr. Zoe Kealoha and her BIOMIST registry but also of Dr. Sophia Abadi.

Beyond her profession, Sophia had a unique background.

Sophia's father had been a professor of archaeology. Sophia had spent her summers in the Middle East from the time she was very young. She was fluent in Arabic, Farsi, Turkish, and Hebrew. Sophia followed in her father's footsteps, getting her own Ph.D. She was already a known and respected name in the small, tight-knit world of working archaeologists.

But she had gone the route of twenty-first-century technology. She was a space archaeologist, using satellite imagery to find possible dig sites of ancient cultures.

When I met Sophia, I learned that ISIS was involved in digging up the ancient relics in Iraq and Syria and was selling them on the black market where a high price was paid for conflict relics.

This was one of the ways that ISIS developed their vast wealth.

Sophia used the satellite images, her expertise, and her contacts to save the cultural pieces as best she could. And that meant she had a network of people who worked in the resistance in Syria, which is where that NSA image of the possible-Kaylie was captured.

It had occurred to me that Sophia could have a contact who knew something about an American woman in the area. She had all kinds of contacts, including the CIA operating in the region, and I thought Sophia's contacts might be the only way we could succeed in a hot zone.

I popped open my door and climbed out of my car.

Brian raised his hand as a hello. His muscles were loose, his smile wide.

Walking over with outstretched arms, I took baby Chance from Brian while he got Turner unbelted.

Sophia held the door wide as we walked up the steps. "Come on in."

Turner squiggled to get down from Brian's arms and ran past his mom toward the den.

"Not even a hello or a hug, Turner?" she called after her older son. She reached out to take Chance from my arms, and after giving him a smacking kiss, she set him down.

Chance toddled after his brother.

"That smells good." Sophia nodded toward the bag in Brian's hand.

"When you said Lynx was stopping by, I thought it might be easier if I just grabbed something." He turned toward me as Sophia planted a kiss on his cheek, whispering thank you.

"There's plenty for you to join us," he said.

"I don't want to mess up your evening. I just wanted to pick Sophia's brain a bit."

"So, she said." He sent me a look that wasn't exactly a warning shot. I'd just call it a "mind your Ps and Qs" reminder. When he focused back on Sophia, he said, "I'll keep the boys busy so you two can talk."

Sophia gestured toward her sofa, and we each took an end cushion, swiveling, so we were face to face. "Chai?"

"No, thank you, I'm fine. Just feeling around a new case that landed in my lap this morning." I reached into my bag and pulled out the printout Zoe had given me with the medical data on the three children. "I got some information that has me perplexed. I'm wondering what you would make of it." I handed her the sheet.

Sophia took a moment to look it over. "Three young children. Each looks healthy." She glanced up. "All in Iraq, according to the GPS coordinates."

"Yes, and it seems that they might all have the same mother."

"Oh." Sophia's lips drooped into a frown. Her finger traced

down the medical information. “Are these all the medical records?”

“Yes.”

“The older children weren’t examined again?”

“Not by this organization, at least. I was looking at the names of the children, hoping you might have an explanation about why each would have a different last name. I don’t know about Iraqi naming traditions. Or if that isn’t the explanation, maybe you understand what that could mean.”

“She’s not Iraqi?”

“American.”

Sophia nodded and stared at the paper. With a deep breath and a long exhale, she said, “With such little data to look at, it’s impossible to say for sure. I would guess that she was captured and is a slave.”

“A slave,” I whispered. Okay, it had crossed my mind that she was captured and held against her will somewhere in the world. Slavery hadn’t been my go-to in this scenario.

“ISIS has kidnapped thousands of girls and women in Iraq and Syria. It’s not only allowed, but it’s also sanctioned. There is a fatwa—a ruling—put out by the ISIS financial chief back a few years ago.”

“Wouldn’t that be an unusual thing for a finance chief to get involved?”

“Not at all. You know from my work that ISIS is a money generating machine. One of the ways they make their money is by organizing the sale of conflict relics on the black market.”

“Yes.”

“Another way that they make a lot of money is through their slave markets. Slaves are a source of needed labor. Many of the ancient archeological tels that are being dug up and sifted through to find the relics for black market sales use slave labor.

They not only use slaves to increase their revenue streams but also as rewards for their fighters. If you join ISIS, you get your very own sex slave. And the higher up the ranks, the more audacious your fighting, the younger and prettier your slave."

"The fatwa said this was okay?"

"It's fine as long as you follow the rules. And those rules might explain the children's names. For example, you can only have sex with your personal slave. If your slave is pregnant, you can't sell her."

"After she gave birth, selling her would be okay?"

"She could be sold, but then the old owner could no longer have sex with her. There's also a ban on a member of ISIS having sex with a slave who was either pregnant or menstruating. If an ISIS fighter got his slave pregnant, he might use her for labor—cooking, washing, tending children or goats, and then procured a new slave to have sex with."

"What would happen with the children?"

"That's the question, isn't it? I know that a woman with children or dependents gets a lower price from the online slave auctions than a woman without. It could be that they sold her away from her child even though the fatwa says that the slaves are to be shown compassion."

"Are these rules that have a tradition in this region, or is this something that ISIS is making up as it goes?"

"According to that document, it's believed that slavery is an inevitable consequence of jihad. These particular rules were written because the fighters were violating Sharia law with their treatment of the women and children they own. ISIS has other documents that talk about how to deal with war spoils gleaned in their attacks in Iraq or Syria, such as the slaves, natural resources, and antiquities." Sophia looked down at the paper for a long moment. "Calculating the time between births and the changes of the names, it looks like her owners waited for her to have given birth and nurse the baby a short while before they sold her or traded her."

"Why would they do that? Why not keep her?"

She shook her head. "Perhaps their wives were displeased. Perhaps resources were tight. Perhaps someone of a higher rank noticed her and requested her. Or there was a debt that needed to be paid, which they could do after she gave birth. Maybe they lost her in a bet. Or maybe the

fighter died, and they passed her on to another owner. It's a volatile and dangerous place to be, especially if you're female."

I rubbed my hands down my thighs. To be taken and sold. To be raped and carry that baby. To then be passed from one slave owner to another slave owner. And again, to be raped and carry his child. And a third time…that we knew about. "The same children are not documented in the subsequent locations. Beyond their having died, can we talk about possible explanations?"

Sophia pinched her lips. "They weren't there the day of the medical review. They were kept by the slave owner's family. Like I said, a woman gets a higher price when she is sold without dependents. The child might be kept as a slave to be raised to do the farm work or to be used for sex."

My eyelids stretched wide. "These are babies."

"They have sex with young boys and girls, too. Seven-years-old is the youngest I've heard of. If the woman you are looking for was a young American woman, she would surely bring a higher price, especially if she was without dependents." Sophia smoothed her hand over the paper as she thought. "It could be that the family kept the child as a bargaining chip should they need something to offer ISIS for mercy or to the Americans for leverage."

"Leverage how?"

"What if American troops took a family member prisoner? The family would have something of value to the Americans to trade." Sophia caught my gaze. "How do you know about the mother?"

"Satellite images. An AI system thought it might have matched her face."

"We could try to find the children that way as well. I have the technology to do that." She focused back on the papers and paused. When she looked up again, she said, "I would try, but I don't see how that would be possible. We don't know what these children look like. No, now that I'm trying to conceive of how images could help, I see that's not possible with only this data. I'm afraid that if you're trying to repatriate these children to the United States, it's going to require someone going in, identifying the children, and bringing them out. And even then, how are you going to identify the children? It's not like they come with a 'made by a citizen of the USA stamp.'"

10

"OKAY, SLAVERY IS ON THE TABLE AS A POSSIBLE EXPLANATION," I said.

Sophia rubbed the palm of her hand into the worry lines on her forehead. "Is this a member of the military or the government?"

"No."

She bit at her upper lip then sighed. Had it been the military or government, some aspects of a rescue might be a little more streamlined. I understood that. But I also thought that from what I'd seen at a fast glance through the files, those resources were not the issue. Iniquus, FBI, CIA, NSA… all had continued the search.

And it looked like the NSA just might have done the impossible. Kudos to them.

"Slavery," I started again, still a little shocked by the idea that that's what had been happening to Kaylie over the past seven years. "Do you know how that would work? I get that an ISIS fighter might be offered a sex slave as a recruiting tool or as an incentive to fight. I can see how women and children could be snatched up when their homes are overrun and used in that way. But what if the slaves came from somewhere else. Does ISIS have a system for buying slaves? How would that transaction take place? Surely, they don't just pull out a credit card and pay."

"Many of the slaves come in from Africa. Niger, for example, is a big provider of slaves to various countries and not only to the Middle East."

I pulled out a pad and wrote: Check on slave trade out of Niger and Nigeria at the time of Kaylie's disappearance. Check on the connection between Niger and Nigeria and ISIS.

I held my pen over the pad, ready to jot down my next thought. "Earlier, I was tasked with finding a woman who disappeared years ago. Now, I realize that there are four Americans who need to be found. For the woman, at least, time is very much on the precipice. I'm wondering if the children's last names might give us more information about her connections. And perhaps…this is a stretch, is there a way that we might be able to follow financial transactions given the names? Do slaves take their owner's last names?"

"I don't think slaves do, no. I can ask my colleagues. The children, yes. Let's start there. In Syria and most of Iraq, the families follow Arab naming ways. The mother would keep her name when she marries. Their children take their father's name. The family name, which is often based on tribe or geography, is seldom used, and looking at this list, it's going to be really hard to identify these men."

I scooted over and looked at the list with her. It was typed out in English.

"The person who did the intake listened to the people say their name and then transliterated the Arabic name into Latin letters. How well this person did depended a little bit on their own language skills. In Arabic, there would be a certain way to spell the last name. The information would have little use if they weren't documenting all of the names in Arabic abjad, the Arabic lettering." She picked up a pad and pen from the side table. "For instance, if I said my name was Hamid. You might also write it Haamid or Hameed. Nur might be written Nour or Noor. You see?" She held up the pad.

I nodded.

"When families are using their name in a country where a different writing system is used, they have to decide how they will write their name. They will typically try to find the easiest way for someone from a different language to pronounce their name correctly."

"I can see how that would be a mess." I pulled out my phone. "Two seconds, do you mind?"

"No." Sophia waved her hand.

I sent a quick text to Zoe.

Me: **The people who were filling out the forms at the medical sites, they wrote the person's name in what alphabet system?**

"As a piece of information, most women in Iraq are illiterate," Sophia said after I put my phone in my lap. "Over half. They wouldn't have been giving anyone this information."

My phone buzzed, and I looked down.

Zoe: **The name is written in Arabic because of variances when translating it to our lettering system. There is a specific way that names are written in Arabic abjad, and we wanted to have record of their official names. It's sometimes tough. The women aren't all able to write their names. We have to depend on the males. If you need the three names in Arabic lettering, I can send them to you in a file. The civil status certificates (like our birth certificates) will be in the official**

names. If they have them. But they'd only have them if the babies were born in a hospital.

Me: **Thanks, I might need that later. I'll let you know.**

That confirmed what Sophia was saying.

A slave.

The thought sent a shiver of horror through my system. I knew what it was like to be held prisoner. My sad tale was just nothing, *nothing* compared to what my imagination was playing out.

I reached out and squeezed Sophia's hand. "Thank you for talking to me."

"Of course." She lifted her other hand to her heart.

"The names. You said the family name is seldom used."

"That's right. The child has a personal name, followed by the father's personal name, followed by the grandfather's personal name. Sometimes they extend out to the great grandfather as well, especially if the father has prestige. It will link the child to their father's success. The convention doesn't include surnames like here in western naming traditions."

"Your name doesn't follow that."

"I'm American born. My mom took dad's last name. My father, Amad Sahla Abadi. Amad, his personal name. Sahla, his father's name. Abadi, his grandfather's name. My father decided to be called Amad Abadi, and Abadi became our surname in America. Had that not been true, then my name would be Sophia Amad Sahla. Sophia, my given name. Amad, my father's name. Sahla, my grandfather's name. You see? It might be hard to match up Amad Sahla Abadi with Sophia Amad Sahla."

"You didn't take your first husband's name. Were you following the Arabic tradition?"

"I needed my name to remain my name as it helps me with my work. My contacts have always known me as Sophia Abadi."

"I think these naming traditions might close a door."

"How is that?" She pulled at her earlobe.

"Going back to the money. I thought perhaps there might be some kind of document trail. Banks, for example."

Sophia stood. "Have you plotted these GPS locations on the map yet?" She walked to the dining room that she had converted into a home office where her computer screens were positioned in an array across the tabletop. "Are they near a hospital? A city center where a bank might be found?" She dropped into a chair and typed her password into the keyboard. "I'd find that surprising. But you never know."

11

I PRESSED THE BUTTON TO START MY CAR JUST AS MY PHONE buzzed. Prescott. "I have information," I said.

"Hopefully, yours isn't as bleak as mine."

A frisson of fear raced up my chest and squeezed my heart. "Tell me." One hand rested on my throat, the other on the top of my steering wheel. I looked out the windshield at the stop sign at the top of Sophia's cul de sac.

"The caravan that was making its way to the refugee check-point was attacked. The satellites tracked ISIS into the area. There are a number of dead. Most dispersed into the hills. We don't know if that woman from our image is amongst them."

"Call her Kaylie," my tone was terse, "and not *that woman*. It's very possibly Kaylie."

"I got your message saying she's alive." His tone sounded braced like he wasn't willing to believe the information and wanted to keep it at arm's length. "Did Zoe find her in the data bank? What exactly did you learn?"

As I drove, I explained to Prescott what I'd discovered since we said goodbye earlier. I finished with, "When I get back to

Iniquus and a secure computer, I'll send you the GPS coordinates and the mapping file as well as the BIOMIST search data. Also," I fell silent as I switched lanes, "Zoe would like to be read into the program, just the part explaining how her information was used to develop the mission and the outcome. She's compiling data on the efficacy and usefulness of maintaining the BIOMIST system."

"Noted." He paused. "It might take me a few minutes to wrap my head around this shift in status. Now we know Kaylie was alive in Northern Iraq eleven months ago."

I flipped on my turn signal and slowed for a stop sign. "It probably won't settle in until you can see her with your own eyes."

"Let's make that happen."

"Working on it." I pressed the gas and slid into the gap between oncoming cars. "When you take a look at the maps, I'm wondering if you can share it with the Pentagon and find out how close our troops are to those areas. In particular, I'd like to know if they already have a rapport. Can we send someone in to get the kids?"

"Get the three children out of Iraq?"

"Well, sure, they're Kaylie's kids. I'm not claiming any legal expertise at all. I just did a quick Internet search about foreign citizenship and what legal papers the children might have. It's not a complete dead end. There's the possibility that the kids had birth certificates and that it might list the mother and father's names."

"Were the biomarkers processed in a city?"

"Sadly, no." My foot hovered over the brake, wondering what this jerk on my right thought he was doing. I let him into my lane and then gave him some space. "I found an article that said there are nearly fifty thousand children who were born in

Iraq who are being denied Iraqi citizenship because they were born in the areas held by ISIS before allied troops were able to push them out. Those children *were* issued birth certificates by ISIS, but the Iraqi government says they're worthless. A, if that's true, there might be an ISIS issued birth certificate with Kaylie's name. B, if that's true, abandoning Kaylie's kids in Iraq would leave them stateless." I pressed the gas to make my left turn, sliding along with the cars and just making it through the intersection before the light turned. "Living in Iraq without being a citizen of Iraq could mean her kids would be denied schooling, medical care, even the right to work or to marry once they're grown. Since these children have an American parent, they're American citizens. From what I read, their US citizenship status doesn't depend on if Kaylie was married to the children's fathers."

"Fathers, plural."

"The three children share the familial blood markers with Kaylie. The three children all have different names. In the Arabic tradition, the children should have their name, then their father's name, then their grandfather's name. The children's names all being different must mean that they are fathered by different men, and these men were not brothers."

Prescott sucked air between his teeth. "Damn," he said under his breath.

"If Kaylie was in a succession of marriages, then her children fall under the 'birth abroad in wedlock to a U.S. citizen and an Alien.' This law says that since Kaylie's a U.S. citizen who grew up in America, if she's the genetic parent, then they acquire U.S. citizenship at birth. And if she wasn't married, they'd still have rights of citizenship under a different law."

"Neither scenario bodes well for Kaylie."

"More?" I asked.

"If she's marrying the men, three in seven years, that sounds like she's acting as a jihadi bride. Getting her home to America means moving her to jail while they try to sort that all out. She'd be treated like a terrorist."

"Sophia Abadi thinks that she might be a slave."

"Wait. You took this to Dr. Abadi?"

"Not *this*. Well, yes, *this* in a way. I didn't give her details about Kaylie. I showed her the readout from Zoe to get cultural information about the names—which I just explained to you—and to see if perhaps Sophia had contacts in the area or could tell me anything from the GPS locations using her unique satellite software. As to the software, she'll look to see if there's anything interesting to report. By interesting, I mean, does she see anything that sticks out to her about these sites. For example, she said that ISIS often uses slaves to dig at tels to find the conflict relics. She can see if there are excavations that happened that correlate with the dates of the children's medical assessments."

There was a long pause. "We don't know what they look like. We don't have fingerprints. Zoe told me that when they were collecting the blood samples, they thought that collecting the fingerprint data would scare people away, and the blood would be a far more useful tool."

Sophia had pointed out the same thing, that we had no easy way to tell which children Kaylie's kids were. I didn't know if the children were together or separate. I didn't know if the people who were raising the children loved them and wanted them or were exploiting them, or something in between.

I didn't even know if they were still alive.

But I had a solution to identifying them.

"That's why I suggested boots in the area. If we had rapport, perhaps they would just tell the truth. Or…we could test the children."

"DNA will take too long and would be cost-prohibitive if there are many of the right gender in the right age ranges." Prescott's voice was still a tight fist. The air barely made it up to his throat. It sounded like he was swallowing his thoughts.

"Granted. But let's go back to Zoe Kealoha and your affiliation with her."

He jumped right in line with my thoughts. "The prototype I was supposed to test for Zoe?"

"Exactly. She developed a device that can do a field rule in-rule out when it comes to familial blood markers. And I have the vial of Melody Foley's blood in my cooler. The problem being, even though it's Zoe's invention, the CIA and DARPA might have something to say about it being out in the field. They'll want to make sure that there's no way that it could land in enemy hands. If our enemies get hold of it and get a look at the software, that puts the BIOMIST database collection at risk. And too, it puts the Middle Eastern population at risk. I was just reading an article about this. Do you remember when they sent that medical team in to try to vaccinate the kids whom they thought might be Osama bin Laden's children?"

"When they hoped to get blood draws and test it on Zoe's machine, yes."

"Apparently, in city centers throughout the region, parents are tepid about getting their children immunized because they think America is up to something that might endanger their kids. Without their immunizations, childhood diseases are becoming regional epidemics."

"But that doesn't affect BIOMIST because they're working out in the rural areas?"

"They collect everywhere there are people. The parents are right to think that something's going on, just not the something that they might suppose."

"Going back to what you were saying, I can't imagine the analyzer being allowed out in the field."

"Unless it's *you* who takes it there."

Silence met that statement.

One hand on the steering wheel, I chewed on my other thumbnail.

The silence was too sharp-edged. I started packing words into the empty space. "If Zoe rigged the analyzer with a remote detonator or some such apparatus," I suggested. "It could be a call-in number, a timer, some other triggering event… The machine has its own power source. Zoe could retrofit the machine to self-sabotage."

His breath came out in a rush. I could imagine him rubbing his hand over his face while he processed. "All right," he said. "I have to go talk to Zoe about this. If she agrees, I'll take it up the ladder for permission, get my team together, and head into the field."

"How long would it take to rig the system? I'm asking because I think it's important for you to leave right away. Thinking this can be slow rolled because the kids are probably okay might be a mistake for this reason, Kaylie's timer's ticking. Having you and your team already in-country, looking for the children, would put you that much closer if we get actionable data on Kaylie."

"True."

"It's an argument in case the signatures you need aren't forthcoming. On the subject of the analyzer and the safety system, I know there are flash drives that, if you put the code in wrong three times, it will release an acid to melt the data. Zoe has an acid system in her WASPs on a micro-level. She should know what to do."

"It's four-thirty—"

I glanced down at the clock on my dash. "She'll be gone for the day. Zoe said she had a personal thing to get to at four. She's usually in her lab by six every morning to miss the traffic. If you were standing there looking all puppy-dog eyed, I bet she'd help."

"Somehow, I don't think that there's any particular look that I could give Zoe that would motivate her in one way or another. But her knowing an innocent woman was in trouble and that we needed to save her kids, she'd at least try."

"Do we know Kaylie's innocent?" I asked, pulling up to the guardhouse at Iniquus and lifting my badge.

My question was met with silence.

After getting a nod, the gate lifted. I pulled into a parking space in front of the atrium door. I had hoped to get back to Iniquus before now. I wanted to talk to someone over on Panther Force. Margot, if possible. I had a theory that I needed to scratch off my page.

Since my question to Prescott had been rhetorical and cautionary, I continued, "Will you be okay getting cleared for a trek to Iraq?" I asked Prescott.

"Even if I'm green-lighted on taking in the blood marker analyzer, I don't think it's going to be as easy as driving up to a house, putting a child into a Jeep, and heading home."

12

WALKING TO THE END OF THE HALL THAT HOUSED PANTHER Force, I knocked on Margot's office door.

"Come in," she called.

I popped the door open a crack and stuck my head in. "Do you have time for a three-minute question?"

She waved me in. "What's up?"

Margot was an ex-CIA field officer. Why she left, I had no clue. She seemed to like to keep her head down. She was friendly but didn't share anything personal. I'm sure that served her well in the spy-world. Here on Panther Force, she made things hum. No task too small, no challenge too big. She was a team player all the way.

I pushed the door shut. "I'm working on a case, and I'm trying to scratch possibilities off a laundry list." I moved to one of the two padded chairs positioned in front of her desk.

She leaned back in her seat, lacing her fingers and letting her hands rest on her chest, thumbs pointing up. This was a body gesture display of self-restraint and dominance, which is exactly what I would expect from Margot. She had the expertise under her belt, but she'd mete it out carefully.

"Black ops," I said.

She tucked her thumbs. Not a subject she was willing to talk about.

"Specifically, the Rex Deus and how their members went from the land of the living to disappeared into the world of black ops."

She moved her hands to the arms of her chair. Okay, she was a little more open to this. "The Rex Deus is a group who are working together for some outcome that we have yet to define," she said. "What we do know is that some of the members were involved in Israeli special forces."

"There was an explosion." I leaned forward. "Everyone was listed as killed in action. If the explosion took place, and there was no DNA evidence to support the theory of their death, wouldn't they be listed as missing in action, presumed dead or some such thing?"

"Not if the government was complicit in disappearing the group."

"Would it have to be the government?"

"It could be insiders who worked for the military who framed things up. But someone had to help them."

"And there was also your Mossad counterpart who was in Paris back when you were with the CIA. She was in a building that exploded and was deemed killed in action. But she was alive and well. She was also doing black ops. Did she join with Rex Deus?"

"She didn't have the Rex Deus tattoo on her arm when Thorn saw her. But we don't know what the tattoo is all about. So her not having it doesn't mean anything. Thorn did put a Rex Deus member to sleep in the men's bathroom in Belgium. That guy woke up and moved on before we could get Interpol involved."

"But you thought this woman was dead."

"Yes."

"In an explosion."

"Yes." She pulled her brow tight. "Is this about a contract you're working on?"

"The contract I'm working on involves an FBI, CIRG team. They thought a woman was dead. It looks like she's not. Obviously, no body."

"And you think she faked her death?"

"No." I scratched my nose. "I don't know what to think. I guess the question came up for me because this woman is a scientist, and she was in Tanzania a while back. Sometimes my brain just picks a thread here and there, and I try to make whole cloth out of it. Working on this case about a scientist, having ties to Tanzania, and I think there was a Rex Deus who was killed in that attack."

"Yes."

"There seems to be some overlap. But there are seven years between these events. I guess I'm trying to rule-in and rule-out possibilities. And one of them could be that the missing woman wanted to vanish. Like I said, I'm checking this possibility off my list—the black-ops. In order for someone to disappear into the shadow world, I suppose they'd have something under their belt, training-wise, that would give them some tradecraft and survival skills. CIA, Mossad, Special ops. Something."

"Almost certainly."

I paused to consider why the men had to go through the subterfuge of the explosion. It must mean that they had family and friends who needed to believe they had died. I couldn't get past the selfishness of it. The meanness. What a terrible thing to do to someone.

Surely, those family members and even their friends spent sleepless nights wondering about their loved one's last moments and what it felt like to be in that explosion.

Melody Foley's graphic description of her nightmares still clung to my imagination. The hot breath of the animal, the sharpness of the teeth sinking in…

That attack never happened; Kaylie wasn't killed or eaten by wild beasts.

Seven years of those nightmares. Not to say that nightmares weren't warranted. Just to say that they should probably have taken a different form.

Warranted…that was an interesting thought I'd bubbled up.

I wondered what Avril would make of that in a therapy session.

Did I think my own nightmares were a requirement of my situation? Did I find it reasonable to assume that—animals or not—Kaylie's falling off the radar screen would necessitate nightmares that tortured her family, as well?

Hearing about Melody's sleepless nights, seeing her in such distress normalized my own situation for me. That was probably another thing I should bring up in counseling.

I sighed heavily.

Margot pressed her lips together and canted her head. "Lynx, are you all right?"

"Why do you ask?"

"You don't look well. You look like you're not getting enough sleep. You seem off somehow. I'm asking as a friend. You have me worried."

I reached up and scratched beside my eye, letting my gaze stray to the abstract painting on the wall. Well, this was the second time today someone basically said I looked like shit. I didn't know what to say to Margot. I hoped she didn't think I was so off my game that I wasn't functioning. I focused back on her with a forced smile. "I've been worried about my Abuela Rosa. I'm going down to Puerto Rico tomorrow night to check on her. I'm taking a long weekend." I stood. "Working weekend. This gal is in the wind and in imminent danger. But I've gone as far as I can. Now, I have to wait to get information in house."

Margot stood as well, keeping us on the same level.

I knew that psychological trick. You don't let the power shift by allowing someone to look down at you.

"You're approaching the anniversary of Angel's death." Margot nodded as if this was all the explanation she needed about my state of mind. "I think it's a good idea that you'll be with his family. I'll light a candle for you when I get back to the barracks."

"Thank you." Emotions pressed against my eyes, making them water. I turned to leave so Margot wouldn't see the frown that tugged my lips.

"I hope you find her, the woman who's in imminent danger," Margot said, as my hand caught the doorknob.

I got my face under control and looked back over my shoulder. "Thank you. So do I. One other question, do you know a CIA officer working in Syria and Northern Iraq named John Grey?"

Her body froze as I tipped open this new box.

This was the actual purpose of my coming here. I just wanted it to come when she would least expect it so I could read her body language. "I need to get in touch with him about this case. Can you facilitate that?"

She sat down.

"It's an Iniquus case." No kidding. But I wanted Margot to

remember she wasn't CIA anymore, and we use our knowledge, wherever and however we accrued it, to get positive outcomes to our directives.

It worked.

She laced her fingers, a sign that she wanted to hold that information caged. "I need to make a phone call."

I nodded and let myself out.

As I walked back to the elevator bank, horror energy swirled around me. Kaylie's case seemed to be one big fat energetic trigger, fuel for the fire that I was already battling in my own psyche. It occurred to me that the exhaustion that I felt from my own shit-mares might make me more porous energy-wise.

I wondered if I hadn't picked up this desperation energy from Melody Foley. The way she looked this morning in the conference room with Kaylie's picture in hand was exactly how I felt.

What I needed to do was go meditate and ground out some of these sensations. I obviously wasn't masking them very well since people were casting worried eyes my way.

So much for my fluffy bunny charade.

Just as I pushed the elevator button to go down to the lobby and head to the men's barracks that housed Striker's apartment, I heard it again, the *knowing*: "*As I was going to St. Ives, I met a man with seven wives.*"

13

STRIKER'S APARTMENT AT THE MEN'S BARRACKS WAS AN OASIS. The floor to ceiling window that created one of the living room walls made this room feel like a tree fort by day with the glittering Potomac River below. At night, it was a symphony of lights from the cars moving on the Washington streets and above them the stars.

Tonight, as the storm raged outside, I had a gas fire snapping in the stone fireplace, flanked by shelves of books. The wisdom of history, the strength shown through memoires, and the glory of art were all there, should I have the time and interest.

My task this evening, though, was to gather more information about the possibilities of Kaylie's circumstances.

Beetle and Bella, my faithful Dobermans, lay beside me as I rested my head on the arm of the leather couch and pulled my knees up. My computer stationed on my stomach. My fingers hovered over the keys.

Angel was in my mind, distracting me. "*Please* come. Please help me."

I had spoken with a priest up at the National Cathedral on

Saturday about how to help a soul that had gone to Hell. The priest said they could perform a mass in Angel's name, but if his soul had gone to Hell, there wasn't really anything that could be done. Did I want to talk about the circumstances of my husband's being rejected from Heaven? Did I want to save my own soul through penance?

I had explained that I wasn't Catholic, and Hell wasn't part of my belief system.

The priest thought maybe those beliefs had landed my husband down with the Devil. After all, Angel wasn't supposed to marry a non-Catholic with a different belief system.

"We had received special permission in order to be married," I explained—one of the reasons our marriage had been held up until the afternoon before Angel left.

"Your marriage is not the reason your husband went to Hell, then."

"I would say not." No, in my mind, it was Angel's own after-life beliefs that had created and sustained his Hell. And as I relived Saturday's conversation with Father Paul, it occurred to me that I might have a solution to helping Angel's soul.

Granted, it was a paradigm stretch. But, honestly, over the last few years, what wasn't?

Since the priest hadn't been able to help, I thought about who else I could turn to for information, a plan.

Then I landed on Herman Trudy, General Coleridge, and Galaxy.

Last year, Iniquus had been under attack. It was then that I discovered the United States military's Galaxy Project.

Talk about a mind blower!

Even experiencing my own psychic skills, and those of Miriam, and even my Strike Force brother Gator Aid Rochambeau, this group still did things that made me question all assumptions about how the Universe worked.

The Galaxy project was developed by the US government in response to the research that Russia was doing into psychic spying. Our own system of psychic spying, known under the scientific term "Remote Viewing," was developed by Stanford University. Our government tasked the Pentagon to develop the program. A military team was composed and trained using Stanford's scientific protocol and methodology. They officially disbanded in the mid-1990s, but there were rumors that it continued on as black ops.

The original members of the Galaxy Project—who were both the scientists and the lab rats—led difficult lives as their work for the military was ended and scoffed at.

Since then, many of the Galaxy soldiers had died, others lived in self-imposed hermitages to try to find peace.

And peace was what *I* was after.

The interesting thing here was that in the world of remote viewing, there was no time or geographical tether. The Galaxy operators had trained to go anywhere along a timeline and anyplace in the universe to observe. Maybe they could even go to Hell and find Angel.

I remembered reading one account of a man who sent himself on a remote viewing task to go back to where a buddy of his had disappeared in a plane crash during a mission. The plane and his body were never found. That pilot had been listed as Missing in Action—presumed dead.

Having met Melody Foley, I could see why this Galaxy operator would want to bring his buddy's family the peace of knowing what had happened to their loved one.

When the Galaxy operators did the remote viewing session, he saw that the plane was under a waterfall, and that's why they hadn't been able to find it. He was also able to talk to his dead buddy. The buddy was happy in the afterlife, and all the more so because he knew that his family had been lifted up and carried by his brothers who had made it home. The buddy thanked him and said he was at peace.

The operator and some friends had spent their R and R down in South America looking for the plane and had been successful in finding it, and the missing airman's remains still strapped into the pilot's seat. From what the searchers found, they could tell the family that the pilot had died on impact and hadn't suffered.

Thank you, God, that the pilot hadn't suffered. Thank you, God, that the family could find relief from knowing this.

Maybe the same could happen for me.

Granted, it was a long shot. But perhaps a Galaxy operator would do a task for Angel, answering the question of what Angel's soul needed to happen to be at rest.

I decided that I'd go talk to Iniquus founder General Elliot.

General Elliot had been in charge of the Galaxy Project prior to starting Iniquus. I wouldn't want to go up and talk to the remote viewers behind the general's back. I'd go see General Elliot about a trip in the morning. Maybe I could fly straight from my visit with Abuela Rosa in Puerto Rico and head up to Wyoming to see Herman and General Coleridge.

Then, like a smack on the side of the head, it occurred to me, I might already have access to some pertinent information.

When Iniquus was under both physical and psychic attack last year, it was by a man who had been an operator with the Galaxy Project; his name was Allan Leverone.

Leverone called himself Indigo.

Indigo had been one of the most dexterous operators who did remote viewing tasks with the Galaxy Mission. An operator's success rate was based on how often he produced correct and actionable information. Anything over fifty percent was considered good. Indigo generally got a sixty-seven percent chance of bringing back useful information from his task.

It occurred to me that that was the exact percentage the NSA AI system had offered up for the correctness of matching Kaylie's name to the woman in Syria.

Sixty-seven percent chance had saved many lives. But they had also endangered them when missions had been planned and executed or not planned at all based on what a remote viewer saw.

Indigo was special. Not only was he entrusted with the secrets of remote viewing, but he was also one of only two people chosen, because of their morality and altruistic outlook, to be trained in remote influencing.

In remote influencing, seeds of thought could be introduced into someone else's brain to, well, to influence their thinking.

During Indigo's training and experimentation, the media got wind of the project.

Americans scoffed and ridiculed the Galaxy's work.

Jokes about men staring at goats turned from news headlines to a satirical movie.

The operators paid a hefty price tag for years of dedicated service to America.

Because their work was considered top secret, their efforts were redacted, leaving them no proof of their high efficacy working in the ether.

Money was withheld from funding their work.

The project shut down.

The Galaxy operators were humiliated and shunned.

When Indigo was relieved of his duties with Galaxy, the things that our government did to him and his family next was beyond horrific. They resulted in Indigo's wife and son dying, his daughter, Tabitha, becoming brain injured by carbon monoxide gas, and Indigo himself spending years of his life being medicinally restrained in a mental hospital.

His family was destroyed, his health deteriorated, his reputation and his chance to work depleted; Indigo struck back at these attacks using the weapons that he had been trained to use by the military—both remote viewing and influencing techniques. His revenge was nearly successful. Not just in taking down Iniquus, but also in taking over the US government.

Scary stuff.

Indigo was dead. He was already sick in the hospital when, by order of the President of the United States, steps were taken to make sure he didn't recover.

Within the day, his daughter Tabitha, AKA Scarlet Vine, who learned the techniques and vengeful ethic from her dad, was killed as well.

It was my hands that wrapped around Scarlet's neck to make sure she was no longer a threat to Striker, whom she had sedated and kidnapped, to General Elliot, whom she attacked, or to the United States.

The thing that thwarted Indigo and Scarlet in their efforts was Indigo's adherence to the science of his work. He kept copious lab notes on every single task and influencing operation that he undertook.

When Strike Force got hold of the scientific logs and was unraveling the long game that Indigo had been playing, one of the things that had been revealed was my role in all of it.

Indigo had wanted to extract revenge on my mentor, Spyder McGraw, as well as Iniquus owner, General Elliot, both of whom had been involved with the Galaxy Project. Indigo felt that these men had failed to protect the Galaxy project and the operators who did the work.

About the same time that Indigo was homing in on me being a vehicle for extracting his revenge on Spyder, Striker had caught Scarlet's eye.

Striker and Scarlet dated, briefly. The problem was that Scarlet thought she'd found her one and only. Striker seemed to have that effect on women. Scarlet started planning a future for them together, trying out baby names, and looking for houses to start their white picket fence lives together. Using the tools that her dad had taught her in remote viewing to see her future, Scarlet wrote out remote viewing tasks and went into the ether to see her pictures. What she saw was Striker asking her to marry him, the two of them standing at the altar, settling into their life of wedded bliss.

The reality was that Striker wasn't there for the long haul. In his mind, they were dating.

Period.

Striker simply wanted someone to enjoy, go out on the town, have some good conversations, and good sex. He was already married to his job. He'd told Scarlet this. She just had a different agenda and believed he'd come around.

Especially after she saw their happily ever after playing out in the ether.

The problem with her data gathering was that Scarlet had written the task herself. She wasn't using the Stanford scientific design that separated remote viewing from daydreaming/fantasy.

She saw what she wanted to see.

The double-blind tasking protocols were in place for a reason.

Indigo recognized the problem, along with Scarlet's delusional thinking, which was a byproduct of the time the government poisoned her with carbon monoxide.

Like any dad, though, Indigo wanted to give his daughter the moon, or in this case, a future with Striker. Besides, Striker was an Iniquus golden boy. He was one of Spyder's favorite people. Why not mess with Striker for a little additional payback?

Tasking information about the situation, Indigo discovered me in the ether, and he discovered my connection to Striker and to Spyder.

It was then that Indigo landed on the idea that Spyder could be punished through me, just like Indigo had been punished through his children. And he set out to do that. For years, he tormented and tortured me. Up until his death, he had been the puppet master, messing with my reality.

The reason I was plowing through these thoughts was that when we were unraveling the situation, I remembered coming across one of Indigo's tasking sheets with my name on it. It read something to the effect: "Lexi was married. But her husband's vehicle will hit an IED. Shit, that would have solved the problem. Lexi and Angel are very well matched and have an intense connection."

Indigo had successfully seen through his remote viewing that Angel would die in the IED explosion.

I wondered what else he saw about Angel and me. I wondered if any of it would be helpful to soothing Angel's soul.

General Elliot had the scientific logs in his Fort Knox-like file room inside his office suite.

Even if Indigo didn't note anything of significance about Angel, his death, and his afterlife, perhaps I could take what I knew and what I had gathered from the files up to Wyoming and ask General Coleridge or his protégé Herman Trudy to help me help Angel.

Since I was already tapping into the unconventional to help find Kaylie and her kids, why not try the remote viewing route to seek out a way to rescue them as well?

14

Having made my decision to approach General Elliot tomorrow morning about going to Wyoming, I reached out to start an Internet search for information that might help me find Kaylie.

My hand stalled over the keyboard. There it was again, my psychic *knowing*.

"*As I was going to St. Ives, I met a man with seven wives.*"

Fine, I'd start there with my searches and try to figure this out.

I first had the *knowing* when I was talking to Miriam about going to Puerto Rico. I was thinking about Strike Force going to Poland, and I was getting a text from Zoe about checking the BIOMIST system. Three possible routes to take.

I started with **Africa and Middle East, Seven Wives,** to see where that would lead me.

Muslim men in many countries in Africa and the Middle East can marry up to four wives. But then there was something called the "fifth wife." The fifth wife being a synonym for a slave. So if the man had many slaves, he would have many "fifth wives."

The more I read in these articles about the plight of the women in these regions, the more horrified I became. Why weren't we talking about this more in the international news? Why weren't our political systems doing something to stop the enslavement of women?

I pulled myself away from that thread.

It didn't feel like the answer to my *knowing.*

I tried another route. **Who was St. Ives?** The articles came up about St. Ives, England. That absolutely felt like a dead end.

I finally found a Catholic Saints site that offered the story. The saint's name wasn't actually Ives. St. Ives meant Cove of St. Ia.

Apparently, Ia, a young Irish princess, was in Cornwall, England, trying to catch a boat back to Ireland. The band of other saints she was supposed to have traveled with had gone on without her. That didn't sound very saint-like of them… "Ia was afraid because she was a young woman, and the journey was hazardous."

Oh, boy. That sentence rang true.

I read it again. "Ia was afraid because she was a young woman, and the journey was hazardous."

Yes, I could feel it in my bones. That was part of what I was to *know*.

Whose journey?

Kaylie?

No.

Miriam?

No.

Mine?

That was a big walloping affirmation.

I was the young woman, and my journey would be hazardous?

Yes.

I closed my eyes. The wind knocked out of me. This last year had been rather calm on the hazard scale. Ever since Indigo and Scarlet died, things had evened out. I would say that things were going pretty well, that I was living my best life, had I not been under the perpetual grief cloud that Angel's death formed over me.

Hazard? I cast the word toward the ether.

Yes.

I read the screen; Ia was grief-stricken over her fellow saints leaving her.

It wasn't lost on me that Ia was grief-stricken over some saints leaving, and I was grief-stricken over an Angel leaving me.

The article said that as Ia prayed, she noticed that there was a small leaf floating in the water. Ia took her rod and poked it to see if it would sink. Instead, it grew bigger and bigger. Trusting in God, she stepped onto the leaf, and it carried her across the sea.

I guessed I was going on a trip. And I'd have to trust in the Fates to take me where I needed to go and do what I needed to do.

If Ia was a saint, it meant she was killed.

I didn't know if that was a part of this. If Ia having been killed had anything to do with the rhyme or with this venture.

We all have to die sometime.

My mind went to the moment I had died out in the desert, looking around, wondering why the afterlife was nothing like I had expected it to be. My team showed up, pulling me back into my body with their defibrillator.

What if they'd just let me go?

What if the pain and the struggles had been over?

I've thought many times since my death that there must be a reason why my soul wasn't ready to leave this body, some task that had gone unfulfilled.

Maybe this was the reason?

Maybe the hazardous journey that was waiting for me, once fulfilled, would allow me to find some peace.

Only one way to find out. I had to walk through the fire.

I'd go to Puerto Rico first, and then, with or without General Elliot's approval, I'd go to Wyoming and task my friends with a remote viewing mission.

I pulled out my phone and texted General Coleridge. **Sir, I'm making flight arrangements to come up and see you and Herman Trudy. If it's convenient, I'd like to come this week.**

I gazed down at my dogs, not thinking anything. Just kind of numb, taking in the new information.

The text startled me when my phone buzzed in my hand: **We already have you on the calendar. The Mrs. has your room at the ranch all set up. Trudy plans to pick you up at the airport. Your flight should arrive on time at 3:40 pm this Thursday.**

They already saw me coming. That was some precise remote viewing if they already had me on the calendar with my flight time and everything.

They knew before I did that I needed them.

This kind of etheric *woo-woo* always threw me off equilibrium.

Thursday evening that would only give me a day and a half with Abuela Rosa. But I was eager to get up to Wyoming and get answers. Both for Kaylie and for me.

The time clock that Prescott had set for Kaylie's survival was ticking down. I didn't want to fail her.

15

WITH KAYLIE BACK IN THE FOREFRONT OF MY THOUGHTS, I focused on the case at hand.

"Let's start with the basics," I muttered as I lined up my thoughts.

"Speculation is not fact," so says Spyder. "Assumptions can eat your time."

Spyder was full of quips that were supposed to be guideposts on my travels down an evidence trail. For example, I knew that there were three children in the Middle East, each with a different last name, who had the familial biomarkers that were associated with Kaylie. I leaped to the idea that these kids must be Kaylie's.

I typed a text to Prescott: **Who are the members of Kaylie's family with biological markers close enough to show up in the system? Where have they been for the last four years? I need to know if any of them has left the United States. Thank you**. I tapped send.

If the NSA image *was* Kaylie, I didn't know why she was in Syria. There were three basic choices:

Kaylie was in the Middle East because she wanted to be there. I shouldn't let go of the possibility that she disappeared because she wanted to.

It could also be that she disappeared against her will but had changed her mind, and now things were hunky-dory.

Or it could be that her circumstances were wholly against her volition.

"ISIS brides from the United States" I typed into the search bar.

I scanned over a story about a twenty-year-old college student who had been attending the University in Alabama. Alabama? Huh. She'd told her parents she was going on a college trip. Instead, she used her tuition money to fly to Turkey. I scrolled up to find out where this interview was done, Al Hawl Camp, Syria. I noted the journalist's name. Perhaps he had seen or heard of another American woman in the area who didn't want to be interviewed. Or maybe he had some resources in the area, people who might have some information. I'd send him an email and feel him out without giving any specific details. I'd need Prescott to sign off on that. Maybe the FBI or CIA already had a backchannel contact with the guy.

The date on the article was four years ago.

I moved back down to finish reading. It said that Hilda had in that time frame been married to three Islamic State fighters.

Three husbands in four years.

Kaylie had possibly been with three men who fathered her children in seven years. So that number wasn't dissimilar.

Hilda wanted to return to the United States. She was sorry she'd cheered on the beheadings in the videos posted to social media. She'd turned herself into coalition forces who were detaining her in a refugee camp in northeast Syria.

There was another American with her. This woman was

much older, forty-six. She'd been a legal administrator. Hmm, whatever that was... But it seemed both were educated women. Women with career paths and potential. To give that up and go to a war zone? This woman was from the Mennonite community and had three adult children. Okay, neither of these women were what I might have pictured.

What would I picture?

Disenfranchised girls. Girls who were sold a bag of goods. Lied to. Manipulated.

The article said that fifty-nine Americans were known to have traveled to Syria to join ISIS. I wondered if I could track down that list. I'd like to check and see if Kaylie had any contacts in common with Americans who had joined ISIS, especially if they had joined ISIS before her disappearance.

I scribbled notes onto my pad.

It didn't feel right. But that didn't mean I wouldn't at least present these thoughts to Prescott and see if he wanted this hunted down. Of course, every time we reached out to someone, chances grew that Kaylie's story would leak.

It didn't seem as though anyone wanted that to happen. Maybe I should ask why that was.

"Oh, look here," I said aloud. "The FBI refrained from commenting on these two cases but said that the Agency built criminal cases against any American who joined ISIS since it was designated a terrorist organization." I noted the refraining-FBI guy's name. Perhaps he had direct contact with the other Americans who were being held and had been interrogated. Since the African case had gone cold, and no one was looking for Kaylie in the Middle East, perhaps this had gone overlooked, especially if Kaylie was told to adopt a different name.

I gathered other possible source names from the article. The biggest thing I gathered, though, was that religion, age, and education weren't predictive, and it seemed that woman's connection to any given fighter was tenuous.

Here was an article that might fit Kaylie's situation. I picked up my pen to take notes. A nurse out of New Zealand, MaryLisa Griffin, was abducted from a checkpoint after her truck had finished distributing medical supplies. Yup, this took place in the same time frame as Kaylie disappeared.

I scanned through, hoping to see what steps they'd taken to find the nurse. Surely, they had mercenaries on task to find her.

I noted: *Is there an Iniquus counterpart looking for Mary-Lisa? Did they get wind of someone like Kaylie?*

It looked like employees of the International Committee of the Red Cross made weekly visits to a detention camp, raising a flag high, hoping MaryLisa would see it and find a way to get to them. I jotted notes. Maybe someone from the Red Cross had seen or heard something, and it was passed up or down some chain of command that didn't reach Prescott.

I was feeling slightly more optimistic as my list grew. Someone had to have seen something or know someone that we could talk to—a spiderweb of contacts spread across the region. Surely there would be gossip.

I put my finger on the screen and wrote: "Camp database. Search and rescue have been looking through those pictures trying to find a match one by one. That's a crazy waste of time." I added thought bubbles as I wondered if NSA or FBI or heck even Iniquus could get a download of those images. We could use our software to quickly run through facial comparison software. If the CIA was involved, they could probably also add that information to the BIOMIST system so that they had not only the blood biomarkers stored but also images for facial recognition. I drew a third bubble and wrote: CIA?

The people in the camp were all escapees from a territory

that fell to US-backed forces. If Kaylie were there, we would have soldiers in the area to assist. Still, that didn't make sense. Why wouldn't Kaylie identify herself if she were in that camp?

There were twenty-three Western hostages known to be held by ISIS, most of whom were released for ransom or beheaded.

I put myself in Kaylie's shoes. Kaylie, an educated woman with plenty of international experience under her belt, would know that being seen as a Westerner would put her life at risk. If I were her, I'd hide my nationality.

While that might have kept Kaylie alive, it also might make it impossible for us to find her.

Kaylie's coloring was similar to my friend Arya's. Arya, who was from Syria, has eyes that were an intense aqua blue-green color. Kaylie might be able to pull it off.

Ah, look, here was a possible answer to my question. For five years, MaryLisa's employer and the government put out a warning not to mention MaryLisa in any public forum. They called for a complete media blackout since any mention of her—or even her country of origin—could endanger her. That had been my guess this morning during the intake. It looked like this article was only written after allied forces had pushed into the area where MaryLisa had been seen. Australia now believed the public could help find her.

I compared the women's situations and decided that, nope, it wasn't the same set of circumstances, and Kaylie's case should still be kept under wraps.

Prescott thought she was still on the run and in harm's way.

Days he'd said.

We have days to find her. Still, I'd forward this article to him, so we could debate the pros and cons.

Here was another interesting thought: MaryLisa was a nurse-midwife.

Witnesses said they saw MaryLisa working in clinics and hospitals under ISIS control. She was using her nursing skills. I wrote "Skillsets—de-desertification" on my paper.

These women—on the run from dropping bombs and ISIS fighters. Captured. Enslaved. Killed.

God.

I was heartsick for them.

Despair wrapped itself around me. The problem was enormous—thousands and thousands of women.

The pictures, the stories, they winded me.

World-weary. Bone-weary. My vision was blurred with fatigue. I checked the time readout. It was just now creeping past twenty-one hours.

People at work were noticing something was off, and that made me unprofessional.

I hadn't had a restful sleep in well over a week.

Even though it was still early, I should get to bed. I closed the lid and moved my computer to the side table.

Beetle and Bella lifted their heads.

"Do you need to potty?" I asked.

They laid their heads back down.

"No? Okay, time to go to bed." My pups weren't pups anymore. I had just turned eighteen when they were born. I was about to turn twenty-three in March. They were middle-aged in dog years. The first gray hairs sprouted on their chins. I reached down to rub behind their ears. "You will always be my babies. No matter how old you get."

I hefted myself to my feet and started down the hallway, the clickety-clack of their nails tapped behind me.

As I brushed my teeth for bed, I considered taking a sleeping pill that Avril had prescribed for occasional use.

The problem was that if I had a nightmare while under the

influence of the medication, I couldn't wake myself up. I had to live there in the scene until Striker shook me back to consciousness.

That wasn't fair to him. He needed his sleep, too. Though granted, he needed a lot less than the normal person. He was the kind of guy who was ready to rocket into the next day after four- or five-hours rest. It said a lot about the situation that he went to bed when I did and got up again when I did. It told me that his five hours weren't restful for him, and he was spending a considerable amount of time with me and my night traumas.

Striker wasn't home yet from the Strike Force security assignment at the Kennedy Center. Tonight, they were protecting the gorgeous Princess of Monaco, a former South African Olympic swimmer. I'd love to hear the scuttlebutt. I wouldn't ask, though. Client information was considered verboten.

Beetle and Bella had already made their way to the bedroom, where their sleeping pads were lined up against the wall next to where I slept. I pulled off my clothes and deposited them into the laundry basket, dropped my nightgown over my head, and crawled under the covers.

"Night, girls," I said. Then as convincingly as I could, I added, "I'm going to sleep for eight hours straight. Tomorrow, I'll be firing on all cylinders."

16

My body jerked, springing me from the jaws of the lucid dream that had captured me like a wild wolf in a forgotten rusty trap.

Lying rigid beneath my covers, my muscles cramped from holding them taut for too long.

Through the night, I'd balanced once again on the razor's edge between being alive and being dead.

I was so sick of this. I hated to sleep. Hated the invasive thoughts and sensations when I was awake.

Once again, I thought maybe it would have been better if my team had just let me die out in the desert. Like Prescott had said, sometimes he saved people that he thought were too damaged to ever be okay again.

Still shaking, I leaned over and kissed Striker's shoulder. He snored softly, one arm draped over his eyes.

Good that he slept.

I felt guilty for all the nights when I've woken him, screaming. He probably got better rest when he was downrange on a mission, sleeping amidst the sounds of war.

Sliding silently from beneath the sheets, I tiptoed across the room, signaling my dogs, Beetle and Bella, that they should stay where they were.

Perhaps I could wash some of this dread down the drain along with the sluicing hot water as I stood in the shower.

While most of my nights, I thrashed with nightmares that were forgotten as soon as I opened my eyes, last night, I dreamed that Angel was calling me to him in the bowels of Hell.

"Help me. Come to me," he commanded. *"I need you here. I need you now. Come now. Come now!"*

Come to him…to Hell.

This nightmare had surfaced each night for about a week now. It was frightening how strong the pull was and how much I wanted to go to his voice. The imperative was so forceful, so vivid, so demanding. It has been hard for me to shake it in my waking hours.

Softly shutting the bathroom door so as not to rouse Striker, I flicked on the bathroom lights and blinked against the sudden jolt of brightness.

This morning, I experienced what going to Hell might feel like—tasted it, smelled it, felt it. A swirl of heated air rushed against my body, loosened the skin around my mouth, flapping it, and letting my drool—cool and moist—fleck against my skin. When I reached a surface, it was grainy and radiated intense heat. Standing, walking, it had been so dark I could barely make out the emptiness around me. Off in the distance, there were wails and ululations. The sounds crept over my skin and made me itch. I didn't want to know why the souls moaned out that way.

Regardless, I was drawn in their direction. I had to see for myself. That's where I belonged.

Angel was calling me to my death so I could be with him.

I'd have to talk this over with Avril when I got back from Puerto Rico. Maybe she'd have some insights. I reached past the glass shower doors and turned the tap, letting the warming water hit against my palm while I waited to adjust the temperature.

As others had been suggesting, my heightened emotions probably had to do with the anniversary of Angel's death. If I could make it to the other side of that anniversary, then I'd probably find some relief.

I peeled my nightgown from my shoulders and slid it down my body to pool on the floor at my feet. The crumpled cloth brought up images from the Nigerian file with the plastic crime scene numbers placed next to a piece of bloody clothing, showing that another piece of scientist had been found.

Perhaps last night's nightmares had something to do with Melody Foley and the vivid descriptions that her psyche had painted of Kaylie's death. Her night terrors sounded an awful lot like mine.

Picking the nightgown up, I gave it a flick and settled it on a hook next to the towels.

The idea of the wildlife feasting on Kaylie's body had brought up my own memories that I had shared with Avril of vultures waiting to turn me into their next meal. How I had imagined the delicacy of my eyeballs and liver.

Avril. "This takes time." "Time heals." "We'll work through this. Just keep with the program. Keep on trying." "One foot in front of the other…" and all the other platitudes.

Under the strum of the shower, my anxiety used more than its share of oxygen. I bent to put my hands on my knees and worked to suck a great lungful of air into my body.

I was suffocating in my fear and horror.

Hell was a terrible place.

Here I was, back on that precipice. Back dancing with the Devil.

This time, though, it wasn't about my soul and me.

It was Angel who was in Hell.

I knew it.

Every time I closed my eyes, I could feel Angel burning up. I could feel him begging me to save him.

17

Dressed, fed, and resolute in my determination to stay focused on helping Kaylie, Striker and I left the apartment hand in hand as we walked toward Iniquus. It was a beautiful Indian summer's day. The air felt like warm velvet. Fall wrapped its crisp, spicy scent around us. Sunlight beamed between the clouds. I tipped my head back so I could catch Striker's eye. "You're a mighty handsome man, Commander Rheas."

He pulled my hand to his lips and kissed the back.

I was still a little rubbery feeling from my dreams, newborn giraffe wobbly as I walked.

When I was alone with Miriam in Puerto Rico, I'd talk to her about my experiences and see if she didn't have some techniques to clear the excess psychic energy from my space.

I've been having trouble grounding and meditating. Whenever I sat and closed my eyes to center myself, I felt a pull and drag toward the Veil and into the ether. Never having sought psychic information from someone who was dead before, I thought answering that call to go into the void might be a big mistake.

One thing I understood; I was to the point where I needed someone's help. I hoped Miriam could be that someone, and if not her, then the Galaxy operators.

It was a problem.

My job was to be a problem solver.

I'm on this! I encouraged myself.

I turned and kissed Striker's shoulder. "I love you," I said, shutting my eyes for a moment to connect with those feelings.

When I lifted my lashes, I found Striker's moss green eyes squinting down at me with that assessing look of his. That brought a genuine smile to my lips. "When I get back from Puerto Rico, you'll still be in Poland." We started walking again. "That's going to be an amazing trip. I looked up Krakow, and the architecture is gorgeous. I want to hear all about the non-security details—the food, the clothes, the sights."

Striker dropped a kiss into my hair. "It would be nice if things lined up differently." He tugged my hand, and I let him guide me off the walking path. "I'd like to go down to Puerto Rico with you and pay my respects to Abuela Rosa."

"I'll tell her. She'll appreciate that."

Our feet crunched through the leaves that carpeted the ground with bright crimson and gold.

The scent of river water rode the breeze. We walked amongst the trees until we were away from anyone's scrutiny. Striker leaned against an ancient oak and pulled me into his arms, tucking me under his chin and smoothing down my hair.

I wrapped my arms around him, wanting to relax into this little pause in our day, wanting to be in the moment and feel his love and support. But what I felt was stiffer, more guarded. "You did this once before. Do you remember?" I asked.

"What's that?" Striker released me from his hug and lifted a foot to rest it on the trunk.

"I was wearing a coral and rose dress." I stepped back and sat on a fallen tree. "You were out of uniform, wearing jeans. I was test driving your car that day, and you directed me to the little park with the pine trees. Word had come down your contact channels that Angel and his team had been pinned down in a firefight, and men had been injured but not Angel. Angel was fine. I imagined you wanted me near something that had deep roots. Something that would give me stability, as you told me the bad news. It feels the same right now. I wish you'd just say it."

"All right." He rested his hands akimbo. "As the commander for Strike Force, I'm worried about your ability to function in your job. As your fiancé, worried doesn't even come close. Your nightmares this last week have been kicking up with a vengeance. They seemed to let up in the last year after Indigo and Scarlet were no longer in the picture. It's been a comparatively calm year."

"Yes, it has. I agree." I smoothed the skirt of my dress, resting my folded hands on my lap.

"Your nightmares are worse now than when I first met you in the safe house two years ago, and I thought those were pretty hellish. Then you were thrashing and moaning, calling for help. Now you're screaming in your sleep that you're in Hell."

"I'm sorry. That's not fair to you." While I responded to the nightmares keeping him awake, I was caught on the fact that he thought I might not be functioning at work. My work helped solve crime puzzles, but my main job was to help the team think through the possibilities that made being in harm's way turn deadly. If I missed something or messed up, my team could be impacted in the worst possible way. I couldn't allow that. I sent him a frown. "I'll stay at my house, so you can sleep."

"Stop." The command was quiet but irrefutable. "This is not

a conversation about me or my comfort. This is a conversation about you and your safety."

I nodded as he moved to sit next to me.

"Every night. Several times a night, you get sucked into these episodes." His fingers tightened over mine. "Have you talked to Avril Limb about this?"

"Yes." I swallowed hard. I did my work at the psychiatrist's office, so I could keep my head on straight. But I couldn't shake my feelings about Angel and his death.

They always struck me as odd. I mean, I had grieved before. My dad died when I was seventeen. My mom died when I was nineteen. I mourned them. I missed them. I thought of them daily, but the things I pulled up were the good memories, the sage counsel, the deeply felt love.

I shouldn't compare grief. That's what Avril tells me. She should know; she's got that Harvard psychiatry degree.

But I still do.

Maybe I couldn't shake the terror and nightmares about Angel because I didn't have with him what I had with my parents. I didn't have time. I didn't have a well of memories to draw from. I barely had anything at all except that three weeks when I felt the relief of finding a lost part of me. Like I was a piece of a broken dish, and I'd been glued back together the way I belonged.

Avril has some ideas about that. She didn't want to detract from my time with Angel, but she wanted me to consider the psychological stress I was under. My mentor, Spyder McGraw, suddenly went off on an assignment. My mom died right after. A few months further along, my home, my belongings, my community was destroyed. And there was Angel. Avril wanted me to consider that the draw and pull I felt might have been influenced by these other tragedies.

Avril wasn't there. Didn't feel what I felt when I saw Angel that first time.

I got her point. She thought the grief I felt over Angel was the compilation of all my grieves stitched together into a quilt of loss.

That Angel was the vessel in which I stored all my pain.

Maybe.

"…saying?" Striker asked.

"Sorry, my mind drifted. What was that?"

"What is Avril saying?"

I didn't want to tell him what she was saying. I didn't like what she was saying.

He waited patiently.

"She sees a correlate between our setting a wedding date and the onset of this new spate of nightmares."

He nodded.

"She thinks that our planning our wedding is percolating old fears."

His thumb brushed back and forth over my hand, a gesture he used to soothe me and help me feel supported. "What do you think?"

"That doesn't feel right to me. It doesn't make a lot of sense. We've been engaged for a year now. It's not like we're rushing into anything. We're living together. We're working together. You've been off-grid on missions. Why would our setting a June wedding date percolate my fears?"

"Something to do with bringing our marriage into focus?" He reached up and combed my hair from my face and tucked the strand behind my ear. "Perhaps when we were engaged, it was a commitment that you felt comfortable with. And now that there's a potential date for the wedding, and we're letting your Kitchen Grandmothers know so we can fly them in… There are probably a lot of emotions mixed with seeing them, joy along with the grief of when you lost your community as your apartment complex burned to the ground. You keep yelling about the flames. Inferno. Hell. That you're burning up. So that's one thing. The other is that you call out that you need to save Angel. The apartment building was exploded by Frith and Wilson at the behest of Indigo. I hope you don't feel guilty for the actions of someone else. Actions that you knew nothing about and couldn't have stopped."

I pursed my lips. "I have a plan that might help me. It's unconventional. But nothing else seems to be working."

He canted his head. "Is this a secret?"

"Not really. I'm going to talk to Miriam to see if she has any psychic techniques, and I'm going to talk to General Elliot about going to see the Galaxy operators. I don't have permission, so I don't know if that will work out."

"If you think it'll help, you absolutely should do that. Maybe you need more time before the wedding? There's no pressure from my end, Chica." He caught my chin, so I'd look him in the eyes. "Believe me, I only want you happy. I don't need an officiant standing in front of me pronouncing anything. I don't need a piece of paper from the government. My commitment to you is forged of stronger things."

"I know." I leaned forward, laying my head on his chest, my hands on his shoulders. "Mine too."

He wrapped his hands around mine. His voice was soft when he said, "I'm going to bring up something that I'm going to admit scares me."

I brought my head up—*nothing* scared Striker.

"I thought maybe going to the funeral for Tony Branson might have been a trigger." His fear sent a shadow across his moss-green eyes.

"Tragic." I frowned. "Heart-wrenching. His daughters. His wife. Watching them at his funeral." I opened my mouth and let out a long sigh. "They lost so much when he decided he couldn't anymore." I frowned and looked into the tree line finding solace. "When his little girls, Riley and Charlotte, were overwhelmed in the church and I brought them to my house—Riley looks so much like her dad, her mom would see Tony in her face every day. In that moment, I wished I had Angel's baby so he could live on. But then I thought about Riley and Charlotte both growing up without their dad. And I think about how Indigo targeted me. What might he have done to my child?" I turned and leaned back against Striker.

"That's an interesting thing to say." He wrapped an arm around me and combed his fingers through my hair. "We've talked about children and building a family, but that was something that would happen years down the line." He kissed the top of my head and stopped to breathe me in. "Have you been thinking about becoming a mom? Are you worried our jobs might endanger our children?"

"It's something to weigh when we get to a point where we think it's the right time. I'll be twenty-three when we're married. To be honest, I don't feel a compulsion to pop out babies. I thought that might be part of my life when we're older. Now, since we're talking truths to each other."

"As we always should."

"Yes, always," I repeated. It was a vow we made to each other when we decided to marry. At least what truths we could share without breaking security protocol. "You brought up Tony's funeral. I think you're afraid to come home someday and find that, like Tony, I've decided I can't anymore and have committed suicide."

"It's a fair fear to have. You have PTSD, and death by suicide is a distinct possibility."

"It is." I felt the energy run through Striker's body like a whip of electricity. "But I've never given it a single thought. I've never imagined how I would do it, when I would do it, if I would do it. It's not part of what's going on for me. Though I will tell you, I signed a contract with Avril that stipulates that I must tell her if I ever did start thinking in that direction. Or if I ever thought that I was in too much pain to keep going."

He shifted around to sit me up and turned me to face him. "Why did she have you do that?"

"It's her normal protocol with people with brain trauma or PTSD." I gave a little shrug. I didn't want him to make a big deal about it. "I could sign the same contract with you. The 'do no self-harm until I make the call' contract."

I tipped back and angled my chin up to watch his face. The muscles in his jaw tightened and loosened, tightened and loosened like he was chewing on the thought. He was working hard at his stoic mask.

"How afraid are you when you go away on a mission that I'll hurt myself while you're gone. Be truthful."

"I'm terrified," he said as an exhale.

"Because of something specific about me or because of the friends and colleagues that you've lost?"

"Both. I know too many strong men and women who just *couldn't* anymore."

"I'm a distraction."

"Since the moment I walked into your hospital room to take you to the safe house, yes."

"One that takes your mind off your work? Because Striker, you know that puts you and our team in danger. I can't have that." I shook my index finger at him. "I *won't* have that."

"There's nothing you can do about the way I feel."

"Except to get better, so you aren't worried." My finger was held up in the air like a weapon I was brandishing.

"Okay, stop." He wrapped his hand around my finger and put my palm over his heart. "You can't get better because you want to. This isn't a wish-it-away condition any more than cancer or heart disease. You're doing what you can."

I swallowed. What he was saying was true. But I didn't want it to be. I wanted to be strong enough that I could conquer my brain. But medical science says that's not how this worked.

"I have boxes," Striker said. "You know that. That's how my brain works. When I'm on task, that's all I see, hear, or think."

"But when you have downtime?"

"Then I love you and worry."

"I'm so sorry." Tears glazed my vision.

He used his fingers to tip my head back. "Go to Puerto Rico. Hug Abuela Rosa." He kissed the tip of my nose. "Let's keep talking. I know you don't want to burden me, so you keep this stuff for Avril." He stood, taking hold of my hand as we started back toward the path. "But I want to be the one you turn to. I want to understand what you're going through and support you."

And I just wanted some peace.

18

STRIKER WENT TO FILL OUT REPORTS ON THE PRINCESS OF Monaco and to work with the team on their security research for the Poland trip.

I went to the Puzzle room to check in with Sophia. She'd sent me a text to call her.

I looked at the computer camera. "Hey there. Thanks for taking the video call. How are the boys this morning?"

"Rowdy. They woke up buzzing with energy. Their poor nursery school teachers." She curled up on her desk chair, one foot on the seat, one tucked under her hip. "I made some calls for you last night. We're going to have to wait while they work their ways to the right ears. I was very circumspect. You don't need to worry. I was just asking for connections in the area."

"Thank you." I pulled my hair up off my neck, quickly securing it with a ponytail holder. I'd already kicked off my shoes and was barefoot beneath my desk. I was in thinking mode. "I was reading some articles last night looking for success stories to see how they found their missing people," I said.

"I bet you didn't find any success stories."

"No. I found some ISIS wives from Europe and the States who are in refugee camps who want to come home. There were also some articles about the children of the ISIS fighters being stateless."

"That might help you to be able to get the kids home without as much red tape."

"I came up with a search possibility. I'm just going to throw it out to you and see what your take on it is."

"Okay," Sophia said.

"There was an Australian nurse that was captured. There are people who say they saw this woman over the years. Every time she's been spotted, it's been in connection with a hospital or a clinic. And then I thought, the woman that I'm looking for has a specialty in saving lands from desertification. I looked up the processes that are effective in the Middle East, and I saw that there are good results with something called 'permaculture.' When I look at the footprint of a small permaculture area, it seems to be distinctive."

"It is, though, I don't remember ever seeing it in my satellite images." Tipping her head, she added, "I also wasn't looking for them."

"I would imagine that if Kaylie were somewhere for a period of time—not nomadic—that she might set up these systems as a way to survive by procuring food, keeping herself busy, even proving her worth in case her life was threatened."

"Agreed." Sophia turned her head as she scribbled on her pad. "It's what I'd do. When I get overwhelmed, I try to make at least one thing visibly better. It helps." She laid down her pen and smiled into the camera. "I'll look up the schematics and give it to the computer to learn. I imagine that I'll need all the variants along a continuum from newly dug or constructed to a permaculture area that's been in existence for many years." She picked up an earthenware mug that was probably filled with her ubiquitous chai.

"As many as seven years."

Sophia focused on the wall and blinked as she had her private thoughts. "Seven is a long time," she said under her breath.

"Agreed."

She took a sip from her mug and set it down. "Last night on the border of Iraq and Syria, the ISIS militants publicly executed nineteen young Yazidi women. They were teenagers put into iron cages and burned to death. Their crime was that after they were taken as slaves, these girls refused to have sex with the ISIS fighters."

"Horrific." It was actually so far from my understanding of how humans should treat each other that I couldn't perceive that as real. Even having experienced inhuman behavior, I still couldn't imagine anyone setting me on fire.

"I have so much compassion for Kaylie and what she must have gone through to stay alive. Sometimes *not* fighting leaves you alive to fight another day. I can't imagine the thoughts those girls must have had. The decision making. Last night, when I was talking to my colleague, and they were telling me the story of the girls, I tried to imagine what it would be like to be thrown into a cage and lit on fire."

"Don't do that," I warned. "Don't go there with your brain."

"Knowing what I know. Seeing what I see…" she said. "I'll admit the plight of those girls lit my night with terror. Brian said he was going to stay here every night he's not on duty, so I can take the sleep meds. He's afraid that my work is triggering my PTSD. He worries about me having another seizure. What Brian doesn't fully understand is that I have a drive to help these people in every possible way I can help them. Things would be worse for me if I tried to stop." She picked up her mug and sipped again. "It's like I was just saying about making one small thing better—one tiny piece of progress. I'm hoping that I can get you something that helps Kaylie. It'll do both you and me a lot of good beyond what it does for her and her family. It's a kind of hope."

Melody Foley had talked about hope and how much it hurt. While I would do everything in my power to help Kaylie, I wasn't sure I should add hope to that mix.

I sat quietly to give Sophia time to decide how she wanted our conversation to go.

"In talking to my colleagues, trying to figure out what might have happened in Nigeria that would land Kaylie in Syria, I thought of one person in particular. This is a man who works in finances. He sees the transactions of men selling women. He told me that the Boko Haram leader in Nigeria swore an oath of allegiance to ISIS. The oath said they would support ISIS in times of difficulty and prosperity."

"I read that. It was about the same time frame that Kaylie disappeared."

"When you mentioned the permaculture food cultivation, I'm reminded of a story a colleague told me a long time ago. It could be significant."

"Can I tape this?" I reached toward the button.

"Yes, sure. Ready?"

"With your permission Dr. Sophia Abadi, I am making an audio-only recording of the story you heard from an unnamed colleague."

"You have my permission. Let me look at the notes I wrote down last night. The notes are about the time period Kaylie was in Nigeria, but they have a bearing on my story." She reached out and tapped her keyboard. Her eyes raced back and forth across the screen as she read to herself.

"This information came from my discussion with the financier. He's asking some quiet questions to see if he has resources in the area where Kaylie's baby was last identified." She reached up and scratched the front of her thick black hair. Her eyes shifted their focus from the camera to read the screen. "I guess I'll get to this in a second." She leaned forward, and her face filled my screen. "When you mentioned permaculture, this story came back to me. A colleague of my father was visiting the United States a few years ago, and I went to his hotel for dinner. They were from northern Iraq. His wife was raving about a tomato she once ate. She said that she'd never had such a delicious tomato before or after. It was a beautiful jewel of a tomato. The skin was perfectly ruby red and warm from the sun. When she bit into it, the juices squirted from her mouth and dripped down her chin. She remembered the taste and how delighted she was. She said the tomato came from an unusual garden, one the wife had never seen before. Rock walls, deep ditches between the trees, leafy awnings to protect the plants. She wanted her husband to construct such an oasis for her."

"Do you remember who told you this story? Can we call them for more information?"

"Sadly, he and his family were killed by ISIS. I can tell you what I remember. Listening to his wife's delight in this tomato gave me a very clear image, and there too was the African connection which I rarely deal with."

She bit her upper lip. "Back to the history part. In Nigeria. Polygamy was not recognized as a civil marriage up until 2000. In southern Nigeria, it's not recognized, but in many of the northern states, they've voted to follow Sharia law. Under this law, a man can take as many as four wives as long as he treats them equally. He can also have a fifth wife to whom he's not married and whom he does not have to treat equally. These are his slaves. My colleague, the one who is in finance, said that the government officials wished for fifth-wives."

"Plural?"

"A fifth wife is merely the term to call your slave. You can have as many fifth wives as you'd like."

"Understood." I leaned forward in anticipation.

"That's the background for this next part of the tomato story. My colleague's wife sought out the woman who had raised such a luscious tomato. She was a fifth-wife in that household." Sophia stopped talking for a moment to take a sip of her drink and leaned back in her chair, cradling the mug against her. "The story goes like this, the government official who wanted fifth-wives sent out a team to gather women from the countryside—men to work the fields and women to serve him in his home. The team followed his orders. They found a group of people, captured them, and drove them, in the back of two trucks, to the border of Zamifara, Nigeria and Niger. These trucks were ambushed by men in uniform."

"Kaylie?" My eyebrows were in my hairline. "Could you have heard this story about Kaylie?"

"It's the right timeline, but the wrong physical description. This woman was of African descent. But it's possible that this woman was in the research group. I say that because permaculture is—as I remember reading about it—a distinctive way to farm. If the research group was teaching permaculture as they moved across Africa, she could have been one of the native speakers that they hired to teach, or it could have been one of the women who had learned. But it seems to me that it would be unusual otherwise for this woman to know the techniques. I'm reaching back in my memory, I remembered how shocked I was that the woman telling the story was fine with the enslavement of the woman who grew the tomato, and rather incurious about how she'd been transported from Africa to Iraq."

"Do you know more about the kidnapping?"

"There were two trucks that drove a group north toward Niger. I can tell you that there is a—there was a very active slave route out of Niger to the ISIS fighters. Work has been done to disrupt the movement. There are fewer Africans being brought to the Middle East now."

"Thank goodness."

"It doesn't solve the problem. It simply shifts to different victims. The ISIS fighters want the reward of their sex slaves. The ISIS command gets those slaves where they can. Thousands of Yazidi have been gathered up and enslaved." She swallowed. "If they don't comply, the women and girls are beheaded or burned to death like those nineteen Yazidi girls in the cage last night."

I nodded. It all felt so overwhelming. "I guess the best we can hope for is that we can destroy ISIS in Syria and free the women." I thought about all the mental health help Sophia and I were getting and how hard it would be to be a victim of such atrocities and have no medical help at all. No medicines. No counseling. No resources.

"ISIS is one of the wealthiest terror groups that's ever existed. Slave trade, black market conflict relic trade, drugs. All they'll do is pick up and move their headquarters to another country. It doesn't have to be Syria. Africa will be next. That's what I think." She shifted around. "Back to my story. The people were kidnapped and in the back of two trucks. The trucks were ambushed. The tomato-woman thought that the ambush was a rescue mission, border guards that had come to save them. The men were in uniforms. It was bad. The kidnappers were all killed in the fight. The men from the group of hostages were lined up, then they were all shot and left for dead. The women were loaded into the trucks, and the uniformed men drove them away. The tomato-growing woman was given to an African man as a fifth wife, along with two of the other women who were with them."

"Seven wives," I said as a chill ran down my spine.

"I was telling you that in many places, a man can have up to four wives, and the slaves that they add are called fifth wives, no matter the number. Four wives and three slaves can be legal."

"As I was going to St. Ives, I met a man with seven wives." I had already postulated that going to St. Ives meant that *I* would go on a hazardous journey. Meeting a man with seven wives could very well mean that I'd come across a slaveholder.

It was possible.

I'd meditate on that later.

"Then she was sold?" I asked.

"She was given as a gift to show deference to an ISIS leader. The leader brought her to Iraq. It happened to so many women. But only so many women would have skills in planting tomatoes in this unique way. Whether or not Kaylie had any part in that tomato story, she had to have known the risks of working in this region. Just like the nurse you mentioned earlier, Kaylie was working in a volatile and very dangerous country as she did her research."

"Like you."

"Hardly. I sit at my desk and observe the horrors from afar. I can't imagine being brave enough to go over to the war zone."

19

As I hung up with Sophia, a tap sounded on the door frame of the Puzzle Room.

"Hey there." I waved to Prescott. "Come on in. Shut the door behind you if you don't mind."

He held a briefcase in one hand and a to-go cup of coffee in the other. "Morning."

I lifted an open palm toward the chair next to mine. "Did you see Zoe this morning?"

He set his things on the evidence table and came to sit. "I did."

"How'd it go?"

"Zoe being Zoe, she had a badge waiting for me at security and had an updated machine sitting on her lab counter."

I chuckled. "That woman has mad brain skills."

"She said that she figured that you'd convince me to go after the kids, make me think it was my idea, and I'd be heading over to Iraq like it was the best thing that ever happened to me."

I sat back with a grin. "No, she didn't."

"I swear on my mother's grave."

"Your mom's not dead."

"Fine. Still. I'm telling the truth."

"Why did Zoe have a different machine for you? Why not just use the prototype you were experimenting with for the FBI?"

"I was part of a working group that was helping Zoe understand how things functioned in the field, what the wear and tear would be on the machines, what circumstances we would be operating under. We were in the developmental stages when the effort was shelved at the request of the CIA." He looked down at my bare feet. "Thinking mode, huh?"

"I go with what works." I grinned. "Zoe told me the CIA was afraid that if the FBI used the information in a courtroom, that a judge could order her to explain how blood markers worked, and that information would then be available to the public. It could then come out that there was a collection center. The fear was that once BIOMIST became public knowledge, it would complicate the CIA's effort to populate the data system."

"Exactly. She was working on a plan to get the machines back in the hands of the FBI to see if they could be effective. And that was two-fold. One, to create protocols for using the system that would not leave it open to discovery in preparing a defense case. Two, to make it so the machine couldn't fall into anyone else's hands for reverse engineering."

"Acid."

"Just like her micro-robotic WASPs only on a larger scale. She has the newest iteration of the analyzer rigged, so if anyone tries to access it without a certain thumbprint, mine for example, then the machine melts the hard drive."

"In movies, the bad guy would kill you and hack off your thumb."

He stilled and blinked. "Thanks for that."

"A pleasure." I laughed. "This machine, you can take over to Iraq without the CIA getting miffed?"

"Zoe got their blessing. They actually want to see if the apparatus can stand up to environmental pressures as well as spit out analysis on the spot. They think that might help them if they capture enemy troops. They can use the information as pressure."

"Wait." I ran through those words again. "Like, they could get the names of the detainee's close kin and threaten their kin?"

"It could be an effective tool."

"I can think of about ten reasons why that particular tool would be a bad idea. But that's not my field of expertise. It does, however, correlate to point number four on my list." I reached over and scratched out that item. "Point number four—" I focused back on Prescott. "When Zoe ran the search for me yesterday, the database was looking for a familial match to Kaylie. The output found the three kids. Given the parameters of the search, the BIOMIST system could not show who the fathers were from Kaylie's blood. But—"

"Zoe could do a BIOMIST search on each of the children and see if she can't identify familial biomarkers from close family members. With that information, we might be able to track those family members down and ask them questions if not find the children."

"Exactly. I must be off my game, or I would have seen it earlier."

"I didn't think of it either, don't beat yourself up about it. I'll call over and ask Zoe to do that after we're done here."

"You have the equipment. What's next?"

"I have a green light to go to Iraq as a four-person team. If the children we find have Kaylie's biomarkers, we're supposed to get a DNA sample for comparison."

"Iniquus can do that in-house and move it to the front of the queue," I said.

"Good, I was depending on that to shorten the time. We're working on a plan for next steps if we identify any of the children as Americans. Our lawyers are consulting on the situation."

"Which child are you looking for first?" I asked.

"Child number two. The three-year-old male. His last known location is closest to an Army base. The baby is in disputed territory. It'll be harder for us to get there. The oldest child has the most time between intake and now."

"With the volatility and population movement, that might prove to be an obstacle. Having more family names from Zoe could help us over that hurdle." I picked up a pen and tapped it against my thigh.

"All three locations on the list are remote. The villagers would have had little in the way of outside interaction. That and a smaller population might make it easier. We'll only know once we're boots on the ground. If we can prove one child has a DNA match—well, DNA is something we can talk about publicly, and BIOMIST most certainly is *not*—then we can get Melody in and give her the information. I'm not sure how the family will react."

"Understood."

I pulled over my list from my searches last night and handed it to Prescott.

He scanned down my notes, nodding his head. "Can I have this?" He raised his brow. "I'll want to take this back and have my teamwork on these items."

"That's your copy."

He stopped with his finger resting on an item. "What's the URL?"

"An audio of a story Sophia told me."

He nodded and kept reading. "How's she doing?"

"She's doing better now that the domestic crazy has been scraped off her plate. She's still in the fight to stop ISIS's exploiting the Syrian relics. And on that subject, Sophia told me she's going to spend some time with the satellite images today. She'll contact me if she sees anything that we might find helpful. She'll also be quietly reaching out to people to see if anyone knows about Kaylie. I mentioned that Kaylie might be hiding her nationality as a way to stay alive."

Prescott slid the notes into his briefcase, nodding to keep me talking.

"I saw in the file that the researchers' passports were all found in the tents," I said. "Whoever drove the group away didn't have proof of their nationalities. That Kaylie was in such a diverse group might have helped her with her subterfuge. Sophia won't mention country of origin as she's checking her resources, simply that we're looking for an educated woman who might have been kidnapped out of Africa about a decade ago."

His focus went to the wall as he processed.

"She was adventurous, obviously. From the photo you showed me with the child, she looks not just fit but like someone who is comfortable using her body—climbing, hiking—is that right?"

"When I knew her, yes. Of the kids our age in my neighborhood growing up, she and Melody were the only girls. Melody stayed inside playing the piano while Kaylie played with us boys. She went at it as hard as we did—and I mean everything: tree climbing, bike riding, wrestling, fort building, football tackles. Nothing intimidated her." He chuckled under his breath. "Her nickname in our neighborhood was Trouble. Or, as my mom would say, 'her poor mother, that child is trouble with a capital T.' Not," Prescott qualified, "because she did anything bad. She was a good kid. She was fearless, and I guess most of the mothers thought Kaylie should try to act more like her sister —bake cookies, sew doll clothes. Kaylie was a paradigm buster."

I paused before speaking, getting a picture of Kaylie's personality and how she might have responded the night the research team disappeared. "That could work in her favor in a survival situation. Is Kaylie multi-lingual?"

"She speaks English, which is the official language of Nigeria, high school and college French, Kiswahili from her time in Tanzania. I imagine she picked up some words of local dialects as she moved west across the continent. But there are over five hundred languages spoken in Nigeria alone. Why?"

"Language and survival often go hand in hand. You can't ask for help or ask someone to turn a blind eye if you don't have the language. While they speak English in Nigeria, the dismembered parts of her fellow researchers were found on the Niger border. If she got across the border, she'd need French. If she's in Syria, the Kiswahili would help her quickly learn Arabic, and that would help her to survive in Syria. You said the photographed woman was in the north. She'd need to speak Kurdish there. But in my experience, once your brain figures out how to learn one language, to listen and speak it, then others are learned quickly."

"To be honest, Lynx," Prescott said, "up until you landed on Zoe and BIOMIST, I couldn't imagine this case going anywhere. But that's why I asked for you. You sometimes seem plugged into the universe in a way that us mortals are not." He gave me a half-smile.

I stiffened. "Your sarcasm is unappreciated."

"That's not sarcasm."

Pressure built in my chest. If I did what he thought I could do, it would mean sending a rescue team into Syria. My findings could put an entire task force right into ISIS's hands. Iniquus, or

CIRG, or both. I'd better be damned sure of myself before I put lives at risk for a shadow.

I pushed my hair behind my ear.

Prescott caught my gaze and squinted his eyes. "You look exhausted. Full workload?"

"I'm fine. I just haven't had my coffee yet."

He shifted his weight from left to right in his seat.

"Spit it out," I said.

"It's coming up on the anniversary of your husband's death. I'm sorry for your loss."

I canted my head. How the heck would Prescott know about my husband?

"Becky is having trouble sleeping, too."

"Becky?"

"Becky Baldwin."

"Peanut's wife," I whispered. "He was in the truck that followed behind Angel's."

"Peanut and I were in the Army together, since his entire team…well, it's landed on the people who knew him before he joined the Rangers to look out for the families. An honor for us to step up."

"Small world." I nodded. "Can I ask you a question?"

He lifted his chin as a yes.

Normally, I didn't bring up peoples' personal lives when I was functioning as an Iniquus employee, but Prescott had opened the can of worms with his noticing I looked like crap. Enough so that he felt compelled to check in. "Did you go to Peanut's funeral?"

"I was there."

"Was it open coffin or closed coffin?"

"Open. The guys over at Dover did a stellar job. They always do. Why?"

"Nothing. Just… did you know any of the other men? Did you go to any of the other funerals?"

"No. Is this heading somewhere? I can see thoughts whirring."

I wasn't sure why I had wanted to ask him that. I decided to change the subject. "Panther Force came in yesterday morning from their mission. I saw Brainiack last night at Sophia's."

"I've worked with Panther Force before." Prescott shot a surreptitious glance at the wall clock. "Do you think they'll be the team assigned to go after Kaylie? General Elliot won't put boots on the ground until they have solid intelligence."

"Right. Yes. I wasn't thinking that. I was actually thinking about Sophia and Brainiack, Zoe and Gage. I was thinking about Tanzania and Randy. I was thinking about Honey Honig and, most recently, Thorn. Do you know what all of those missions have in common?"

"Lives on the line, I'm guessing."

"Scientists," I said. "Scientists who applied their brains to puzzles of world importance like Kaylie."

He scrubbed a hand over his face and exhaled. "It's jarring to hear you use the present tense when I've thought of her in past tense for almost a decade." He planted his hands on his knees and leaned forward to stare at the tip of his shoe. "I could have done more. I obviously should have done more."

"Like what? You were acting under orders."

He nodded, unconvinced.

"The scientists that Panther Force cases have involved weren't just smart, they had a knowledge base. They had creativity. *And* they had fitness. That's an equation that adds up to a better shot at survival. Kaylie was alive eleven months ago. Granted, eleven months is a long time in a war zone. But it's possible we can get to her in time."

Without saying a word, Prescott stood, pulling his lips tight. Briefcase in hand, he turned and strode off. Two steps toward the door and he called back over his shoulder. "It's like rocket fuel." He pointed at the to-go cup he left sitting on my table. "Maybe you should lay off the coffee for a little while. I tried to drink that cup on my way up to see you, and I don't think I'll ever be able to sleep again."

20

I TWIDDLED MY PEN IN MY FINGERS, REVIEWING WHAT PRESCOTT had said about me.

People were noticing I wasn't on my game. I lived with and slept (sort of slept) with Striker. Of course, he saw what others didn't. But Margot? Prescott? Not just noticing, but it being so obvious that they felt compelled to share their concerns over my welfare.

My not asking Zoe to do separate searches of the kids? That was a ridiculously obvious next step. Why didn't I catch it while I was at her lab?

I had to fix this.

Me.

I had to fix *me*.

I checked the wall clock. It wasn't quite time for me to meet with General Elliot, but I was going to head up there now.

I slid my feet into my kitten-heeled shoes, closed the Puzzle Room door behind me, and decided to take the stairs as I walked to the Commanders' wing.

I thought best when I was moving. I worked through a lot of

issues on my daily run. If need be, I'd pace back and forth in my office with bare feet. It got my thoughts flowing.

As I moved toward the stairwell, I was thinking about Striker.

My psychiatrist had another theory she wanted me to consider. Striker might be part of the problem. And the reason I'm getting worse, not better.

As if Striker could be a problem.

Absurd.

Though, Striker wasn't really what Avril was suggesting was the problem but my relationship with Striker more specifically.

And yeah, I admit it, I've had emotional Striker issues from the moment I met him. We met as two different people. First, I met him when I was a teen, training under my mentor, Spyder. That's when I was Alex. Alex could have been a boy or a girl or completely without gendered parts because Alex was a silent ghost who was secretly crushing on Striker Rheas the demi-god and completely drool-worthy.

I pushed through the door to the stairs and caught the handrail as I made my way up.

Early Striker had been fantasy Striker.

Then, when I was attacked by Travis Wilson, I was a very wounded Lexi Sobado in the hospital. That's when Striker became 3D as part of the team that was meant to help protect me and solve the case.

He was a person, not a myth.

In my tumultuous fight to survive Travis Wilson, Striker was a resting place. A moment of peace. A life vest thrown into the turbulent waters for me to cling to.

With Angel gone and Striker right there, I'll admit, it got confusing for me. Like I was tied to Angel but belonged, somehow, to Striker instead.

And there was a metric ton of guilt surrounding my confusion.

It was strange. And this was something that I'd never found an answer to—one of the few things that my therapist didn't postulate a theory about: While I thought I felt guilty about my feelings when I was under Striker's protection, it was a sense of guilt imposed by how I thought others would be judging me. Like I was caught with my hand in someone else's cookie jar kind of guilt.

Though, nothing physical ever happened between Striker and me while Angel was alive.

I rounded the landing and took the next set of stairs.

After Angel's death, those guilty feelings changed.

I remembered the *exact* moment.

The night the IED exploded the vehicles transporting Angel's Ranger unit home from a mission, I woke up in shock, unable to think, to process. I knew on a cellular level that something horrible had happened.

I later determined, that sense of shock, the one that seemed to lift me up in the air and throw me down on the bed, waking me up into a place of suspended animation, was the exact moment Angel blew up with the IED.

I knew that that day, the military would send their representatives to inform me of Angel's death.

But that wasn't when the guilt shifted.

It was on the flight to Puerto Rico, two days later, with Angel's coffin in the luggage hold of the plane. I was going down to bury Angel per his wishes. Strike Force was with me. And I was still numb. But up under the numb came the sensation of guilt, deep-down guilt that had more to do with purposefully breaking a bond. *Deciding* to break a bond.

What was that all about?

Certainly, I had never cheated on Angel. Striker and I had never even kissed. We hadn't made love until we were engaged almost a year later. It was two years since Angel's death. Two years of this broken-bond guilt.

Did I think there was some way that I could have kept Angel alive? Something I didn't do that would have helped him survive? I thought that the look on Prescott's face when he was confronted with Kaylie's survival was familiar to me. It was a feeling that I carried around with me.

Baggage. Too much baggage. Too many woulda, coulda, shoulda.

I crossed my fingers, whispering, "Please, General Elliot, let me go to see the Galaxy operators. I don't know how else to help Angel's soul."

I pushed through the heavy door and stepped onto the carpet, sinking my heels into the deep pile.

I loved Striker. My future lay with him, of that, I had no doubt. Any doubts I had about that were cleared from my mind when I was dying in the desert after the plane crash. I hesitated about our relationship during my crash recovery for fear that I was just too big of a horror magnet, too big of a problem to impose my cloud of bad juju on anyone. But Striker convinced me that he was a big boy and could make decisions like that for himself. If he was willing to tie his cart to my stampeding horse, it was a personal decision that he made willingly. Then he laughed as if that image was comical to him.

I didn't think it was funny.

But I let go of trying to regulate and manipulate our relationship and allowed it to be what it wanted to be.

As I moved up the corridor, I felt Angel call to me through the ether, *I'm in Hell.*

I put a steadying hand on the wall, dropping my head as I tried to take a breath. Anxiety sucked.

I worked to shift my thoughts away from Angel and onto Kaylie, but Kaylie, too, had kissed her family and flown away, never to be seen again. Now, a judge told her family that their beloved Kaylie had been gone long enough to pronounce her dead.

They'd buried the essence of her without seeing her body.

That was very much like what had happened to me.

The parallels in our stories, the grief, and horror that Melody was swimming in, made the tempest waters roar louder through my system, foaming up into a night of fight-mares, of terror-mares, of adrenaline-soaked guilt-mares.

I set out walking again, heading straight toward a smiling Leanne.

Angel was distracting me from my work.

Angel was *dead*.

Kaylie, though, had a shot at survival.

Prescott had thought we had a week to get to the woman in the photo. But after the attack and the band of refugees scattered… Who knew if they had food? Or water.

You can't live without water.

Her time frame could be down to days, in that heat? Hours.

And here I was, fighting to stay effective.

21

I FINGER WAVED AT LEANNE. "HEY THERE, THE GENERAL SAID I could have five minutes of his time."

"Let me check and see if he's ready for you." Leanne worked her way around her desk, taking mini-steps in her tight pencil skirt, expertly balancing in her Louboutin stilettos despite the thick carpet. That took some core strength. I bet she did Pilates.

As she shut the door to the General's office behind her, I stared over at the prisms of the Tsukamoto mobile, *Gateway to Nirvana*. I let it mesmerize me, heal me. If only I could stand and stare at one of Tsukamoto's incredible works all day long, I thought, I'd be just fine.

Leanne stepped from behind the general's door before I wanted her to. "Lynx, he'll see you now."

I walked into General Elliot's office and right into his arms that were outstretched for a hug.

He planted a grandfatherly kiss on my head. "Well, young lady. It's not often you come to visit me."

"I don't want to wear out my welcome."

"The Mrs. was talking about you just this morning." He

moved to the wing chair and sat down stiffly. "She wants you to come around to dinner. I thought you might be showing up this morning because you *felt* her invitation, and you just wanted to know what time to come." He chuckled as he shifted around to a comfortable slouch in his chair. Then waggled his hand toward the chair opposite his.

I liked that General Elliot knew I had psychic abilities. He was one of the very few who knew the extent of them. And he appreciated how it was both a blessing and a curse.

To him, my skills were mostly a blessing; they'd saved him from a psychic attack by Indigo and Scarlet. A militarily trained attack that left the general in a coma.

"I would like that very much. Maybe once I've got this Kaylie Street case wrapped up."

"Kaylie Elizabeth Street was one of Iniquus's early cases when I left the Galaxy project, and we started up our international hostage response team." He pursed his lips. "Always bugged me that case. The pieces didn't fit together right."

"I had a thought," I said, finding my place on the very edge of the chair. "I'd like your permission to pursue it, though."

He leaned back.

"What if I took a trip up to Wyoming?"

He rubbed his bottom lip between his index finger and his thumb. "To see my friends from the Galaxy project? You want to work with remote viewers?"

I found myself clutching at the sides of my thighs like I was trying to hold myself together. I *needed* his permission. "I know it's not the way we normally work—"

"There's a reason for that. We'd be out of business if the Pentagon got wind that we utilized remote viewing intelligence. The brass has painful memories of the time that we tried to combat the Russian parapsychologists and remote viewers with our own. When the program came out in public, it made for a political and budgetary scandal. The military became the butt of public ridicule. Reputation is everything in the military. The same feeling pervades the other alphabets."

"I understand. I do." That sure sounded like a no. "Just to briefly catch you up on what happened yesterday with the Kaylie Street case, if that would be okay?"

"Good." He patted his knees.

"When Iniquus decided to pro bono protect Zoe Kealoha from the would-be kidnappers, she has never forgotten your generosity. Her BIOMIST system helped us in France when Panther Force needed answers, and her BIOMIST data was able to help us again with Kaylie. In both cases, Zoe was providing the information off the books. You should know what an asset she's been."

"Noted. We'll keep tabs on her and make sure Zoe has what she needs when and if she needs us. Just that much information tells me that Kaylie survived Nigeria and somehow found herself in the Middle East. She must have gone through a hearts-and-minds medical check."

"No, sir, she did not. But there are three babies who did."

His brow pulled together. "Kaylie's children?"

"Yes, sir."

"Are we getting them out? Special Agent in Charge Damian Prescott is on the case, right?"

"Yes, sir. There's a connection. One of those, 'wow, it's a small world' things."

"Oh, you know better than that. You travel in the ether. You know how things are aligned."

"I know how I make things seem reasonable in my mind." I smiled. "How it all works? No, I don't have a good grasp on that.

In this case, though, I would agree. It seems that things are lined up. Damian Prescott grew up in the same neighborhood as Kaylie Street. They played together as children. He was surprised when his CIRG unit was sent to Nigeria to find that his childhood friend was one of the missing scientists."

The general frowned and nodded as he listened.

"Flash forward a bit, and he was here in Washington D.C. when he was asked to be involved in the development of a hand-held field blood analyzer. They were giving feedback on a prototype for Zoe when the project got put on a shelf so the CIA could protect the BIOMIST system. Zoe knew Prescott and sent him an SOS from under her bed when the kidnappers were in her apartment. Because of their history and his work with her on that blood biomarker prototype, Zoe's given Prescott permission to take her hand-held analyzer into the field, with the CIA's blessing, to see if he can't track down Kaylie's children. He told me just now that he's been given the green light for a four-person team. They're suiting up to head downrange. They should be in Iraq by tomorrow."

"A step forward." He laced his fingers, steepling the index fingers and putting them under his chin. "What about Kaylie herself?"

"Prescott told me last night that the group of people who were making their way to the border—the ones picked up by the NSA images—were attacked by ISIS fighters. Many of the refugees were killed. The ones who survived ran into the surrounding hills for shelter. To begin with, we don't know if that was a picture of Kaylie that the NSA flagged. Second, we don't know if that woman was one of those caught in the explosions. We need boots on the ground, but that's a non-permissive environment."

"What are we doing about it?"

"I spoke with Dr. Sophia Abadi last night. At my request, she's reaching out to her Syrian contacts to see if anyone has heard of an American woman in the area. And of course, the CIA is also involved."

"But you want to head up to Wyoming."

I smoothed out the skirt of my dress. "I'm going to be honest, sir. I decided that I wanted to go up there because I was hoping they could help me with a personal matter. But now I'm thinking it might be the best shot we have for finding Kaylie Street. Two birds…"

"When were you thinking of going?"

"I'm flying to Puerto Rico to see Abuela Rosa for the anniversary of my husband's death. I'll stay in contact and work remotely if I'm needed. But with the Kaylie Street case, I'm in a holding pattern, waiting for information to come in. I was planning to fly to Wyoming on Thursday, straight from Puerto Rico."

"If I said no to your using Galaxy operators to look for Kaylie?"

"I still need to go talk to the Galaxy team." I wished I had a glass of water. My mouth was so dry, my lips were sticking to my teeth. "As I said, I have personal reasons."

His head bobbled while he thought. After a moment, he said, "One of the problems that my men and women had as they developed their remote viewing skills with the Galaxy Project was that there was a whole lot of noise that was hard to clear. Lots of psychic vibrations and information." He shook his hands near his head. "A thinning of the veil. There aren't many people who could commiserate with what they were experiencing. Not many people who could intervene when they needed help." He stroked a finger along the edge of his jawline and rested it on his lip. "Yup, it's there around the outside of your eyes and in the way you're pursing your mouth, like your trying not to show pain while a needle is being jabbed into a nerve bundle. I recognize it."

I shifted around. Seemed like I wasn't doing a great job hiding my problems.

"I know you have Miriam Laugherty in your corner. She's good at what she does. I have the utmost respect." He shook his head. "But it isn't the same. She can't do what you can. And you can't do what the Galaxy soldiers can. But I bet they have some ways they can help you ease your burden. They had a gal that's been working with them since we noticed this problem with our remote viewers. Sort of a psychic doctor, if you will. We just call her Doc. Not a very imaginative code name. She's rather a practical gal. The name fits." He pursed his lips. "I think you should make it a habit to go up and see the others. Talk things through. Get checked out by Doc. I'm *ordering* you to do that. I'll set up an account with General Coleridge to cover the costs of training, counsel, whatever they want to call it. You're to go up and check in on an every-other-month basis. More if need be. We need you whole and healthy. You're an asset to Iniquus." He bent forward to pat my hand. "And you've got a special place in this old guy's heart. You hear?"

"Thank you." I squeezed his hand.

"You take good care. I'd like you to stop by my office when you get back."

And just like that, I was cleared to go.

I hope this works.

"One more thing, sir."

He lifted his brows.

"Indigo had been doing remote searches on me when he was alive. I was hoping to look something up from his lab notes I saw in passing."

"About the attacks, he was orchestrating against you?"

"No, sir, it was actually about Scarlet Vine and her obsession with Striker. When Scarlet was getting confused about what she saw during her remote viewing of Striker, she asked her dad to do the same task so she could compare notes. I saw something I wanted to review."

General Elliot didn't answer right away. "You have to be careful. These aren't oracles. The remote viewing findings have just over a fifty-fifty chance that they're right." He dipped his chin.

"His conclusions were accurate on this particular point, sir. I wanted to see the tasking sheet to see if there is more information about how he reached his conclusion."

"Can you tell me what situation we're talking about?"

I held his gaze. "I'd rather not, sir. It's personal in nature."

"To do with Striker? Your team?"

"No, sir. To understand the circumstance of my husband's death."

"His memory haunting you?"

I looked up to find sympathy in his eyes. Not exactly the norm for this man. General Elliot wasn't the sentimental type by any stretch of the imagination. He was a diamond in the rough, in the sense that diamond is the hardest material on Earth.

His sharp edge was honed in the Vietnamese jungles.

I'd trust him in anything. Follow him anywhere.

But I wouldn't let his sympathy sink into my psyche.

I thrust my shoulders back. "That would be a fair way to put it, sir."

22

"I'LL DIRECT LEANNE TO TAKE YOU TO THE FILE ROOM." General Elliot spread his feet wider and pushed on his knees as he stood. "The lab notes have been digitalized and are searchable. For tight security's sake, they're only stored on the one computer designated for that singular purpose. If you need the original copies, they're stored on a shelf in there, off to the side. Leanne can set you up in the file room. Oh, and here." The general got a trickster-gleam in his eyes. He stalked over to his sofa and picked up a throw pillow. "I'll tell Leanne that if you decide to take a nap in there, that it's A-Okay."

He was poking fun. Probably more at Leanne than at me.

One of the times that I had gone into the file room, I had fallen asleep on the floor. Granted, I was recovering from the plane accident, and Leanne had thought I'd passed out. She called the medic. And Striker. The problem with the situation was that only one person could get through the security system to the file room at a time. And I was that "one." The files were protected with gates and alarms.

Striker had to stand in the doorway calling to me, trying to get me to rouse so I could stumble out on my own.

Had it been a real emergency, and had Striker hustled in to save me, we would have been trapped in there with no equipment and no easy way to get out.

Obviously, Leanne had ratted me out to General Elliot, or he wouldn't be having his fun by handing me the pillow.

I wriggled my knees as I waited for the general to phone his directives to Leanne. General Elliot's office was always considered high security, and Leanne was not allowed to monitor by camera or audio.

If the General wanted Leanne involved, he would have chosen his meeting room one door down from here.

I left his office to join Leanne, who was standing outside, ready for me. She looked down at the pillow and blushed as we walked through the suite.

"You remember how this works." She tapped in a code, and the wall slid to the side to expose the hidden door. "I have to go in and get the research computer booted up. There's no Wi-Fi connection in there. You can't send files anywhere."

"It's okay. I just wanted to read something. And you know, take a little nap." I laughed.

While I waited for Leanne to get through security and set the computer up for me, I made mental notes for next steps. I needed to throw a bag together with both hot weather clothes for Puerto Rico and cold weather clothes for Wyoming. And maybe I could take a piece of my art to Mrs. Coleridge as a hostess gift. Striker and the team would be gone, but Nutsbe from Panther Force was crazy about Beetle and Bella; I needed to find a pupsitter.

It seemed Leanne was taking overly long in there. Of course, my anxiety was pretty high, so that warped my perception.

When she re-emerged, she tapped the code panel again.

Everything closed down, then opened back up with a yellow light shining over the door.

Leanne opened her palm toward the antechamber where my biometrics would be read, reaching to take the pillow from my hand.

The space was about the size and shape of a closet, and I didn't like the idea of being trapped in there anymore this time than I did the other times I've walked through this process. With my hands at my side, I opened my eyes wide, trying not to blink.

There was a flash of green light, then a panel glided open. Stepping up, I placed my palm on the scanner. Again, the light flashed green, and this time the file room door slid open. I turned to Leanne. "Will the alarm sound and the gate slam shut if you hand me the pillow?"

"He was joking," Leanne said. "You aren't planning on passing out again, are you?"

"I really don't think I passed out last time. But I had a rough couple of nights, so I might just take advantage of my time under the Tsukamoto bliss mobile and take a power nap."

She gave me a half-smile.

"I'm actually not kidding."

Leanne turned the pillow on its side and handed it straight out. There must be a hole in the infrared security system so files can be handed to someone to put into place; otherwise, I wasn't sure how one could get papers through the system.

"You have to hold the pillow up and turn three-sixty," Leanne explained. "Wait for the light to flash again. Security is monitoring."

I had forgotten how James Bond this all was.

I went straight over to the desk and sat in front of the computer screen, typing ANGEL into the search bar.

The number of entries that came up was a surprise.

Scrolling back to the beginning, I was also surprised at how early his name appeared. Angel's notes started well before Angel and I even met.

But why?

I scanned along: Scarlet wanted to marry Striker, and, in tasking to look at Striker's future, Indigo saw I was the woman who Striker would marry. I thought back to what I knew of Striker's relationship with Scarlet. And yes, that lined up. Gator told me that Striker and Scarlet had dated a year before the team had met me. Scarlet had thought that Christmas she'd get her engagement ring. When that wasn't the case, then she thought new year, new relationship, she'd get her ring on New Year's Eve at midnight. But no, instead, Striker had broken up with her. All the while, she'd been doing remote viewing, trying to see their future together. And so had Indigo. Instead, he saw Striker and me happily married. He tracked me down. Found out where I lived. That was right after Spyder had gone off-grid and mom had died.

I read through the pages that followed. Task after task, Indigo gathered more information.

Some of it correct; some not so much.

The trick I had learned with remote viewing was that you pick a subject matter you wanted to learn about, and you view it repeatedly. This repetition increased the probability that what you were seeing was correct. A sixty percent accuracy could rise into the mid-eighties. And that was a significant shift in probability, especially if you could then get eyes and ears on a situation to verify like Indigo did. And yes, here were notes that his henchmen Frith and Wilson had been helping to stalk me for information.

Over and over, the tasks were viewed, attacking the question from different angles.

It was the same way I went about solving puzzles. The macro is rarely the thing that solves the puzzle; it's the micro-information where I succeed in coming to an understanding.

It was in this early time frame that Indigo wondered how I came to know Striker, thinking he could just thwart that meeting. But he saw I had already met Striker through my connection to Spyder and to Iniquus. He was seeing me as Alex from the description of the gray hoody and glasses, making me look like the Unabomber, sans mustache.

Whew, that lit him on fire. Pages were filled with his rage. Even in transcription from his notebooks to the computer, his words held onto the power of his wrath. I didn't want them polluting my already overwrought system.

I moved quickly forward in the file.

As Indigo's fury settled to a seething poison, he noted that he wouldn't let General Elliot or Spyder steal another morsel from his daughter. Not a single bite of her future. Not only would Indigo stop me, but he'd also use me. He'd extract his revenge through me.

This was where my nightmare began with Indigo's decision. It's lasted all these years, and I've never been able to rouse myself and shake it off.

It was Indigo all along.

Emotions bubbled along the surface of my skin like the blisters of black plague, dark and deadly.

I forced my gaze onto the screen. Forced myself to read on.

Indigo searched the ether for another "mate" for me.

He found Angel.

He noted that Angel was part of my "warrior learning group" along with others. "Warrior learning group"…huh. I leaned over the pad Leanne had laid out and scrawled notes to take up to General Coleridge.

Indigo said that as a member of my learning group, Angel would already feel familiar to me. He simply needed a way to tweak the role we played in each other's lives this go-round. Indigo had no idea how to make that work; he'd think about it.

Scanning down, I saw where Indigo noted how he used his military connections to find out who Angel was, where he was on deployment, and if he'd get home alive and whole, "*or no point in pursuing this avenue.*"

And then oddly, he noted:

I TOOK Daisy to the vet to have her spayed. They said that while they were performing the surgery, they'd like to do a gastropexy because Great Danes are prone to die from bloat.

THAT NOTE WAS a strange thought to add here. It was out of context enough that I took a picture of that screen. And again, this next thought seemed off:

MY FIRST EXPERIMENT WAS SUCCESSFUL. I was able to make an incision. I think I'll watch it for a day or two and see what happens. I'll call this experiment GEMINI. And perhaps I should write this part in code. Tabby Cat, you know what they say about curiosity.

TABBY CAT, Tabitha Catherine Leverone, Scarlet Vine's birth name. There was a highlighted notation here that the person transcribing the lab notes couldn't type parts of the notebook because they were written in an alphabet that they couldn't identify. Please see notebooks AZ6. AZ6, I wrote on my pad, then looked toward the shelves on the far side of the room. I'd get pictures of those pages. Maybe one of the other remote viewers knew how to read that information.

"I need to get Angel and Lexi in the same location at the same time," it said. He traced down Abuela Rosa. He tracked down Angel's deployment. He sent a note to Angel as if he were Abuela Rosa asking him to please come and visit when he was stateside.

"Angel responded," I gasped, one hand over my throat, the other over my mouth.

Angel wrote to Indigo, who was feigning to be Abuela Rosa; of course, he'd come. I thought of Red Riding Hood and the wolf posing as the sick grandmother. Indigo as Abuela Rosa.

I CAN PUSH up the date of burning her nest. I can get Wilson and Frith out to monitor the Angel-Lexi meeting. The plan is afoot. It's fun to play God!

WHEW! This was crazy! I had to keep looking at the dates and times. This was…wow.

This was my timeline. This was how it all unfolded.

I had met Angel in an inferno. It was the hellish night when the apartment complex where I was raised was burned to the ground, and with it came not only the destruction of tangible things but also the end of our tight community that had lived there together.

I always said that I had been raised by a village. Everyone at the apartment complex had treated everyone else like family.

In the complex, I had the mentorship and tutelage of a group of older women whom I called my Kitchen Grandmothers. They came from different countries, spoke different languages, but their warmth and kindness had no boundaries. One of these women was Abuela Rosa. She escaped from the flames, thanks to her great-nephew Angel Sobado, who was apparently tricked into place by Indigo's letter.

I was barefoot in the freezing night, clutching the two boxes I'd grabbed as I ran, filled with my parents' sketchbooks, journals, and photo albums. I didn't register the weight or the burden. It was all I had of them in tangible form.

Angel took my boxes and drew me to his truck, where he tucked me in and blasted the heat.

There was a picture in the D.C. paper of that fire. The photographer happened to catch the moment Angel came up to me. We looked into each other's eyes, and our fate was sealed. I was his. He was mine. It was as if we'd always been and always would be together—two pieces of a whole.

I remember the relief of finding him.

I remember the peace amongst the chaos, standing under the precipitation of ash and fire hose mist.

Three weeks to the day after that, we were married by a justice of the peace. One day after I said I do, I said good-bye. He loaded onto the transport, and off he went to war—a Ranger.

He was supposed to come back a year later.

Instead, he came back in nine months. In a coffin.

That peace, that connection, it wasn't real.

"It wasn't real," I whispered, pressing my fingers against my lips as if to stifle the words. Goosebumps covered my skin as a cold wash of horror dowsed me.

Indigo had done something to me. To *us,* Angel and me.

Indigo had contrived my connection and my marriage to keep Striker free for Scarlet.

I thought I was going to vomit.

Grabbing at the trash bin, I leaned over. My stomach churned, and my gag reflex spasmed.

My mind whirled. I was *supposed* to be with Striker. Angel was *supposed* to be a friend.

Somehow, Indigo had tried to change our destinies.

I hugged the trash bin tightly like a floatation device as my head swam.

I bet that whatever it was that Indigo had done was the reason I've lived in this state of anguish for so long.

My body became electric. A distress message zapped up and down my nervous system, now that the brain fog, buffering me at first from full clarity of Indigo's words, was burning off.

With shaking hands, I pulled my phone from my lap and took pictures of the screens to show to Herman and General Coleridge when I got up to them.

Maybe whatever Indigo had done could be undone.

I scanned forward and read again about how he saw that Angel had died. In the notes, he had tasked the question, "Next milestone in their marriage?"

He came upon me at Angel's funeral. At the end of the summation, Indigo had written on the next page:

Angel's death is actually wonderful news. I hadn't thought this through. This will give me an opportunity to observe Lexi's state of being and the result of the experiment. Yes, I should have thought of this earlier. Striker's job is very dangerous. If Tabitha does marry Striker, and he were to die, what are the ramifications?

. . .

A NOTE WAS ADDED on December 20th two years ago, weeks after Angel's death, just days before Spyder came back to Washington D.C.

ADDING this in here to have data for a hypothesis. My question was: if one dies, will the other die too? That's obviously not the case. Frith says he's checked on Lexi with his own eyes. She's alive and in mourning but not so much so that she isn't coping. She's still useful not only in understanding the ramifications of my experiment but also in enticing Spyder out into the open. Things will need to escalate to accomplish the Spyder goal. Obviously, a stalker and his attacks on Lexi weren't enough to get Spyder home. It will have to be something much worse. What does that worse look like? I'll have to come up with something truly horrific and yet make sure Lexi stays alive, so I can keep an eye on the Gemini experiment.

WHATEVER INDIGO DID PUT it within the realm of possibility that if either Angel or I died, the other would also die.

What did he do to us?

There was a reference for a notebook entry by the transcriptionist.

My rubbery legs had me clutching at the file cabinets as I made my way to the far corner of the room where the Indigo notebooks were cataloged. I sat on the ground, reaching for the correct reference numbered notebook.

AFTER PHOTOGRAPHING THE SQUIGGLE-FILLED PAGES, I took the general's couch pillow and placed it under the mobile that

Tsukamoto constructed of prisms. I laid down and let the gentle movement of color and shape mesmerize me.

Did I love Angel because Indigo had manipulated us into loving each other?

How could I possibly tell?

"It's a puzzle, Lexi," I said aloud. "You do this for a living. You can figure this out. One step, then the other."

How would I ever know for sure? I lifted my hand and looked at Angel's rings, wondering if Indigo had made them into some kind of black-hearted charm. But no, that couldn't be an aspect of how Indigo trapped me. Striker was having my rings redesigned when I was kidnapped and taken to a prison in Honduras. I was there for months, and my feelings for Angel had never wavered.

I knew Indigo had the capacity to seed thoughts. That wasn't noted in the pages that I could read. Perhaps, they said something in the squiggle pages that would clear things up.

It very well could be that Indigo did something in the ether that could account for how my psychic connection was so attuned with Angel's while he was alive. And how even after he died, Angel was very much still a part of me, keeping me company in my nightmares and stopping me from moving forward with my relationship with Striker.

I knew that both Indigo and Scarlet had tried to influence Striker, but they weren't successful. He was so solid when they had tried to plant thought seeds with him, they'd found it impossible.

But me?

I was a mess. I often felt susceptible to the ether, vulnerable to circumstance.

I might have been fertile grounds for those seeds.

Did I believe that? Maybe. Maybe not. There hadn't been

anything in what I'd read so far, I reminded myself, about influencing and seed planting—just some experiment.

They did a lot of experimentation in the Galaxy Project, trying new things, working to make progress in etheric manipulation.

Angel and I had been Guinea pigs.

To Indigo, I was a microbe in a petri dish, part of some trial.

Here was the real question: if Indigo had trapped me, could I get free?

Thank goodness General Elliot had signed off on my going to see the Galaxy folks. They might have a way to unwrap me from the spell. And there was that person he mentioned, Doc. Maybe there was an etheric cure.

What a horrible thought that my love for Angel and his for me was just a madman's ploy.

What a sick, sick, *sick* thought.

And yet. It made all the sense in the world.

23

STRIKER SAT BEHIND THE WHEEL OF THE INIQUUS HUMMER AS WE powered our way to the airport.

As he maneuvered through the traffic, I was jotting notes. Remote Viewing Tasks: 1) How do I stop the nightmares? 2) What is my connection to Angel? 3) How can Angel be helped? 4) Best method to locate and save Kaylie.

These tasks were poorly written.

The best way to get a good remote viewer reading was to make it as clear and as nebulous as possible at the same time. And then to do it as a double-blind experiment.

I tried again. 1) How do I make it stop? 2) What happened? 3) Best action? 4) How?

I lifted a lip as I read them over. I had very little idea about what I was doing with the tasking questions. One thing I did know was that I had digested the Indigo information as best I could and decided there was nothing to be done until I got to Wyoming and could ask if someone could read the logs. If they couldn't, I'd hire a cryptologist. I bet it was just a matter of figuring out the new alphabet. I didn't think this was a new language.

On those pages lay the information I needed. Until I read them, I wouldn't let myself jump to conclusions. Instead, I planned to try a Striker technique by putting those thoughts in a box and setting the box on a shelf. Out of sight, out of mind for the moment.

Striker had insisted on driving me to the airport. Now, he insisted on carrying my suitcase and holding my hand.

"You're acting like a mother hen," I said.

He didn't smile. "I want to be there for you in Puerto Rico. I don't have a choice." He let go of my hand and wrapped me in a possessive arm. "They contracted me by name, not just our task force."

"Because you're the best of the best." I smiled up at him. "I'd ask for you by name, too." I was quiet for a step or two before I asked, "This isn't a woman, is it?" The last time he was requested by a woman, it was Scarlet. She drugged Striker and drove him into the sunset to start their happily ever after together. "We don't need a repeat of the Scarlet Vine scenario."

"Three men and a woman. All executives. It's going to be an easy assignment." He pushed the door wide for me to pass into the airport lobby.

I checked in at a kiosk, then we made our way up the stairs and down the hall.

As we approached the security line, Miriam hustled over to us. Dressed in yoga pants and a flowing tunic, her blonde hair cascaded in curls down her back. "Hola!" She grinned, sandwiching my other hand between both of hers, and closed her eyes. After a moment, they popped back open. "This is good." She turned to Striker, nodding her head vigorously. "This *feels* right. This is the path that needs to be taken."

Striker's brow drew tight as we formed a klatch by the wall. "What are you two up to?"

"Me?" Miriam opened innocent eyes. "This is partly a working trip and partly personal. I'll be visiting Abuela Rosa and spending time with Lexi. I've planned some time down by the water." She turned to me. "Lexi, what are you up to?"

"Miriam," Striker was using his no-nonsense voice, "you said path. What path are you two on?"

Her grin fell off, and she looked Striker in the eye. "The path to peace, I sincerely hope." She squeezed my hand tight. "Maybe going to spend some time at Angel's grave will be helpful. Abuela Rosa mentioned talking to their priest and arranging a Mass said in Angel's name."

I hadn't talked to Striker about Angel being in Hell and my needing to save his soul. I hadn't meant to keep it from him. I'd explain when Striker and I each returned from our trips and were back in Washington D.C.

That is *if* I hadn't solved the problem by then.

I sincerely hoped I had solved the problem by then. I wanted to cross my fingers to give that thought a little extra good juju, but Striker held one hand, and Miriam was holding the other.

Striker eased his posture a bit like he was laying his hackles back in place. I bet he'd imagined that Miriam was dragging me into a crime scene that would put me at risk. He didn't want me to go behind the Veil to gather crime information like I had when I was training under Miriam a few years ago.

I focused down at my tennis shoes, searching back along my timeline. I had been training with Miriam for years in doing extra sensory detective work. Everything had been going fine. Then one night, a police detective had gone to her house, photo in hand. A known predator had kidnapped a young woman from the mall parking lot. The woman was in imminent danger. The police had no leads. Could Miriam help?

Miriam was very good at what she did, but her talent was in things that had already occurred.

Man, I was off my game. I had forgotten to ask Prescott if there were any objects that had been collected at the spot where the body parts of Kaylie's fellow researchers had been found. At this late date, knowing what happened there probably would have no bearing on our ability to find and save Kaylie, but who knew? Never say never.

Tucking those thoughts to the side, I reached for the glimmer of an idea that had sparked when I thought about Miriam mentoring my psychic work. In the notes I'd read in General Elliot's file room, there was that lab note…

Sending a smile toward Miriam, then Striker, I pulled my hands free and dug my phone from my pocket. I scrolled through the photos I'd taken until I found the lab note: *My first experiment was successful. I was able to make an incision. I think I'll watch it for a day and see what happens. I'll call this experiment GEMINI. And perhaps I should write this part in code. Tabby Cat, you know what they say about curiosity.*

I focused on the date and time. Indigo had written about his experiment, then two days later, Miriam had come to my apartment with the lost girl's photograph. I put it in my hand, and I flew out of my body to get the shit kicked out of me in the ether. I was brutalized just as the girl was. Fortunately, I had kept just enough awareness on the mundane side of the Veil to tell Miriam what I was seeing. She sent the information on to the police. The police found the girl and saved her life.

Indigo had made an incision. Was that in me, somehow? Is that how this ability of mine to merge with a victim became a thing? Was it the reason I was so hurt as I tried to help?

That could make sense.

The time, it lined up.

"Chica!" It was Striker's voice from far away. I lifted my head, and his face swam in front of me. Gripping at both of my arms, he held me up as my legs went out from under me.

"What's happening?" he demanded.

Miriam took my phone from my hand and read the photograph, then held it up to Striker.

"That's from Indigo's lab notes," I muttered. "I think he did an experiment on me. And it occurred to me just now," I regained my balance and Striker's hold softened, "that the thing that happens to me when I go behind the Veil might be the result of Indigo's experimentation."

"What?" Striker's voice sizzled.

My focus shifted from Miriam to the phone and back to Striker. "I'm going to try to figure it out. I'll be flying up to Wyoming on Thursday. I think they might be able to help me."

"Indigo experimented on you?" Striker let go of me with one hand to take the phone and read the image again. "When did this all start?"

"The crazy things that happen to Lexi when she goes behind the Veil?" Miriam asked. "That started at the beginning of November, three years ago, just after her mother died. I thought that might have been why things had changed. It was before the fire, before Angel, before the stalker. Indigo. Oh, baby." Miriam pulled me into a hug, then pushed me to arm's length and looked me in the eye. "This is all you know?"

"I don't know that the lab note pertains to me. I refuse to jump to conclusions." I leaned back into Striker's chest. He was solid. A boulder. So stable.

"That's the smart thing to do" Miriam focused up on Striker. "We'll figure it all out. Try to." She lifted her hand to read her watch. "Right now, we've got to get into line. I'll let you two say good-bye." Off she walked, tugging her boarding pass and ID from her pocket.

I spun in Striker's arms, offering up a smile, so he knew everything was okay. "It was just a thought," I said. "Nothing changed from last-minute until this except a hypothesis formed."

"Agreed. But I feel better that you're going to spend some time with General Coleridge." He kissed the tip of my nose. "We're heading in opposite directions again. I want to go with you. Figure this out *with* you."

I lifted my lips to him, and he gave me a proper, toe-curling kiss good-bye. "You're always with me," I whispered, laying my head on his chest. "You live in my heart."

As I dragged my carry-on toward security, I thought that Striker was with me in a natural, healthy, wonderful way. His living in my heart felt nothing like getting sucked toward the abyss by my connection to Angel.

I couldn't go on this way.

I was going to free myself from this torment or die trying.

24

Abuela Rosa sat at her pink Formica table with wads of tissues bunched into her arthritic hands. She had aged since I saw her last year. She had a fragility about her that I had never seen before. How much of this was Angel? How much the effect of Hurricane Maria? Or was this just age creeping up? Abuela Rosa was in her late seventies now.

Sitting quietly together, Miriam was sketching a forest scene on a pink paper napkin.

Every once in a while, Abuela Rosa swiped an errant tear or dabbed under her nose. "I'm so glad you're here." She pressed her hands to her heart.

"Me too." I reached out and squeezed her arm. "I'm going to make you a coffee. Decaf since it's almost time for bed."

As I bustled around the kitchen, pouring the grounds, reaching for the sugar and mugs, I knew exactly where Abuela Rosa liked to keep everything.

When I was a teen, as part of the Kitchen Grandmother rotation, every Friday afternoon, I'd help Abuela with her chores, and in return, I learned.

Abuela liked her house to be full of people. The family members would arrive in the evening. At these gatherings, I studied singing and guitar, I practiced swaying my hips in Latin dances and using my lashes to send flirty looks to my dance partner. From the Sobado family, I became fluid if not fluent in Spanish and learned to cook foods from all over the Caribbean. Fun. So much fun. It was an honor to marry into such a wonderful family.

I couldn't get over how much Abuela had changed in these last two years. Weathered. Worn. Tired. She looked as tired as I felt.

"Are you not sleeping, Abuela?" I asked as I set a mug, filled mostly with warm milk and a splash of coffee, in front of her.

"Better to stay awake." She patted my seat. "My dreams are not pleasant ones. You said you're heading right back to the mainland." Abuela hefted herself to her feet and made her way over to a stack of papers on her counter. "I would wait. But it's getting late. I need to make phone calls if you agree."

I lifted my chin, then sent a glance Miriam's way.

Abuela Rosa shuffled back to the table, sat, and tucked the papers onto her ample lap. A lap where I would rest my head for comfort when I was younger, and she would stroke my hair and hum. Lying there, I told her all my teenaged angsty problems. So kind. So patient.

"I have been troubled for over a week now with terrible nightmares about Angel," she said. "They cling to me even when I'm awake."

My breath caught and held.

"He tells me he is in Hell and needs help." When she made a sign of the cross, I realized she was holding her silver rosary with the tiny silver beads. "Angel says I should please send help to him."

Abuela, too.

"I have been to the priest." She let the rosary tumble until her thumb and index finger trapped a bead, and she began to work it back and forth. "They offered up Mass in his name Sunday. Sunday night, the nightmares grew worse."

"Yes." I clasped my hands together. "That's what's been happening to me. What do you think it means?" I leaned forward.

"That he's in Hell." She moved to the next bead. "He didn't go to confession before he died." She lifted the crucifix and kissed it.

I pinched my lips together.

"I prayed about what I should do. I prayed the rosary twice. That night, I had another dream that said you were coming, and I was to do this thing. I only did *this* thing because right after the dream, I got phone calls from Miriam and then from you that you were coming. It felt like the answer to my prayers. And I had this shown to me by my guardian angel." She paused. "You're going to think I'm terrible." She snatched up another tissue. "I thought. I think..." She covered her eyes behind a shaking hand. "It has always bothered me that I never saw Angel's body."

I nodded my head vigorously, posting my forearms on the table and leaning closer.

"I understand that the Army thought his body was not viewable after the explosion. I wanted to anyway. I wanted—what do you say in English?"

"Closure," I whispered.

"Yes, this. Closure. My dream told me that I was to look at Angel. I went to the government building to ask if this was possible. My guardian followed along each step." With a frown, she lifted the papers from her lap to the table. "I have the documents here." She slid them to me. "We can have my Angel dug up. We can look inside the coffin and see him. The priest will come. He'll bring incense and holy water. I need Angel to be at rest."

I didn't take the time to read the papers. If Abuela needed this. This would be done. I tugged a pen from my pocket and signed at each of the little sticky note arrows. "When do you want to do this, Abuela?" I asked softly as I pushed them back to her.

"I want you with me. I arranged everything so that if you agreed, we could go to the cemetery in the morning. There's a service that comes to help. I paid the deposit."

I nodded. "Make sure that I get that bill. That should be my expense." I flicked my gaze over to Miriam. I was glad we'd talked through what had happened this last week with me and my nightmares about Angel so she could follow this new twist. "Can you come?" I asked.

Abuela turned to Miriam, too. "I thought if you could touch him, you might be able to tell me what happened that day." She sent a pleading eye toward Miriam and then dipped her chin. "Maybe, even, you'll get a sense of what Angel's soul needs to climb from Hell and go to God."

"Of course, I'll come. It's an honor to be included in such a profoundly personal moment." Miriam reached out to lay her hand on Abuela's arm. "Thank you for asking me."

And just like that, the plan was formed. I was going to go to the cemetery and dig up my husband, so Abuela and I could get some sleep.

"It's getting late. I should let the peoples know."

Abuela made phone calls to the cemetery, to the exhumation specialists, to the church. My laughing, singing, fun-filled Abuela Rosa, I had never seen such determination in her eyes.

She was going to save her beloved Angel from the fires of Hell.

I hope her guardian angel was right.

I picked up the papers and read about the circumstances under which a body could be exhumed—some of the words I didn't recognize. Whoever had helped Abuela up at the government buildings had highlighted the parts that pertained to her, and that's where I focused my attention.

It had been less than five years.

His widow had agreed.

The body hadn't been embalmed. It was all good.

Well, not good.

It was legal.

Leaving the papers on the table, I walked quietly, so as not to interrupt Abuela's conversation, to the living room where I snagged my suitcase. I took it into Abuela's bathroom to get ready for bed.

After wiping off my makeup, I changed into a nightdress, then hunkered over the sink, brushing my teeth.

I was a widow. That was on the paperwork I signed—Angel's widow.

For two years, I'd been trying to figure that out.

Trying to develop a concept of widowhood.

Trying to integrate my beliefs about life and death into what I experienced in my daily world.

I was a widow. And yet, I've never accepted that label.

That was probably because I never saw Angel's body. I completely understood Abuela's distress.

From the moment when those two officers had shown up at Iniquus with their hats in their hands to tell me that Angel had died in an IED explosion of his vehicle, I had divorced myself from the idea that Angel had been reduced to a portion of a body.

Now, I was going to see his remains. This could very well make everything worse for both Abuela and me.

I spat into the sink and rinsed the foam of toothpaste down the drain.

Pulling the elastic from my ponytail, I reached for my brush.

Angel had gone away on a mission. He was supposed to come back.

They gave me a flag-draped box and said, "Here he is."

But I didn't see him.

And part of me didn't believe them because I *felt* Angel in my daily life. I felt him near me every day since we met.

That horrible day when I pushed myself against the walls of the sound-proof room and howled with pain at the news of his death changed nothing for me.

The spirit of Angel had never left me.

At night, I slept in Striker's arms. I wore Striker's engagement ring. I promised my future to him. It was time to plan the wedding.

And I couldn't.

Now that Zoe was planning her ceremony and asked me to be part of it, it was going to be harder for me to ignore the fact that something in me would *not* let me think about flowers and dresses and a cake with all the trimmings.

I made promises to Angel, standing before God. To have and to hold until death do us part. And to me, Angel was.

He just was.

Or maybe this just *was* the unfortunate results of a madman's science experiment not going to plan.

The brush caught on a tangle, and I yanked it free, glad for the brief bright ache.

Until I could move myself forward. Until I could accept that

Angel was dead and gone, how could I possibly consider making vows to Striker?

25

I HAD PLANNED TODAY DIFFERENTLY.

I was going to wear a black sundress with sandals and carry the little pink plastic rosary that I'd been given when I was in prison in Honduras. I imagined cleaning Angel's grave, reciting that rosary, and decorating the tombstone with the spray of flowers I'd ordered.

Instead, I was dressed in a pair of shorts and tennis shoes. I'd never been present when a body was exhumed before. I imagined it would be dirty work.

Miriam was present when a body was exhumed from time to time with her job. She was describing the process as she drove our rental car through the traffic out to the countryside, where Angel was buried in the cemetery that held generations of the Sobado family.

The grounds workers had started their work ahead of us. As we approached, I saw that they had placed a tent over the area with two flaps down, guarding the view from anyone who happened to be visiting their kin that day. There were some chairs set up too.

As we stepped closer, I could see that Angel's tombstone had been moved to the side. There was a mound of dirt under a draped carpet of green AstroTurf.

Two men lounged on the chairs in loose dress trousers and button-down shirts, laughing with each other.

I turned toward the crunch of gravel under tires. Father Julio, the priest who had performed Angel's funeral, climbed from his car and headed toward us.

Surreal, I thought.

I hadn't truly imagined what we were actually doing.

But here it was, all prepared for us.

I was close now and could see that the hole they dug around Angel's coffin was large enough that someone had been able to get down and put the straps in place for the machine that lowers the coffin into its grave. This time they'd be pulling the box up. They'd unlock the coffin, lift the lid, and there would be the blown-up remains of my husband.

My mind flashed back to the images of body parts of the researchers that had been eaten and scattered by animals in Nigeria.

A photo was one thing. Having remains lying there in front of me was another.

And Abuela Rosa had asked Miriam to touch them and gather insight.

Miriam was unphased. It was part of her job, just like it had been part of the FBI's and Iniquus team's job to find the researchers' pieces, catalog, identify, and care for them.

They'd had emotional distance from their task.

I most certainly did not.

While I wanted to focus on Abuela Rosa and make sure she was okay, I admitted to myself I was wigging out. I wanted this very badly. Wanted the closure for myself. It felt like the end of an era—the last steps on a three-year-long marathon. I stumbled toward the finish line.

"My suggestion," Miriam said. "Is that I move your chairs out of the tent once we're ready to raise the lid. I'll look first and describe what I'm seeing. And at that point, you can decide if you want me to do my work and let Father bless Angel's remains while you stay where you are, or if you might do better seeing it for yourself."

Neither Abuela nor I responded.

"I can tell you that the remains of our fallen war heroes are cared for with honor," she said. "I had a friend who went to Dover once. He saw the soldier buffing each of the buttons on the deceased's uniform. He said, 'The family will appreciate the care you've taken.' The soldier answered, 'They'll never know. The sergeant has chosen to be cremated.'"

Abuela nodded. Leaning heavily on my arm, she rocked her body to get her stiff limbs to round to the other side of the tent wall.

The two men lifted chairs and brought them to us.

After a time, there was a whir of the engine.

The people spoke reverently under their breaths.

I petted Abuela's arm.

Miriam came out and crouched in front of us. "You should come and see. There are a boot and two boxes. One holds a tooth. One holds his dog tags. There's nothing grizzly to upset you."

She stood and held out her hands to Abuela Rosa. The three of us moved under the tent. There, without the breeze, the temperature had started to rise. The respite from the bright sun and beating rays was still an improvement.

We stood at the coffin staring in. Silent. It wasn't a whole boot. It was just the top part with the laces, scorched black. I tipped my head to see that the bright metal was Angel's second dog tag laced into place.

They had told me that they had identified Angel by his dog tags and his dental records. They meant a single tooth with a filling. I had to assume there had been more of him out in the desert sand. Probably separating his pieces that came apart in the blast from his fellow Ranger's pieces would have been difficult. Impossible. They probably sent a team in to gather what they could. The mere act of someone finding his tooth and piece of boot meant that other soldiers had put themselves in harm's way to fulfill their obligation that no man be left behind.

I sent those men who had dug through the grizzly aftermath a gift of gold light. I wondered about how that had affected their minds and lives. How picking up Angel's molar had changed them.

It had to have. How could you package a tooth to send home to a widow and not think about it and the fragility of being as you brushed your teeth in the morning?

I had, anyway, after they told me they identified him with those dental records.

"Abuela, shall I begin?" Miriam asked.

Abuela sat down with a nod.

I stood beside Abuela Rosa, holding her hand, not willing to take my eyes off the inside of the coffin and the little boxes.

"I'll start with the tooth." Miriam picked the tooth out of its box and placed it in the center of her hand. She ducked her chin, and the wind rose around us, swirling her blonde curls into a wide halo and hiding her face.

"I am in the back of a vehicle. It's dark, and there is the smell of sweat and unwashed bodies. In the distance, there's gunfire. Angel feels anxious to get out of the truck and help. His brothers are in trouble. They're pinned down."

Doubt crept through my mind. This was nothing like the story I was told about Angel's death. I had hoped so much to know. I had trusted Miriam to be able to see. This wasn't right.

"The truck is picking up speed heading in. The men are readying their weapons. There's a plan to get on-site and jump out of the truck, then run forward."

No. That was all wrong.

"There's a call over the radio. They need the PJs to come in. They're saying some are dead, some badly wounded."

I wished Miriam would stop. My anger at this false picture she was painting for Abuela stomped angrily through my system.

"They're standing. Jumping. Running. Angel was at the back of the truck and was the last to jump out. On the opposite side, as the men were gathering, an RPG hit. The concussion threw Angel down. He hit his jaw against the corner of a crate." Miriam lifted her hands and gathered her hair out of her face, and turned to us. "I'm sorry. The tooth was lost in the week before he died. It was knocked out. It had been lost in the truck. The truck later was exploded in the IED, but it wasn't the truck Angel was in."

I closed my eyes, trying to let my anger slide down my legs into my feet and deep into the ground.

Miriam's story hadn't been fabricated, after all.

Just before Angel died, Striker had gotten word that his unit had been pinned down in a firefight. There had been soldiers who had been killed and injured. Striker thought that I might be picking it up on my "psychic network," and he'd been right. I had.

Striker had gotten confirmation that Angel had not been injured. And I knew from Angel's shrapnel in the shoulder story that Angel didn't like to tell the powers that be about his injuries, lest they take him out of the fight, and he wasn't there to support his buddies. Of course, Angel wouldn't have reported losing a tooth.

The boot, though, and the dog tag would be different.

I braced myself. Abuela clutched at me.

This time Miriam was silent. I guessed she thought that the last story she told us had taken a toll.

She put the dog tag back in the box, then put her hand onto the boot laces. She stood there for quite a while, moving back and forth between the impressions she was picking up from the two. She did this when she was trying to verify the impressions she was picking up in the ether. I'd also seen her do this when she needed a moment to gather her thoughts to share a story that she knew would be tragic for the family.

She wouldn't lie. She'd tell the whole story. But word choice and inflection mattered.

One had to be sensitive when working with the families of crime victims.

I recalled the raw pain that Melody Foley had displayed in the conference room. Could that have been just two days ago? Crime did not affect one person but an entire community. A soldier's death, Angel's death, it affected so many, so much.

Miriam made her way over to us and dragged a chair around, so we were sitting in a circle.

"This is what I saw," she said. "There was a woman sitting next to Angel in the back of the truck. They were in a truck with cloth walls. There was the metal truck with Angel's tooth behind them."

That would be right.

"They had been on a successful mission. But it wasn't to kill anyone. It was to rescue the woman who was sitting next to Angel. She was important to a group. She had been taken. It was Angel who was tasked to get her back to her family group. This was supposed to help them get the information that they needed for a different assignment. That assignment isn't clear to me. There was talk in the truck of meeting someone at the crossroads, and the men should go ahead and get ready. The woman covered her eyes with a cloth, and Angel stripped down to naked. The clothes he put back on, I couldn't see, but I got the sense that they were designed to allow Angel to blend in. Angel put his dog tags on top of his folded uniform, rolled them, and shoved part of it into the top of his boot. There was more rumbling. Stop and go. Then the explosion."

Abuela nodded. "Fast then."

"I can only tell you what imprints were left with the objects I touched. I would like to tell you it was fast. That Angel didn't suffer. That he had been there one moment and a free soul the next. But I can't speak to that. I'm so sorry. I do know that the truck was moving, then there was a massive explosion. From my understanding of events like these, it is very unlikely, putting these two pieces of information together, that Angel suffered."

I thought about Melody Foley and how they tried to put her sister's memory to rest by putting photos and diaries into the coffin and burying it. I doubted that felt like closure to them.

This whole event wasn't satisfying in the least.

"Father, would you?" Abuela said.

Father Julio came to the coffin and began his rites, praying for Angel and that his soul would find peace.

In my mind, I went over the story again. After every mission, Angel sought absolution from his chaplain. Miriam said this mission hadn't been about killing people but rescuing someone.

If that was right, and Angel hadn't killed anyone since he'd last confessed, why would he be in Hell?

I listened to Father Julio, chanting his prayers. The stress on Abuela Rosa's face had eased.

The last time I sat out here in this graveyard, they handed me the triangular-folded flag. "On behalf of the president of the United States, the United States Army, and a grateful nation, please accept this flag as a symbol of our appreciation for your loved one's honorable and faithful service."

I watched as Father Julio stepped back, and they lowered the lid and locked it.

The mission had been a success. The men with their hats in their hands had told me so.

I guessed they were right. In a way, the Rangers had captured the woman back. Was that better? I mean, she would have been in the truck and exploded, too. Was that the best thing that could have happened for her?

Sitting there, processing all of this, I thought of Kaylie, and what Prescott had said to me at intake about pulling people out of situations so broken, he thought it might have been kinder had they not survived.

26

My flight from Puerto Rico to Atlanta was over in the blink of an eye. It was like that sci-fi book I'd read where the scientists had learned to fold Interstellar space, making their starting point and ending point side by side. In this way, ships didn't have to traverse the entire expanse of a galaxy.

I was there kissing Abuela Rosa and Miriam good-bye; the next thing I knew, I was checking my ticket in Atlanta for my next gate.

It was a little shocking not to have any remembrance of events happening and time moving forward. I'd done this in my car but for minutes, not hours. I called it driving on autopilot.

Then, it happened again between Atlanta and Wyoming.

I remembered walking toward gate twenty-four with my ticket in hand. Then the time-space continuum flexed, and voila! Now, I was walking out of the secure area, dragging my carry-on behind me.

Herman Trudy stood with his shoulder pressed against the wall, watching me progress up the ramp.

He checked his watch. "And there she is, three-forty, right on time."

According to my ticket, I was supposed to have arrived at three-ten. That was the closest ticket that I could find to match up to the time frame that the general had noted on his calendar.

I checked my phone. Sure enough, three-forty on the dot mountain time. "You're remarkable," I said, falling into an easy walk beside him, leaving Herman the extra personal space that helped him stay comfortable.

He slid his hands in his camo pants pockets. "Before you say anything. You shouldn't."

"I shouldn't what?"

"Say anything. You're here to figure something out. We knew that. But what it is, we don't want to know. You don't want to mess up the double-blind. So keep it to yourself."

"How are you?" I goosed my stride to keep up with Herman.

"World of difference last time we talked until now. After that whole mess with Indigo, I took your check and the money I got from selling my house. It was enough money to buy a piece of land. I built close to General Coleridge and put some of the rest of it in the bank for a rainy day. The general hired me to work for him doing research. The pay's better than when I was flipping burgers, for sure. We have a grant from a group that wants to fund solutions to stop and even reverse climate change. It's interesting to try to take a look at various projects and see if we can't remote view outcomes. Like this one project, we just looked at. They wanted to know whether or not to allocate funds to the Great Green Wall across Africa. Heard of that?"

"The shelterbelt of trees that extends fifteen kilometers wide and goes from the east coast of Africa all the way to the east coast in Tanzania. Yes. The goal is to slow the winds and help preserve topsoil, providing shade as well as homes to diversify the animals and bird populations."

He looked down at me. "I don't want you to tell me how you know that. I don't want to know."

"I guess as far as conversation goes, that leaves us with, how's the weather?" I smiled.

I almost got a chuckle out of him.

Mrs. Coleridge was bustling around the kitchen where she loved to be. I was in the den with Herman and the general in front of a crackling wood fire.

"Okay, how did you know I was coming today at three-forty?" I asked.

"I tasked it when we met," Herman said.

I had my hands wrapped around a ceramic owl mug of chamomile tea. "What was your task?"

"Next time?" he said.

"I love how cryptically you write these tasks. Broad and yet, when you know what they refer to, very specific. I've noticed since we worked together, that's a lot like the *knowings* I get. They are so broad as to be all but useless. In the end, they're as clear as clear can be. Getting them at least tunes me into the idea that I needed a warning."

"You have a warning brewing now?" the general asked. He was leaned back in a recliner that looked like a child's chair under his height. His legs dangled over the footrest.

"I do, actually. 'As I was going to St. Ives, I met a man with seven wives,'" I chanted.

"Yup," the general said. "That could be a task. I'm assuming since you said it aloud, you don't want us to look at that."

"I have other priorities." I set the mug on the wooden floor, pulled out my phone, and scrolled through the pictures. "Herman, did you know that Indigo had a dog named Daisy?"

"It was a Great Dane. Nice dog. She got hit by a car, and Indigo had her euthanized. It happened when you were in the prison."

I showed them the photo of what Indigo had written about his dog being spayed into his lab notes. "Does that mean anything to either of you? I know that before your team was defunded and disbanded, the operators in the Galaxy Project were working on the idea of hiding a name or a story to make it unsearchable in the ether, was there anything else your team was trying to work out?"

The general frowned down at the phone then handed it off to Herman with a shake of his head.

"That doesn't ring any bells with me," Herman said.

I took the phone back and swiped. "How about this. Can either of you read this writing?"

I handed the photo showing the squiggled writing on lined paper to Herman.

"That's the Galaxy alphabet," he said. "When we're developing the protocol for something new, we'd write it like this. All the squiggles in the lettering are supposed to give it a doorknob effect, the kind of thing that would distract an enemy if they became proficient enough to read our work off a page. I'm a bit rusty, but I can work on this and get you a transcription."

"I'd be interested in reading it." I accepted the phone back. "It's not all the pages from Indigo's notebooks. Just the ones that had to do with my reason for being here. I—"

Both men brought their hands up and their chins down as if they were holding off a barreling car.

I stopped. "I wasn't going to tell you. Geesh," I said under my breath.

The general stood to his full height, reaching out his arm. He reminded me of Baloo from the animated Jungle Book, and I was the thin-limbed awkward Mowgli in this moment.

I slid into his bear hug.

"Awesome, Lexi. We'll have fun with this. I'll tell you what, Herman and I'll go over to the office out back. The Mrs. can point out the way for you. While we get set up, why don't you go into the kitchen? I can smell the cobbler coming out of the oven now. Have yourself a bowlful with some ice cream. By the time you're done eating, we should be ready. And you can talk over the best way to get the viewing tasks worded with her. Get the envelopes all numbered up. The Mrs. knows what to do. Then come slide the tasks through the mail slot. That way, we don't have any clue what's going on. We'll go see what there is to see." He stopped to grin. "With a more or less sixty-five percent chance, we aren't handing you a load of hooey."

27

I WAS THE ONLY ONE IN THE RANCH HOUSE. THE GENERAL AND Herman Trudy were back over at the office. Last night they'd each done two remote viewing tasks.

This morning they planned to switch and see how their answers compared. One thing I knew was that Herman, when tasked with "How do I best help the woman?" came back with the conclusion: "You should go looking for Trouble."

Trouble in my mind was Kaylie; that was her childhood nickname. I saw on the paper Herman had written it with a capital T, a proper noun. I also had the *knowing* telling me that I was to go on a hazardous journey.

An American woman in Iraq and possibly into Syrian ISIS territory? I imagined that fit the bill for hazard.

Of course, now I'd have to convince General Elliot to let me go.

It was interesting to me that the Kaylie task was the only task conclusion they'd let me read.

"Give it time," General Coleridge had said.

No clue what that meant or if it meant anything. I was getting paranoid.

I hoped they could come up with something because even if Father Julio waved the incense and sprinkled the holy water, these last two nights, my nightmares were off the charts bad.

Mrs. Coleridge had sat with me while we ate our breakfast porridge. After I helped her wash the bowls, she'd checked the clock then went off to check on one of their cows.

It had seemed like a subterfuge when she left. Now, with the doorbell ringing, I was convinced they'd left me here alone for a reason.

The Coleridges lived in the middle of freaking nowhere. A chance visitor was almost an impossibility.

I pulled open the door to find a woman of about the general's age. Her features were masculine and angular. She stood a head taller than me, and I imagined, in her prime, she had been a formidably sized woman.

"Hi, Lexi. My name is Dr. Martha Granger." She pulled a hand from her parka pockets for a shake. "They call me Doc." She was wearing a pair of too big bib overalls and a buffalo plaid flannel shirt under her unzipped jacket. Her white hair was cropped short and windblown. Her cheeks were ruddy under laughter-filled blue eyes.

I both liked and trusted her immediately.

Stepping back, I held the door wide to let her in.

She hovered over the plastic mat in the entryway where outdoor shoes were lined up in a neat row like soldiers on a parade field. Reaching down, Doc yanked off her muck boots. "This morning, General Elliot called over and asked me to swing by and have a talk with you." She curved lower to rearrange her pants legs. "I was actually already heading this way to chat with you. Crazy how the universe works."

"General Elliot told me about–"

"Elliot wants us to do a regular check in. I told him I'd see if we meshed. I think we're meshing fine." She waggled her hand between us. "There's an affinity. Didn't know that last night, though, when I got the midnight call from Coleridge. That man doesn't have the good sense God gave him to wait until the morning, and a body was awake and ready to listen."

Doc put her hand under my elbow and made her way into the den, guiding me in front of her.

"Coleridge wanted me to look at the tasking report that Herman did for you." She pointed toward the back of the house. "I went around to his office earlier and took a look at the picture he drew. Wanted my opinion. My opinion was that I didn't have enough information, but for sure, it was weird."

Weird to someone connected with Galaxy? That didn't bode well. I grimaced.

"My background," she said, dropping her hand once I was in front of a chair, then moved to one beside it and plopped down. "I have undergraduate degrees in religion and sociology. I joined the military to pay for my medical school, surgical. I ended up with psychiatry as well because I was doing research into the effects of war—the mind-body connection, and the effect of a spiritual intervention on surgical outcome." She tapped her head, then swept her hand down to take in her body parts. "Sit," she said.

I realized I was standing there, staring at her. I picked up the decorative pillow and sat in the chair near hers. We were almost knee to knee.

"I worked a lot with our elite teams—SEALs, Green Berets, Delta, and so on—studying their well-being, looking at metrics of the physical, mental, and spiritual bodies. Fascinating stuff. It was good work." She sent me a wink. "Probably would have been great work being around all those hyper-fit bodies if I were interested in males, but I've found they're not my type."

"Yes, ma'am."

"I've traveled around the world talking to, studying, and practicing with spiritual leaders, ranging from small indigenous tribes to the Dali Lama. Then Galaxy operators started having issues. 'Ether sickness,' I call it. Their issues were and still are unique. Bottom line, I'm a psychic physician."

"That's…amazing. How did you get involved with Galaxy?"

"The first case, I got called in because I had served with General Elliot, and we'd had many a fine discussion about his experiences in Vietnam. We kicked around ideas of spirituality and the things I'd learned traveling the world. One night, Elliot called me up. He wanted to pick my brain when one of the Galaxy operators became exhausted. This poor fellow could barely get out of bed to crawl to the bathroom. He'd urinate then have to lie on the bathroom floor and take a nap to have the energy to crawl back to bed. He couldn't chew. It took too much energy, so he was living on protein shakes."

"Wow. That sounds awful."

"The western doctors tested him for everything they could think of. They decided it was a psychological condition, and I had the great privilege of being called in to work with him. The Army asked me to help him get his head screwed on right. He was doing primo work for the project up until that point. His specialty was pinpointing locations. They needed him back functioning. How do you know Elliot?"

"He's my commander at Iniquus."

She leaned her head against the chair back and looked at the ceiling. "Ah, okay, this is making more sense to me now."

"What was wrong with the Galaxy operator?"

She lowered her gaze to mine. "Healing sickness. He was

using white light, which is something people should never do. It's much too high a frequency for the human body." She popped her eyebrows, making sure I got her point: Don't play with white light. "When the remote viewers went on a task, they saw terrible things. This particular fellow wanted to make things better, so he would spend extra time on task, trying to heal the situation. The goal in healing is to run etheric energy through you." She lifted her hand toward me like she was warming herself over a fire. "It feels to me like you know this, you were trained in Reiki?"

"I was. And I was taught never to use my own energy."

"Who was your Reiki Master Teacher?"

"Miriam Laugherty."

"All right. Good. I've met her. She's very solid in her abilities. More importantly, she knows her limits and stays within the bounds of her capabilities." Doc crossed her legs, resting her ankle on her thigh. Her socks were black with silver ghosts. "You'd be surprised how rare that is. Everyone wants to push the envelope and gain more dexterity. Sometimes enough is enough. Like this fellow, I was talking about. He couldn't stand the suffering he saw. Even though he was trained in the scientific methodology, he figured it couldn't hurt if he projected healing energy into the situations. Did it without telling anyone. And little by little, he depleted himself of his life force. It was a great learning experience, though. Everyone could plainly see what had happened to their colleague. Everyone was afraid that it might happen to them. When I started training the group on the importance of observation only, that became part of the protocol. I think it was an important thing to learn."

"Absolutely. I'm very curious about why General Coleridge wanted you to look at the tasking conclusions."

"He saw something he didn't understand. Coleridge

suggested that it might necessitate some research in the Akashic Records. A peek at some of the contracts and agreements you've made for this lifetime." There was a pause. "Coleridge assured me you were okay talking about what he terms the '*woo-woo* stuff.'"

"Yes, it's fine." I offered up a smile. "I've traveled behind the Veil, and I've been studying the *woo-woo* language for a while now, not to say that I'm fluent. I can find my way to a bathroom and can order off a menu."

She laughed. "Okay then, so the tasking question was, 'How do I find peace?' It's a wonderful question in general. We're all seeking peace, but there is something specific that you want to find peace from, not make peace with. That's my impression."

I nodded.

"The picture that Herman drew in his conclusions looked to me like cell division in the telophase stage. Each cell had everything it needs to survive on its own. The DNA was replicated. The cell was finalizing its division. It's almost there but not quite."

"Huh."

"Yep, very interesting."

"Off the top of your head, what would you guess that meant?" I asked.

She slapped her hands onto her knees. "That's not how we do things."

"Granted. But a scientist would form a hypothesis."

She swizzled her lips around like a man gathering spit from his chewing tobacco. "I'm not approaching this as a scientist but as an investigator. I'm here to get your permission to go on a research trip."

"Okay." I paused to let what she said sit for a moment so my mind could process it a bit. "I'll ask you what that means in a second, but I'm going to push you here. Just looking at the picture, just applying your understanding of biology, what would you hypothesize? When you go on your research trip, you have to be looking for something in particular."

"Fine." She tipped her head and brought it up, like she was being forced to do something against her will or best judgment. "I'm wondering if you were a twin in utero, the twin failed to develop, and you absorbed those cells."

"I've heard of that. People have operations on what they think are tumors, and they end up having hair and teeth." My body convulsed. Was I carrying around my absorbed twin with me? How gross was that? "I'm forming some pretty disturbing pictures." I tried to laugh it off. "Let's say that's what happened. Why would that be a problem?"

"Again, just throwing spaghetti at the wall to see if it sticks. This is one of the things I want to study. If there was a design for you to be a twin, and there was a change of plans. Something happened—"

"Something did happen. When my mother was pregnant, she was attacked. I don't know the circumstances, and I don't know how she was hurt, but she almost lost the pregnancy. I was told she was on bed rest, and my father refused to leave her side."

"That makes this more possible. But let's not set it in stone." Her hands wrapped the ends of the chair arms. "The idea would be that something thwarted that soul's journey. That soul's cells were absorbed into your body, and the soul decided to come along for the ride instead of just letting the opportunity go."

"Living through me vicariously?"

"Or maybe not so vicariously. I could imagine that another soul might have their own agenda and try to manipulate the energy to get their life's goals accomplished."

"Whoa. I…back up. Where are you researching this?"

"When I was an undergrad, and one of my religious classes was on the Old and New testaments. In both, the "Book of Life" was referenced. Many, including the Christian Psychic Physician, Edgar Cayce, believed that the Book of Life was another way of saying the Akashic Records. In fact, these records are mentioned in many religions. Most religions. I like to think of it as the computer over at the NSA."

Interesting that she'd bring up the supercomputer at the NSA since that was the AI system that put us back on the trail toward Kaylie Street.

"The Akashic Records is a system for storing all of the information about every single person who has ever lived on the Earth. Every word, deed, feeling, thought, and more importantly, intent."

That intent part was important to me. It was why I didn't think that I would go to Hell, even if I killed five people. My intent had been pure. It was also why I didn't think that Angel could really imagine himself going to Hell, even if he thought he needed to be absolved of his sins by a priest. I didn't see them as sins. His intent was pure—to save innocent lives and protect the defenseless.

"The interesting part to me," Doc said, "and one of the things I wanted to look at is the circle of souls that you're training with. In my understanding of the universe, everyone has a study group they work with life after life."

"That's what I think."

And Indigo did too. He said that Angel was part of my warrior study group.

Doc shuffled around until her head was cradled in the corner where the wing and the back of her chair came together. "In each life, the individual soul will take on different roles in order to learn new things. General Coleridge mentioned that you're having trouble moving on from the loss of your first husband, and this is affecting your relationship with the man you're engaged to. The decisions you made in your planning group before entering this lifetime will have an enormous impact on your everyday life, your feelings, relationships, and even your belief systems. That we're even having this conversation tells me that you decided on a spiritual level to allow me to come and chat with you. You decided to allow me to say these things. And you can imagine or even believe that what I'm saying is correct. To others, it would be blasphemous. But then again, there are many belief systems that are unimaginable to me, as well."

I heard the words, but they slid around like bumper cars at the fair, banging and jostling each other. "Sorry, I tuned out that last bit. I got stuck on what you were saying about my first husband affecting my ability to move on. The general said that to you?" I hadn't said that to the general.

"Not in words. I picked up the clairvoyant pictures during my conversation with him. In the Akashic Records, I'll look at the contracts you've signed. And we can come up with a plan."

"Okay, I'm with you so far. And I've studied Edgar Cayce, so I have an image of what is possible in the realm of a psychic physician, I guess." I felt my nostrils widening, trying to suck up oxygen to fuel my brain and grasp the ramifications of this conversation. "By going to look at the records, are you gathering information so I can better understand and align myself with some inevitability? Is that what you're saying to me?"

"They'll help me understand what draws you closer, what repels you. It will help me to see what molds and shapes your consciousness. It isn't predictive of the future, however. The decisions and agreements we've made, the contracts we've signed, they help to guide us toward where we need to be educated."

My brows drew in tightly.

"Our lives are supposed to transform us," she said. "We're supposed to work to be the very best we can be. This isn't a play where the lines are written, and the movements are blocked by a director. Our futures are fluid with an array of potentialities as we interact and experience, and make body-level decisions. We are always at choice." She held up her index finger then lowered her hand back to her lap. "The choices we imagine presented to us might seem limited. But truly, our choices are vast. When I look at the tasking sheet and compare that information to your record, I'm simply going to come up with some ideas on what can be done and how I can help as a psychic physician, like my first Galaxy patient with the healing sickness. He was being poisoned by the energy of all the white light he had used to tried to revitalize himself once he'd started depleting his natural resources by healing others. I simply popped the bubble and drained the white light out like a huge boil."

"Gross."

"Yeah." She sighed. "It actually was."

"All right, for clarity's sake, you plan to go and look through my record. Will that affect anything? Can you mess anything up? Move anything around?"

"I can't go without your express permission. Or let me put it this way, I wouldn't do anything to someone else's life story out of fear of what would happen to my own soul."

I'd heard of people doing this. I'd met some. Though they were well-meaning. Talking to them, I felt like a grown-up playing tea party with the kids. Doc? She was the real deal. I felt it even before she told me her connection to General Elliot, General Coleridge, and Galaxy.

"How does this work?"

"The records search I do in advance. When I do my work as

a psychic doc, I don't like the person I'm working within the same room with me. I prefer to get them on the phone as we hook up in the ether. This lets me speak to both their physical body and their spiritual body. I give them information and options. They tell me what they want to do about it."

"And General Coleridge saw the tasking sheet and thought I needed a psychic doctor?"

"He said he saw something that has him flummoxed and, to be honest, a little alarmed."

"Wow, this feels like I'm at the doctor's office, and they've just told me they found a concerning lump that needs to be biopsied."

"Is that the metaphor that came to you? That's interesting." She sat very still. This was what Miriam did when she was seeing things clairvoyantly.

I shifted back and forth on my thighs, wondering what she was reading in the ether.

"I guess where we are right now," Doc said, "is this question—should I open the file and do the research?"

"Yes. Thank you. I don't know when you'd have time to do it. But I'm leaving here in just a bit to fly to D.C. From there, I'll be heading downrange as soon as I possibly can. I'll have a satellite connection. I'd like to get answers as soon as you're able."

Her eyebrow arched. "It feels like this conversation has stirred the pot, does it?"

"More like it's stirred a wasp nest. My psychic distress is off the charts."

"Isn't that telling? That means the energy knows that things are about to change. Good for you. That's brave." She gave me a nod. "Some people feel that doing anything in the psychic space is hazardous. I, on the other hand, think that not doing things with our psychic selves is the hazard."

Just like Doc thought it was telling that I'd had the biopsy metaphor, I thought her choice of the word "hazard' not once but twice was telling.

Ia was afraid because she was a young woman and the journey was hazardous.

Was *this* the journey that my *knowing* warned me about?

28

On the plane ride back to the East Coast, I tried to distract myself from my conversation with Doc.

Not an easy thing to do.

I spent the extra money to get an Internet connection and was doing searches for Kaylie's case. I needed to convince General Elliot to let me go downrange.

Funny thing, I wasn't even worried about going.

It almost seemed inevitable, like this had been written into my chapters a long time ago. Maybe it was one of those agreements that Doc was talking about.

No matter what I thought about the inevitability, I couldn't get myself over to Iraq without the proper paperwork. Could I convince General Elliot to send me to the Middle East despite my contract?

The more arguments I had in my back pocket, the better.

I developed a possible travel trajectory from the point that the NSA took the picture. It was the northeast border of Syria, near where the Yazidi lived. The nineteen Yazidi women who had been burned to death in the cage flashed into my imagination.

What a terrible place to be.

This group, had they completed their trek, would be crossing into Turkey. Kaylie could still be aiming that way. Could we flag officials to watch for her? Was that a safe thing to do, or would it put a target on her?

I'd asked Margot for contact information from a CIA officer in that area, John Grey. She'd sent me a text that she'd hit a brick wall. He would have known the area and would be able to answer my questions.

Maybe Sophia would know. She had colleagues in Turkey.

Turkey was shipping the refugees around to various countries, trying to spread out the sheer volume of people. The Syrian population had been twenty-three million about the time Kaylie disappeared, and this statistic said that eight million had sought refuge in other countries in the ensuing years. Seventy-five percent of whom were women and children.

The refugee camp where the possible-Kaylie was headed was now moving the people on to Tajikistan.

A lot of those showing up were kids by themselves. Their mothers were imprisoned, charged with being associated with ISIS, and were awaiting trial.

How could they tell if these women were voluntarily with ISIS or simply trying to save their own lives as slaves and prisoners of ISIS?

What a nightmare.

Would Kaylie be facing trial? Could her kids have been swept along in this human tide? Prescott, I needed to reach out to him when I landed. Granted, it was Friday night here in D.C. It was the wee hours of Saturday morning for him. I had last seen Prescott on Tuesday. That wasn't a lot of time for him to make progress, but it was also day five on the ever-ticking Kaylie clock. Prescott said it was a seven-day window.

He was searching for the children. The weight of finding Kaylie was on me.

Herman said my next step was to go find Trouble with a capital T. And then General Elliot had come back with virtually the same message though for a different task: How do I set Angel free? While he'd written "Trouble," his sketch was of a Middle Eastern-looking compound with down arrows and a helicopter.

They let me see the tasking sheet that Doc had mentioned. Even though it looked like two bubbles to me, fear painted over me when I saw it.

Prescott had said that Kaylie's nickname growing up was Trouble. According to Doc's theory, Prescott wouldn't have offered up that little tidbit had it not been something I needed to hear.

I focused back on the article. Eighty-four minors from Iraq underwent medical checkups. I looked at the dates. This was just last week. I wondered how often the BIOMIST system updated. Was it automatic? And if these kids were landing, was our medical team involved? Would they have captured the children's blood markers? I made a mental note to ask Zoe. She had texted that she had an updated file for me based on the new parameters of Prescott's search request. So possibly new leads. New answers.

Ah, look at this—UNICEF was trying to repatriate those kids to their mother's nation of origin. I pulled out my pad. I had a lot going on in my brain right now. I didn't want to let any of this slide onto a back shelf to be forgotten. One, Zoe. Two, tell Prescott about UNICEF repatriation.

I thought about all the children in the war zones, separated from their families. Families who were trying to seek asylum away from their hell. I thought about Zoe's BIOMIST system applications. If only it weren't a secret, think how it could be applied in our own country at our own borders. Then folks seeking asylum here in the US could be tracked, families reunited more easily. Of course, safety nets would need to be in place to keep the system from becoming something it was never meant to be. It was complicated. It probably needed the attention of professional ethicists.

I went back to the article to see if it mentioned a specific liaison at UNICEF who was involved with the repatriation of minors. If Prescott found Kaylie's kids, they'd already know the process for getting the children to America. There in the last paragraph of the article, it said that some kids were in prisons because their mothers didn't grant permission to repatriate their kids.

While I had questioned if Kaylie wasn't revealing her nationality to stay safe, I hadn't spent much time on the idea that Kaylie simply didn't want to be found. Didn't want to come home. Didn't want her kids to be raised as Americans.

What if Dr. Kaylie Elizabeth Street *was* a jihadi bride?

"Oars in the water," I told myself. "We have to find her to ask."

29

I DROVE RIGHT FROM THE AIRPORT TO SOPHIA'S HOUSE. A TEXT from her dropped as I was making my way to the garage where Gator had left my car.

Now, I was sitting on her couch, my right leg tapping the floor impatiently. Sophia wouldn't tell me about her update on the phone. I needed to come talk to her.

Then, Sophia decided we needed tea.

It was a stalling tactic.

Finally, Sophia emerged from the kitchen, balancing a tray. "I have a contact who's willing to help you," she said without preamble, setting the tray, laden with plates of snacks and mugs of chai, on the coffee table.

"That's a funny hitch in your voice." I reached for the mug and napkin she stretched toward me. "Thank you." I put my nose over the steam and inhaled deeply. "This smells delicious."

"The reason I asked you to come over," she ran her hands down the back of her thighs as she sat down, "I spoke to one of my contacts, a woman in Syria. She knows a story about an American woman." Sophia took her own mug and settled back into the throw pillows, nesting in. "She guesses it's an American woman, at least." Sophia blew across the surface of the hot liquid. "That woman spoke Arabic with an American accent."

I leaned forward in my seat, balancing my mug on my knee and trying not to get too excited. "When was this? Where was your contact at the time?"

"My contact is a woman named Mushkila."

"Mushkila?" I pulled my brow together. "Her parents named her Mushkila? Like 'problem'?"

"It's her military call sign. The ways it's used, it means Trouble. As in, 'If you stand against me, you will meet Trouble.' It comes from a local saying."

Trouble with a capital T. Two different tasks given to two different remote viewers. Both had come up with the same answer. I was supposed to go looking for Trouble. And now there were two Troubles—Kaylie and this Syrian contact. I'd call that an affirmation despite the thirty-five percent probability that everything I'd been told was flat wrong.

"Where is Mushkila?"

"Right now, she's on the Syrian-Iraqi border. In the Kurdish region where the allied troops have cleared most of the ISIS fighters. She's willing to wait there if someone's coming quickly."

"Do you trust her?"

"I knew her before the war. We were friends. I've helped her with her work. I trust her to get a job done." Each short, clipped sentence was delivered in a staccato beat. Sophia obviously was uncomfortable with what she was saying.

"Mushkila and her husband were both educated people and had been part of the resistance that was trying to protect and save the antiquities. Her goal is to stop the free flow of money to ISIS. She works to interrupt the trade routes for both relics and drugs, but she has a harder time interrupting the slave routes. If her unit attacks, too many innocent people are hurt or killed. This then makes slave trading a safer money stream. These are businessmen. They weigh their risks. A human commodity can sicken or fail to perform. Drugs and relics don't need to be kept alive, but the resistance will try to stop the drug and relic trade to stop ISIS from funding their war. The slave market makes the resistance fighters think twice about their attacks. They won't use flyovers, for example. You can see how this becomes a problem for the resistance. Every success Mushkila's unit has in helping me with the relics means she and her fighters are encouraging slavery. She says it's like the whole country is on fire, and all they can do is stomp on the coals to try to put it out."

"You said, 'her unit.' It's amazing that she's in the fight given the gender roles in that part of the world."

"ISIS captured and beheaded her husband, crumbled her village, and killed the families. She'd been away visiting friends during the attack. On her route home, she came across some men, fleeing on foot. They warned her away because ISIS had captured the other young women and girls. Mushkila went to the village, took her uncle's rifle and what bullets she could find, and went after them. She ended up killing the ISIS guards and freeing most of the women. The mothers took their daughters and sought refuge in other villages. But many of the young women had nowhere to go. They decided to form a unit, train, and fight together."

I frowned. "Mushkila must be an incredibly brave woman."

"Not the way she tells the story. She said saving the girls was an accident."

I shook my head, not understanding.

"When she discovered what had happened in her village, she wanted to curl up in a corner and die. She tried to commit suicide, put a gun in her mouth, but she couldn't bring herself to pull the trigger. She decided she'd get the ISIS soldiers to kill her."

I could understand. I'd been in that mental space for brief flashes in my own life. "Wasn't she terrified she'd be taken prisoner and sold as a slave instead?"

"Exactly." Sophia took another sip of her drink then put the mug on the floor by her feet. "But she didn't feel that she had a choice. And that's why the story unfolded the way it did. She went after the ISIS unit wearing her uncle's clothes, hoping that as a man, they'd shoot her. She even sought out the group with the RPG, thinking that would be a faster, more definite death." Sophia talked while watching out the window instead of looking at me. "As she was shooting, she decided she'd kill as many of the ISIS fighters as she could while waiting for them to kill her. Lo and behold, in her rage, she killed them all and saved the others. Mushkila's unit is absolutely fearless." Sophia turned her focus back to me. "Savage. Soon other women with the same aim came to fight with her. An army of women. It's tricky to focus on killing the men when the fighters hold so many women and children in front of them as human shields."

"You spoke with her? She thinks she can help us find Kaylie?"

"Her unit was doing reconnaissance in the same GPS area as the coordinates you gave me from the NSA. Her unit saw the women were in danger from an approaching ISIS group and were trying to get word to them, warning them to disperse into the hills and travel in smaller groups. Before they got to them, the attack began. The women who were doing the reconnaissance work didn't have resources to help."

I scooted to the edge of my seat. "They saw the attack?"

"The ISIS fighters hit them with RPGs, then rounded

everyone up who was still capable of walking. They left the others to die of injuries and exposure. Mushkila's group was going to go after the women who were captured, but the fighters moved the women further north before the unit could act. They were waiting for drone information from a CIA contact when I talked to her last."

Silence fell. I could feel Sophia debating, weighing, unsure. Since I didn't know any of the circumstances, I sat quietly and let her process.

"My contact thinks she can help you find the women." Sophia's voice was so soft I could barely hear her.

"That's wonderful."

"No, you don't understand. My contact thinks she can help *you.* She won't work with a group that's led by men. She only interacts with women-led groups. She's learned to be leery of men and their motives. She knows the U.S. won't send in a military group, that this will be paid contractors who are trying to find the American. It's my fault. I was playing up your role in this rescue attempt to get Mushkila to trust the situation and the idea of working with a unit. I thought it would be enough that you were directing them from the United States."

"All right. I can do that." Maybe. Hopefully.

Her gaze held steady on me. "You're considering this?"

I swallowed. Yeah, it sounded crazy. What did I know about going into a war zone? And if I went, would my lack of skill put our task force in more danger?

"Weigh into that decision, the goal of the unit isn't to stay alive. If you do go, you should understand that. They're okay if they die, and they're okay if you die trying to save other women."

Well, then…that was scary. But, according to Herman Trudy's remote viewing response to how to help Kaylie, I needed to look for Trouble with a capital T, that coupled with my *knowing*, I thought in all probability (well—better than probability, sixty-five-ish percent) this meant I needed to do it in person. Along the Iraqi-Syrian border.

"St. Ia was a martyr," a tiny voice whispered from the back of my mind.

I pushed back against those thoughts—two women named Trouble in the same part of the world? What should I do about Kaylie? Go looking for Trouble. How can I help Angel's soul? Trouble, written with capital T.

It seemed like that was the place to be.

Destiny was destiny, right? I felt little bubbles in my veins as my survival instincts took notice of my thoughts.

"Mushkila has a CIA officer that she works with. He provides her with intelligence analysis to help her unit in the area. You know how this works. In this non-permissive environment, without a verified identification, the CIA will not bring in special operations. They won't even get a plan in place for someone else to intervene. If you go in with an Iniquus mission force, and things go badly, they most probably won't act to get you back out."

"You're worried. I get that. We won't know what things look like until we get there. Does your contact know where ISIS took their captives?"

"Her reconnaissance has been on-site watching. The captured women are being warehoused. The field reports said the ISIS fighters were pulling the women's veils off and taking pictures."

"For a slave auction?" I asked.

"Exactly. They'll probably sort them, too. After they see the women without the veils, certain ones will be set aside for the fighters' rewards. Others will be sold for whatever the owner wants to do with them. I'm trying to identify the website. If I can find it, we'll have all the photos of the women, and we can tell if the woman from the picture made it through the attack. If she's dead, your case would be closed."

"If I got Iniquus researchers involved, would they be able to help find the auction site?"

"It's probably easiest if I work my contacts."

"I appreciate it. I'd imagine if Kaylie survived and was warehoused with the others, that the only way to get to her is to get to all of them."

"That is exactly why Mushkila is willing to wait and willing to help. But she said it has to be you."

"Okay, thanks. Sophia, I had been given a clock to save this woman. That timetable got messed up when the refugees were attacked. I think you've started a new one. If we're going to get to the possible-Kaylie, I'll need to do it before the slave auction closes and the women go off to their new owners. Finding out about that auction, not just for the picture but also for the timing, is important." I stood and set my mug on the tray. "I need to go talk to General Elliot about all this."

"I'll do what I can," Sophia said as she gave me a good-bye hug.

I headed to my car.

I met a man with seven wives, my *knowing* sing-songed in my ear.

"I've got it. I'm going already!"

30

I STOOD IN GENERAL ELLIOT'S HOME OFFICE, MY NOTES FROM these last few days in my hand.

St. Ia had tapped the leaf and created, out of magic, a conveyance to get her from where she was to where she needed to be.

Perhaps I had done a similar thing by gathering these leaves of paper to hand to General Elliot.

He sat behind his desk, his face unreadable.

I'd briefed him on everything I knew, everything I thought I knew, and the much bigger chapter on what I didn't know about this case and about me. I held nothing back.

The most I got back from him in return was a stone face.

Now I sat silently listening to his wall clock's soft tick, tick, tick.

Finally, he laced his hands and put them on his stomach. "It says in your contract in plain English that you're not a field operator. You haven't been trained the way these operators have been."

"And yet I've operated next to them since I was eighteen."

"Not the same thing as a war zone. In that part of the world, females are at greater risk. I could see possibly sending you in to meet with this woman at a base. But you're a bigger prize than the men if you're caught. Imagine the damage you could do to America if they paraded you around and cut off your head on a video. Or like those Yazidi women you were telling me about, Can you imagine the effect of ISIS locking you in a metal cage and lighting you on fire?"

I pursed my lips.

"I only say that because I know it's an argument you might hear. You wouldn't listen to me if I said you shouldn't put yourself in harm's way."

"While we let the men?"

"Can't say I'm the misogynist type. I was thinking more about their training versus yours. All of my operators are SERE trained."

"I'm SERE trained. On the job training. For me, survival, evasion, resistance, escape wasn't a school acronym. I never had the luxury of knowing I could tap out or that I had a hot meal waiting for me at the end of the week, a soft bed, and a slap on the back. For me, it was do or die."

Ha! Sometimes things just smacked me in the face. There was a concept that Miriam and I discussed where the accumulation of life's lessons, both good and bad, formed steppingstones for what was needed next. Who knew that my time in prison would allow me to understand with compassion these women's fates? (And be so grateful that I got off so easy.) That my time in survival mode would give me the key (I hoped) to getting General Elliot to let me go into my next lesson. I *had* to believe I was ready for this. That I could use what I trained and learned along the way to do good. But more importantly, I thought Fate had positioned me for my next big test. The next huge ah-ha.

In theory, I was up to the task.

After all, brave in the face of personal adversity and brave to protect loved ones were different than the brave it takes to put one's self at risk for a stranger. Everyone on Strike Force had that altruistic kind of bravery. It was probably past time for me to test my own mettle.

"Here's why I'm the one for the job—when I went to see General Coleridge, the task said I had to go looking for trouble with a capital T. Did you know that Kaylie grew up in Special Agent in Charge Damian Prescott's neighborhood? They were childhood friends. Kaylie was a tomboy, and she had a nickname."

"Trouble."

"Yes, sir, and what's more. Sophia Abadi's contact, the one who said she could help a female-led unit is named Mushkila, and that's Arabic for—"

"Trouble."

"More or less, yes."

"They are only showing you images. You already knew that Kaylie's nickname was Trouble. They could have been picking up on that in your psychic space."

"I understand. And I get that it could be a coincidence that the two women are called Trouble. Who knows how many strong women are given that nickname? But anything better than fifty-fifty means we have to consider acting. The NSA picture had a sixty-seven percent chance of it being Kaylie. If it weren't for that photo, if someone didn't think, 'Hey, it's a long shot but let's send this out,' then Special Agent in Charge Prescott wouldn't have been knocking on our door. Everyone thought Kaylie was dead. We'd never know about her children."

"You think that the wheel of fortune is turning, and there's momentum to get you where you need to be."

"And that's all I think it is. I think it's the wheel, the vehicle, the thing that is positioning me for where I need to be for the next thing I need to do to accomplish my contracts in this lifetime."

An actual smile wrinkled General Elliot's leathery cheeks. "Ah, I see you've been talking to Doc." He stilled. Sniffed. "All right then. Grab your jump bag. I'll make some phone calls to see about getting you over there. I'll reroute Strike Force, and they'll meet you in the sandbox."

31

"YEP, THANKS, LEXI." DOC'S VOICE CAME OVER MY PHONE speaker. "Now that we've moved through the salutations, you need to take a moment and ground yourself before we get into the fat of this conversation."

"Alrighty then, freak-out it is!" I forced a laugh.

"This is information. That's all it is."

"Sure. Okay." I was lying on the bed in Striker's room. Beetle and Bella were stationed on either side of me, lending me their heat while cold washed me from head to foot. "Do you have information from my Akashic Records?"

"Not yet. When I'm doing something that involved, I have a team with me, keeping the space safe. I'm working on getting it scheduled. Right now, I'm calling to share some of the notes that Herman Trudy has transcribed. I wanted to check in on your Earth-plane experiences at times these notes were written."

"Ready," I said and crossed my finger to undo the lie.

"You have your laptop up?"

"Yes, ma'am," I said. It felt like I was in one of my doctor's appointments for my brain injuries. I was always braced for bad news.

"Good. Jumping in then. Indigo mentioned, in the logs, about making an incision before he changed to write in Galaxy print, the squiggle writing. Do you know what I'm talking about?"

"Yes."

"I'll send all the notes to you that Herman transcribed, but these next few are the ones I want to go over with you. I'm sending it over in legible form, one section at a time. I'll read them aloud as I do. That way, we're on the same thought wave."

There was a *ping*. I pressed the accept button on my secure computer.

Doc began, "It says—'I traveled to her and found the girl in a strange state.' This is Indigo talking about a remote view of you, Lexi, two months before you met Angel. Three months before you married. Interesting courting timeline. Pretty short for a lifetime commitment."

"We married quickly, yes. We wanted to make our vows before he deployed."

"Gotcha." She continued, "'She wasn't sleeping. She wasn't in a coma. She was, how could I express this? *Gone* is what I'd say. Her body seemed injured, beaten, and yet it was not. It was like there was an odd veneer of someone else's injuries on her body, and she was recovering, weak, and open.'" Doc paused. "Do you know what that could mean?"

"Yes, I think so," I told Doc, briefly, about that first time I went so fully behind the Veil, leaving my body to join with the kidnapped victim. How the punches and slashes had bruised and cut my body. How I'd gone into a recuperative sleep. For three days, I had no awareness. When I woke up, Miriam and I discovered that the battle wounds had been like shadows. They weren't part of my real body experience. I had no vestiges—no scars, no discoloration, no aches nor pains, nothing. "When I was in that recovery trance," I told Doc, "I would have been weak, and I also suppose open—if he meant that in an etheric way. The dates line up."

"I can't imagine the Miriam Laugherty I know allowing you to do that," Doc said.

"She didn't. We were both shocked by the turn of events."

"That had never happened before?"

"Exactly. Something changed. Possibly it was this thing Indigo was trying." I swallowed hard. "Indigo had written in his log, 'My first experiment was successful. I was able to make an incision. I think I'll watch it for a day and see what happens.' From that passage, do you suppose he could have cut into me somehow? Into my aura or my…I don't know, into something?"

"I don't know. Lexi, breathe. I'll take a look at that clairvoyantly. I may have more questions for you later about that experience."

"What does that mean, the Gemini experiment? A Gemini is a twin." I blinked at the bedroom wall. "I'm wondering if he found a way to make—I don't know—a copy of someone's experiences?" My mind raced.

"Speculation can cloud the truth. Let's not follow those thoughts right now. Give me time to check your records and see if that is even a possibility."

"Yes, ma'am." I both wanted to know and didn't. A little courage here, Lexi, I chided myself.

"Looking further down the page," Doc said. "We're reading from the next step that starts, 'I couldn't have found her,' That's you."

"Yes." I had my arm over my eyes, trying to come to grips with the idea that mad-hatter Indigo had experimented on me in the ether.

"'I couldn't have found her in a better condition. She was ethereally vulnerable. And at the same time, the boy.' That's Angel."

"Are you sure?" I asked, my hand moving to wrap my throat.

"Yes, Indigo spells it out later on the page. He writes, 'And at the same time, the boy seems to be under anesthesia as they repair something in his shoulder.'"

I searched back in my memory. I was at the gym with Angel. He was wearing a tank top. My fingers had traced over new scars. "Angel told me that he had a shoulder full of shrapnel before Thanksgiving that year. He'd been afraid they'd send him stateside to recover. He didn't want to leave his team in Iraq a man down. I don't know the exact date of his surgery, though. That timeline could make sense. Me and my out of body experience. Angel and the shrapnel. Striker and Tabitha, AKA Scarlet Vine dating, I think this was about the time when she was trying out Sebastian Rheas as a baby boy's name."

"It's noted that whatever Indigo did, it was timed so that he could observe the effects before Indigo arranged for you two to meet."

"The beginning of November until the end of January. There was a time difference of not quite three months. The night Angel and I met, Indigo had his henchmen, Frith and Wilson, set my apartment building on fire. I guess Indigo specifically picked the date of the fire to match up with Angel's visit with Abuela Rosa. And perhaps he was waiting to see if Striker gave his daughter an engagement ring. Tabitha thought Striker was downrange on assignment, but when she saw him at a party, he ducked her." Out of loyalty to Striker—not wanting Doc to think badly of him—I added, "Striker had broken up with Tabitha that December."

Doc said, "Let's look at this next part. Indigo wrote, 'It's done! I feel a bit like a mad scientist. I have to admit it was like being a Nazi doctor conducting human experiments. Soul be damned.' That's the last that he wrote about that. Then moving forward, I'll post another section to your screen now."

"Soul be damned"? His or mine? Angel's? Was *this* why Angel was in Hell?

The computer dinged. I tapped and brought up the new passage.

"Got it?"

"Yes, ma'am." *Soul be damned*? My lips were buzzing.

"Here Indigo says, 'I'm going to get Spyder back to Washington. It's as if the universe is aligning to help me. It's all so perfect.'"

"You can almost hear the evil scientist with his bwahaha!" I said.

"It's evil. We agree on that. Okay, we're on the second paragraph. 'Maybe there is such thing as Karma, and now it's finally serving my needs. The boy is finally on leave and coming to see his great aunt. On the Earth level, I can see if this is the way that I can get Tabitha what she wants from a relationship with Striker. If I'm right, what a great night! Frith will be burning down the nest, forcing the baby bird away from the clucking hens, making her vulnerable to Wilson's attack.' Sounds like Indigo's been giving you a rough ride for years now."

"Yes, ma'am." And it seemed his influence continued even after his death.

"Then he wrote, 'Lexi will call Spyder in to save her. The boy will have arrived, but he won't be in the picture to save her from Wilson. Angel will be right back in the field. Three weeks. According to my tasked views. Will this be enough time? Note: make sure Frith sees the boy arrive. I want the reaction of Lexi and Angel's meeting captured on video. The ramifications of this experiment can be immense!!!'"

"Three exclamation points," I said.

"He was rather excited about what he did. Yep. Crazy. I will tell you I looked clairvoyantly at what happened after Indigo's death. His essence has been sequestered from his learning group. Essence being the word used when it's no longer a reincarnating soul. Some people just call it a "being." He'll be sequestered off and no longer be allowed to manifest in a body form. He's done."

"I can't say that gives me any comfort."

"I assume not. Ready for the last part?" Doc asked. "This one speaks to your ongoing issues now that Angel died."

"I'm *not* ready, but go ahead, anyway."

"Indigo writes, 'I looked forward in time, Lexi is receiving news that Angel is dead. I hadn't thought of this. I'm not sure what will happen to her now. It's a part of the experiment that I hadn't considered, and yet, what a great test to see how things work out on the body level.' You have no idea what this could be?"

"I do. Indigo and Tabitha, when she was calling herself Scarlet, were trying to psychically influence Striker and make him love her and marry her."

"She's not in his learning group. I know because I worked with Indigo when he was on the Galaxy project. I researched his learning group, his family, his fellow Galaxy operators, and so on. Of course, his wife, son, and daughter were part of that. Spyder was not. Elliot was not. I was not. Having contact doesn't mean you're from the same group. But we have sister groups, if you will. Groups that like to bump up against each other and cross-pollinate our storylines. Sort of like good genetics, it's important to mix things up to keep everyone healthy."

"Miriam taught me a bit about that but in passing. Nothing in-depth."

"It's a whole spiritual study. You don't need to worry about it. Just that Tabitha and Striker didn't have the potential on the soul level to marry because they're from different learning groups. Let's read on. 'Striker has a dangerous job. He's not searchable in the ether, just like Spyder and Elliot aren't—they're too dense. Same with Angel. It was fortunate, and I think divinely constructed, that Lexi and Angel were vulnerable in the same time frame. A time when I felt compelled to go and check on them. God is on my side. It's interesting to note that when I try to check on Angel, I could find him when he was in the German hospital and when he was visiting America, but when he's in the Middle East, the psychic pollution coupled with his own protections make it impossible. Lexi, too, when she's not in crisis, can't be read. Fortunately for me, she is frequently in crisis. I just need to send myself on the right task, making sure that I don't compromise the data by having the desired outcome in mind. That's what's been tripping Tabby Cat up as she's been looking at Striker. I'm merely there to observe and counsel. Except for my little experiment. In that case, I'm God's right hand.'"

"I should be more frightened hearing this than I am," I said. "This has a familiarity to it."

I stopped to weigh those words and decided they were accurate. "Reading these notes, we know Indigo did *something* in the ether. If it was meant to hurt me, I don't think I'd be able to tell the difference in mental pain that November. My mother had just died. I thought my grief was what opened me like that to the psychic connection behind the Veil. I can say for sure that things got markedly bad—emotionally, psychically—when Angel deployed. The day we got married, though, was my first note from stalker Wilson. I had a nightmare almost every night. From the time Angel took off. But after he died, the connection was different. The pain of being his wife has never eased—these last ten days. I honestly don't think I can survive it. I don't want to go through life feeling like this. It's torture."

"Interesting you should use that word," Doc said. "Putting up the next section."

Ding, the computer sounded. I tapped the button.

Doc read, "'The torture of Angel's death is compounded by Lexi's own physical circumstances. She is trying to form a real-world relationship with Striker, but I can see that the energy of her ties to Angel is preventing this. Interesting note: in remote viewing sessions, I'm shown the picture of Angel and Lexi in the judge's chamber taking their vows. It's a sticking point. I even see Striker and Lexi want to make vows at a future time, but Lexi will be unable to say those words to him. I have decided that I won't attempt this intervention on Tabitha and Striker. It seems that it would cause her too much pain even after death. Curious. I wonder why that would be. I have a hypothesis: Dead Angel is connected to live-Lexi. Though Angel's body was buried, that is but a life vessel. Angel wouldn't need a physical body for his soul as long as Lexi is alive. Lexi is the vessel that transports her soul, and hence Angel's as well. Ergo, Angel is both dead and alive. His soul can't rest until Lexi dies. I'll continue to watch this. It's an interesting twist. Following along with these thoughts, I postulate that the problem for Lexi marrying Striker is that she swore an oath to Angel, 'until death do us part.' How little does she realize that's exactly right. Until her body is dead, she will be tied to Angel. Actually, I don't know if that's true. It could just as well be true that they will always be bound for eternity. Perhaps not even death can separate them. Still, I need to find a way to change the future for Tabby Cat and Striker. I have an idea. My next experiment will be on General Elliot. If this works on the general, I can work on Striker next.'"

Well then. I lay there silently. That was when he started thinking about influencing General Elliot. Not just as an experiment on the general but as another Guinea pig to trap Striker.

"Lexi? Are you okay?" Doc asked. "I've been sending you golden light to help you through all this."

"I can feel it. Thank you. I know this should boggle my mind. But I'm oddly okay. Well, okay, in a horrifying kind of way. It all lines up his notes and our experiences. My feelings. Knowing that there is a cause and effect is helpful. Doc, have you ever heard of anything like Indigo's experiments before?"

"It's all brand spanking new to me."

"Here's the more important question, is there anything you can do as a psychic physician to help me?"

32

I SHUT THE DOOR BEHIND NUTSBE. HE HAD A DOG BED UNDER each arm as Beetle and Bella flanked him, walking down the hall to the elevator. My bag was on the chair. Sophia had lent me a niqab, the veil that covers a woman's whole face except for her eyes.

She also handed me an indigo-colored burka. I found that to be ironic, given the prevalence of Indigo in my thoughts. Sophia said this would be the safest way to hide my pale skin and blue eyes. It was like throwing a huge sheet over my head and looking out through a mesh window. I'd need to practice with this if I were to wear it. It was disorienting to me, and there was no peripheral vision.

I was rinsing my breakfast bowl in the sink when my phone rotated on the counter as it buzzed.

I was surprised to find it was Prescott. He sounded exhausted. "We have the boy," he exhaled.

"What?" I couldn't believe it. "That's amazing. The machine found a match?"

"I used the analyzer for Zoe's research. But I didn't need it.

This kid's the spitting image of Kaylie as a kid. Blond hair, blue eyes, sunburned fair skin."

"What about the people he's staying with. Did they tell you the circumstances of the child not being with Kaylie? Are they mad that you're taking him away?"

"The village was abandoned ahead of a band of Taliban. The old guy and his wife had decided to stay where they were. The rest had headed toward the mountains. That was back in the spring. The couple found the boy outside of his house abandoned by the family. The guy and his wife took him in."

"How horrible. I wonder why the family would abandon a little boy that way."

"I told the couple I'd take the boy back to his mother's family. And that was fine with them."

"Nothing about Kaylie?"

"Nothing good. Kaylie was with the group of ISIS fighters who had come to the village to take food and supplies. Kaylie gave birth while she was here, and her milk didn't come in. A neighbor who had just had her own baby offered to feed the boy. They call Kaylie's son Ameer just like on the intake forms. The second two names were the names of the neighbor's husband. They didn't know Kaylie's name. The man said Kaylie abandoned her child, so the infant could be fed. She left with the fighters."

"Wow."

"The man didn't know anything beyond that."

"What happens next?"

"We're sending Ameer back to the States on a medical flight. This military post is nowhere for a three-year-old kid to be. He's in the infirmary now getting checked out. He'll stay with the nurses so my team can head back out to the field. Right now, though, I'm going to have a shower and get some sleep. Our next focus will be on the oldest daughter."

"That's incredible. I'm thrilled. How long do you think that nap's going to be? I'm heading your way, and I'd like to compare notes."

"Here? To Iraq?"

"I'm a strap on a flight out of Norfolk with a SEAL team. I'm heading down the stairs now to throw my duffel into my car." I checked my watch then went through the apartment, turning off lights.

"You and who else?"

"I'm not enough?" I tried to sound offended.

"Iniquus is a team sport."

"Strike Force will beat me in. They're already in the air. I'm bringing their equipment in with me."

"Iniquus wouldn't have a team here unless you have actionable intelligence." His voice had the edge of excitement.

"Actionable enough to put us in place. There are some contacts that need a face to face." I took a moment to explain the slave auction and what would happen if we didn't get there in time.

"Are you leaving this up to Sophia to find the auction site?"

"Iniquus is searching for it, too. If they find something, they'll run it by Sophia." I hefted my duffel strap over my shoulder.

"Even if we identify that woman from the NSA photo as being on the slave market site, the FBI CIRG isn't going in unless we can prove she's Kaylie. It's going to end up being on Strike Force's shoulders. I don't think a single mission force is going to be enough for this kind of an operation."

I grabbed my keys from the bowl and pulled the door shut

behind me. "As of now, this is the way Iniquus is going to handle the situation." I headed toward the elevator. "We're not contracted with the FBI. We're merely supporting each other's efforts. Our focus is on fulfilling our contract with the insurance group."

"Understood." He was recalibrating. This time he and I were working side by side but not hand in hand. We each had our own agendas. Now, his words were carefully measured. "I appreciate the strategies, information, and resources that Iniquus has shared. The FBI values the ongoing partnership on this case as well as the many other cases we have in common. I hope you feel open to continuing forward in the same vein."

That was quite the change in tone. It was interesting that I'd set Prescott back on his heels momentarily. But that's not where I wanted him. I had wanted to set boundaries, so he didn't feel like he had command of me or my mission. I needed to warm the air between us a bit. "To be successful with the Kaylie Street mission, I think we're going to need all the friends we can get."

33

I HAD NEVER FLOWN ON A MILITARY PLANE BEFORE. THAT wasn't true. I had never flown on a military plane while I was conscious. I had a pill in my pocket, so that would be true this time too.

It was a thirteen-hour flight, and the men in the area were talking about their traveling latrines and pointing to plastic bottles on their pack. I had a plastic food container with me that I guessed I could use if life became unbearable. I'd limit my liquids intake and make sure the last thing I did before stepping on that plane was to find a restroom.

That sounded darned uncomfortable. Not that I was complaining. I was just glad to be able to get wheels up so quickly.

I wouldn't think that slave auctions would be held open for bids for too long.

We couldn't miss this opportunity.

Mushkila was waiting for me at the border. And my team would have already landed and found bunks in the contractor tents. I wondered what they'd think of my being in on a mission.

Sure, I'd done domestic things with my team. I've dressed up like an escort, planted bugs, spied, lied, and coerced. I've killed in action before, shooting at bank robbers when we got caught up in a wrong place/wrong time scenario. Well, from the perspective of the people we saved, right place/right time. But I've never gone overseas on a mission. Or to a conflict zone.

Would they be pissed?

I sat on the ground in a corner, trying to stay out of people's way. All these people in their uniforms and short-cropped hair were trained for combat. I was a stealth walker, a martial arts girl. I had skills. But not these peoples' skills.

There was a very intense Malinois who made his way over to sniff me, scrunching down and dragging his handler at the other end of the leather lead. I seemed to pass the test when he smelled Beetle and Bella on my legs and knew I was a dog person.

His handler looked at me with curiosity but didn't start a conversation. It might be my lack of uniform. Or my lack of confidence.

I wasn't trained to play team sports. Spyder had trained me to act on my own. A one-man band. Well, a one-woman band.

Civilians went into hot zones, I reminded myself. Linguists, journalists…

I did have Arabic language skills. I'd learned from my kitchen Grandmother Jadda. While she was from Turkey, she married a man from Morocco, and they spoke Arabic in the house. My accent might be a problem. And most of my vocabulary had to do with cooking. But who didn't like to talk about food?

I pulled out the booklet Iniquus had for their contractors heading to Iraq.

These rules didn't seem too hard to remember. Stand when someone older than you walked into a room. Avoid sitting, so the soles of your shoes are pointing at anyone. It was an insult. So was crossing your legs when facing someone.

I looked down at my crossed legs and wondered what I was supposed to do with them. I pulled them around and tucked my feet under me. That was uncomfortable. Maybe in the Burka, my legs wouldn't be an issue.

If someone offers me something or made a gesture of kindness, I was supposed to protest. I shouldn't accept the offer until they insisted. Huh. I wondered about Kaylie and her newborn. When the woman offered to nurse Kaylie's son, surely, Kaylie wouldn't have said, "Thank you, but that's too kind. I wouldn't put you out." Surely, Kaylie just took her crying baby and pressed him into the stranger's arms, knowing that, in all probability, she'd have to leave that baby behind if the person who owned Kaylie told her they were leaving. A life and death decision when baby bottles and formula, or even water, might be scarce to non-existent.

Horror. I simply couldn't imagine the horror and the inevitability of that non-decision.

I swallowed hard. This wasn't the place to tear up.

I tried to focus back on basic Iraqi etiquette and the separation of hand duties, the left being used for washing and cleaning and not to be used for pointing or touching people. I read that three times. I was still visualizing Kaylie and the infant. Kaylie walking away.

Startling when my phone rang, I checked the screen. Doc. "Hey there."

"There's a lot of noise. Where are you?"

"I'm waiting for them to load the plane. I'm heading to Iraq in just a few minutes."

"I was working on your case this morning. I got a message for you with clairaudience. It said you're on a journey to find one person, but your path will take you to another," Doc said. "It makes sense that I found you at the airport."

I stuck my finger in my ear to block some of the ambient noise. "I'm not following."

"Hold onto that message. Clarity will come." She chuckled. "In hindsight, it's usually crystal clear."

"*That* I understand. It happens to me all the time. I have a *knowing* about going to St. Ives that I'm still chewing on. Any insight there? '*As I was going to St. Ives, I met a man with seven wives.*'"

"Nope. You're on your own with that one. It's good that you understand that sometimes things need to unfold in a certain way."

"My mentor, Spyder McGraw—well, you know him. You've mentioned him before. Spyder likes to remind me that I should sit aloof when things happen. I find that I have not yet mastered aloofness." I pulled my earbuds from my pocket and stuck them in my ears, then attached the cord to my phone.

I picked up on Doc's response with, "...few do. Though understanding the concept means, at least, it weighs into your processing to some degree. Are you meeting up with your team?"

"If their plane was on time, they just landed in Iraq. It means they'll leave me with an upper bunk since I'm later coming in. I may actually know what your message was about. I'm hooking up with a resistance fighter who might have information or contacts to move us forward in our search for a missing woman. Did you pick up anything about her on your woo-woo channel? I'm guessing that's what you meant when you said, 'you're on a journey to seek one person but to find another.' Anything about the outcome of this little adventure?"

"I haven't seen hide nor hair of a missing woman in your clairvoyant images."

"That's a shame." I spun around so I could guard my words better from any listening ears. "Speaking of teams. Were you able to get your friends together? I'm feeling anxious to know what Indigo was up to."

"That's what I'm calling about. I've been researching your case in the Records. In particular, I was looking at the people you're working with in this lifetime. I think it's best to have them on a team with me for our next step. I picked out Miriam Laugherty and Jean Marie Rochambeau."

"We call Jean Marie 'Gator.' Or 'Gator Aid.'"

"Ah, that explains that picture." She chuckled. "Let's cut to the chase. It looks like we need to do some work with you on the etheric level."

I stalled, not sure what that encompassed.

"My plan right now is to set up a secure Internet connection. Miriam can be at her home."

One hand on the wall, the other gripping at the phone, I reminded myself, it's just another step forward. I reached for the aloofness we'd just been talking about.

"I see that Gator is damned protective of you in the ether. I'd like him to be physically with you. Or, I'm afraid he'd intervene when he shouldn't."

"Okay. In Iraq? Or should we wait until everyone's back stateside?"

"My sense is that this has become urgent. I would even call it a crisis. Don't ask. I don't know why."

"You said you were doing research. Can you give me any information about that?"

"Some cool stuff," Doc said. "You'd better make sure you're sitting down for this."

I pulled my knees up and rested my forehead against them.

"Angel and you are, of course, from the same spiritual group—the ones that are supposed to learn lessons together. The two of you would have had a natural affinity for each other."

"Yes. That's one of the notes from Indigo that Herman translated for me—Indigo had looked at my soul group to find someone who was a male and the right age to marry me. This was taking arranged marriage to a ridiculous level. Indigo called soul groups "pods." In his notes, he speculated that he needed to choose someone from there, so I had a 'natural affinity.'"

"When Herman read that over, he remembered that he had done some remote viewing for Indigo. It had nothing to do with you, but it was written up in a notebook. And Herman found the notebook and transcribed this new information."

"Oh, boy."

"Yep, it's a doozy. It turns out that Indigo, in his early remote viewing tasks on the subject of his grand experiment, had been shown pictures about blood types. From there, Indigo extrapolated that if he tried to connect two people, the souls would reject the connection, like a poorly matched organ donation or incorrect blood type."

"Blood types?"

"It's a metaphor. I'll explain. Indigo noted that Tabitha wasn't in Striker's pod, and this raised concerns about rejection and what that might look like if he tried to surgically conjoin their spirits."

"Surgical… Sew them together? Holy moly," I whispered.

"Let me read this part to you. He said, 'I might take up the experiment on someone else, conjoining two random people just to see what would happen next.' He's talking there about choosing two arbitrary people from different learning groups who therefore didn't belong together to see what would happen if they were attached, in the hopes that he'd be able to form an attachment between Striker and Tabitha, who are not from the same soul group."

"I'm following."

"Then Indigo wrote, 'Lexi is too precious of a commodity. If this surgery kills her, I won't have my weapon to torture Spyder and drag him home.'" There was a pause. "Gator," Doc said with irritation. "Move over."

There was another pause, and I tried to imagine what was going on.

"Gator's here in the ether, listening to us, and he's crowding me. You and Gator are in that same group. But I can see that you've already determined that. I bet when you got word that Angel died, everyone on your team took that death hard. Especially Striker."

"They did, which I thought was touching but odd since they'd never met Angel. I assumed it was compassion for me. Why especially Striker?"

"In their past lifetimes, their relationships have been very close. Not brothers, but brothers in arms. You're all in the same warrior clan."

"I can see that being true." This was such a weird conversation to be having, sitting on an airport floor. Well, to be having anywhere, really.

"I saw in your contracts that you and Striker had agreed to marry in this lifetime. And I know you're wearing his engagement ring. Despite what Indigo has done, you seem to be on your right path."

I reached my thumb to spin Striker's engagement ring. Then I remembered I'd left my rings at the apartment for safekeeping. "I'm sorry," I said. "My mind is back on Indigo's dog. When Indigo had his dog spayed, was that an ah-ha moment when he figured out how to stitch Angel and me together? I didn't have a twin, did I? What General Coleridge saw was how I was conjoined with Angel?"

"I have to say, you're mighty calm with that thought."

"It's the first time I've thought it, but it seems like I already knew. I'm not shocked. Maybe I am shocked, and I'm just not processing the freak out right now. Right now, I feel like I'm handling things okay. I'm assuming the procedure you want to do in the ether is some kind of psychic surgery to separate us back out?"

"Exactly. It's a decision that you need to make. Probably with your loved ones putting in their two cents. I've never come across a case like this before. And anything I do will be experimental. I have no idea of the consequences. I'd set up a meeting as soon as you get to your team. I'd like Striker, Gator, and Miriam on the line. The more questions asked in the beginning, the better, I think."

"This connection to Angel is making my life difficult. That's too mild a word. I don't have the right vocabulary. I'm not the only one suffering. Angel has been telling me he's in Hell, and he wants me to save him. I'm sure you wouldn't have contacted me if you didn't have a plan. I don't need that plan right now. That can wait until everyone is talking together. But do you have a projection for what would happen on the other side of your psychic surgery?"

"Once I get you two separated, it's going to take time to readjust. I'd imagine you'll feel bereft. Maybe even phantom pain. In my mind, I'm thinking of this like an amputation. If that's the case, you'll need to rediscover the boundaries of your own aura. You and Angel are both going to have to learn to stand apart on a spiritual level. It's going to be a period of recalibration, rebalancing. No matter what—I can't say this in more rigorous or direct words—do not reach out to him in the ether. Do not walk behind the Veil to help him in any way. Hell or no Hell, that's on his soul and for his spiritual helpers to figure out. You're not to even check on him clairvoyantly. I feel so strongly about it that I would like you to make that vow to me. For a year and a day, you will not seek Angel in the ether. Agreed?"

"I so vow." When I said it, my whole system felt like it had been set on simmer. I flushed and perspired as energy bubbled through my body. I wondered if that was me realizing I'd signed a soul contract with Doc, or if this was my electrical system freaking out.

Doc did one of her low deep chuckles. It reminded me of Spyder and his roll of thunder laugh. Spyder said it was important to have a belly laugh every day, no matter the circumstances; it helped to balance the dark with the light. Doc's chuckles had that kind of feel to them. Like they were a tool for reminding her about aloofness and releasing an attachment to an outcome.

"I just blew your calm right out of the water, didn't I?" she asked. "Now I can see what was under there. You're doing fine. Let those emotions come up. We can't heal them if they're hidden." Her voice took on the timbre that Spyder used when he hypnotized me. "Whew, you're full of emotions. I can see you were pushing down the shock and anger. I can see how you're trying to be pragmatic and stoic. I agree with you, though, that Angel needs to be saved from his Hell."

That was exactly what I was thinking. Angel didn't deserve to burn for a year and a day simply because I made a vow. His soul was attached because of Indigo and me.

Angel was an innocent bystander.

"This psychic surgery might do the trick. It might not. Either way, you made a vow. You'll need time to settle into your body, so you can understand what your unmanipulated relationship was supposed to be."

"Did you see that contract? If not my husband, what was Angel supposed to be to me?"

"For this lifetime? You were supposed to be a brush past. Someone whose company you enjoyed when you happened to be in the same room. A vague contact."

"Psychic surgery it is. When?"

"Let me catch up with Miriam. You need to talk with Striker. Just like any other surgery, you need to talk about the risks. They aren't to be taken lightly. You need some time to process. It isn't something you can put off for long. There's something ticking. A timer. It has to be done before the buzzer goes off."

"Kaylie? The missing woman?"

"That doesn't ring true. It's something else."

"Okay, great. Two timers ticking then."

"Gator, thanks for holding space for us," she said. "When I'm doing surgery, you can't push on me like that. Understood?"

I didn't hear Gator's response. He must have made one because Doc said, "Thank you. And Lexi, you have a lot going on right now. Striker has a process of compartmentalizing so he can stay present and focused. You'd do well to mimic that too. You're not exactly sipping champagne on the beach over in Iraq. Head in the game."

"Yes, ma'am. Head in the game."

34

My bottom was numb. Now I knew what it meant to fly as a strap. I'd been given a metal bench to sit on with a kind of plastic netting behind me.

Pallets and equipment were secured in place by strapping them to the netting.

One of those palettes was Iniquus equipment. Strike Force had gone to Poland as a security detail. They'd worn suits that had been specially designed to look upscale but were made of fabric that wouldn't dampen, soil, or wrinkle. Their clothes, from button-down shirts to suit coats, were made of a material that would stretch with movement. Each accessory had a purpose, from the survival belt buckle—that hid a compass, high lumen flashlight, and knife—to the tie clip that served as a body cam. It was all cutting-edge cool.

But it wouldn't serve them well in a conflict zone.

I not only had their Iniquus uniforms with me, but a whole array of ammunition, weapons, computer systems, and other equipment that would help us write another success story. I hoped.

The people on the bench with me were likewise strapped in. We had all popped our Rx sleep aids and had slept most of the way here.

The SEALs got to string hammocks up. It was their resonant snoring that had roused me.

That and the Malinois (I found out his name was Bungee) panting in his crate.

We must have been descending. My ears were painful. I yawned to pop them.

The landing gear rumbled into place under my feet. The plane tipped nose up. There was a screech of the braking system, and we were here.

I was anxious to see how my being down range was going to play out with my team.

I was equally anxious to know what Striker and Gator were going to say about my Indigo discoveries.

The first time I kissed Striker under the mistletoe, I knew I was home.

Mistletoe was a parasite, I thought as I unhooked myself from the netting. And Angel's soul was a kind of parasite. Wasn't that a sick little concept?

"Are you gonna barf?" The guy next to me was trying to give me room should I need it.

I wondered what kind of face I was making. "I'm good." *Wish that were true.*

I SHOULD NEVER HAVE WORRIED about my team. There they were, in their shirts and slacks, looking a little warm on this ninety-degree day, but otherwise wonderful.

There was a round of high fives to welcome me. Then the

guys got to work on dealing with the equipment like I'd done this a million times before.

Striker didn't kiss me, didn't reach for my duffle, or take my hand. He wasn't exerting any claiming body language. It was a hundred percent professional as we strode through the forward operating base to the contractors' corner.

He showed me the tent. I had a section blocked off with a tarp at the back. There weren't any other female contractors on the base right now—no one for me to bunk with.

"How was the flight?" Striker asked as I sidled back to stow my bag.

"I was medicated."

He laughed. "That's for the best. General Elliot said you've done another one of your magic tricks, and we might just be bringing the dead back to life."

"He caught you up on the case?"

"Prescott did when he brought Kaylie's son in." Striker pulled the tarp down, so we were in the back of the tent alone. He pulled me into his arms and kissed me like we'd been apart for months, not days. I didn't mind at all. I wished it could go further, a lot further, but I wouldn't be so indiscreet around my team.

"Do you have a next step?" he asked as I cuddled into his chest.

"I'm reaching out to Sophia as soon as I unpack my SAT phone. In the meantime. I have a GPS and a phone number for her contact, Mushkila."

He held me tight against him. "Mushkila, 'problem?'"

I leaned back to catch his eye. "Sophia says 'Trouble' that it's from a local phrase." I bet he'd be glad to get out of that button down and into his usual compression shirt and tactical pants. I wouldn't mind helping him with that process. I grinned, remembering that Striker and I had once had a heartfelt conversation about the dangers of horniness in a conflict zone. It was a throwback to our caveman preservation ways. And look, my body was proving the theory. Too bad they didn't give me a women's shack somewhere.

"Stop looking at me that way, Chica. You're making it hard—"

"Oh, am I?" I reached out my hand to paint over his zipper, grinning at what I found there.

"You're making it hard for me to behave. The guys are going to be back in just a—"

The door squealed.

"Second," he finished.

"Poo," I grumped.

"Exactly." He dropped a kiss onto my head. Then louder, "Mushkila?"

"I'm hoping Mushkila has data from her CIA resource. If she doesn't, General Elliot said Iniquus would reach out to Langley. Sophia is trying to get us a time frame for taking action."

"We're changing into our uniforms," Deep called so I'd stay put.

Striker sat on my cot and pulled me onto his lap. "A lot happened in the last couple of days. I'm anxious to hear about Puerto Rico and Wyoming. How is Abuela Rosa?"

"Better. But that trip took an unexpected turn. Let me tell you that story when Gator's here. I need to share some information about Wyoming, too."

DRESSED in an Iniquus gray camo uniform, I stood out from the others because of my gray niqab. It had its benefits. For example, it kept sand from between my teeth when the wind picked up. The breathing thing was strange. Like wearing a medical mask under a heat lamp. Now that the temperatures were cooling, it wasn't quite as claustrophobic.

Maybe I'd get used to it.

I hoped I wasn't here long enough to get used to it.

We were loading up provisions and water. We planned to spend the night. But they said to always be prepared for worst case. No one was going to drive out to this particular location and give us a ride home if anything were to go contra to plan.

I didn't weigh in. I didn't know anything about anything. My plan was to snap to when asked to do something and be zero problems.

Okay, my track record on the problem part was pretty bad, but still. Today was another day to try.

With satellite oversight that Nutsbe was monitoring for us from Panther Force war room back at Headquarters, we drove to the Iraqi-Syrian border.

Normally, Deep was the Strike Force computer and logistics guru, but the team hadn't needed that for Poland. General Elliot had rerouted the entire team as soon as they put their executives back on their private plane bound for New York.

Our team was divided between two armored vehicles. Blaze drove, Striker sat beside him. I was bobbing along with the rough terrain in the back seat next to Randy. This was Randy's first mission back following his death-defying recovery from a terrorist attack last July. It was good to see him here. He was obviously in his element.

Behind us, Gator was at the wheel. Jack was shotgun. In the back seat, Deep and Axel.

Blaze swished the windshield wipers to push some of the dirt to the side. Up ahead was a large village that had been pitted by bombs. I had no idea if this destruction was done by the U.S. or ISIS. It looked dangerously uninhabitable, with tall buildings ready to collapse.

When Blaze pulled the vehicle into a shadow and turned off the engine, I sent a message to Mushkila in Arabic: **We're here**.

Sophia said Mushkila spoke Kurdish and Arabic as a second language.

Our car was air-conditioned. When I opened the door, it was like sticking my face into an oven. The dashboard said it was only ninety degrees. Striker and the other men had been drinking bottle after bottle of water and had been pressing me to catch up. Heatstroke could be deadly. None of us was acclimated to this heat. The guys, though, would be much better about it than me. After all, they'd served long years here. They'd fought days-long battles in a hundred- and twenty-degree weather. Blaze was just laughing about the time when he'd been on a roof in his ghillie suit, doing overwatch with an IV of saline solution dripping in his vein to keep him functioning.

"Speaking of overwatch," Striker said. "How about you and Randy find some nests."

"Nutsbe to Strike Force Actual." Nutsbe's voice came over the comms.

Striker keyed the mic on his chest. "Go for Striker."

"I have about twenty figures due north. They've been there for about an hour. Looks like they're just sitting."

"Any other movement or vehicles?"

Gator pulled up beside us and shifted out of gear. The men popped open their doors—heads on a swivel.

"Not that I can make out," Nutsbe said.

"Copy." Striker turned to face the team. "Here we go."

My teammates stacked up, rifles in hand. I didn't know my place in the pecking order.

"Lynx." Striker looked at me. "We didn't have time to teach you tactics. I want you to let us get ahead of you, and you're to shadow walk behind us, working from cover to cover."

Shadow walking was a skill set that I'd learned from my martial arts master as a small child and honed with consistent practice. It allowed me to move like a ninja without being observed. The technique has served me well and saved my life on more than one occasion. I was glad to have this skill out here. And would happily employ it.

"If you see movement, disappear. If there's any gunshot, I want you to stay invisible and make your way back to the overwatch. Clear?"

"Yes, sir." I didn't usually "yes, sir" Striker. But here, I wasn't his fiancée. I was a teammate. I wanted to be clear that our roles changed with the circumstances.

My SAT phone buzzed as I got a reply that we were welcome and then a string of numbers to tell me the GPS location within a meter of where she stood.

First, entering the coordinates into our systems, including waypoints back to the vehicles and our overwatch, we trekked through the cubist surrealism of demolished urban landscape.

Rubble was tied with ribbons of wire. Charred wood. The remains of a cooking fire. Hard surfaces were softened by the litter of colorful cloth, quilts, pieces of satiny clothing.

Here, a flash of lilac or scarlet. A moment of magenta or salad green. There was a leg, bare but for its shoe, dried in the heat, blooming with fungus. In the fire lay a ribcage, surely human at some earlier point.

Up ahead, a wall of barrels was topped with sandbags to shoulder height. It would stop most rounds. They were safe enough as long as the enemy wasn't firing an RPG or something bigger.

"They're around the next corner to the south." Nutsbe's voice was in my ear.

Striker waved me forward and whispered, "You're lead."

I flipped my rifle onto my back and held my hands where they were visible as I rounded the corner. "Greetings from Sophia," I called out, seeing no one.

A blue bedsheet flapped in the wind over an opening. A moment later, it was thrown back.

A woman emerged. Her waist-length hair was braided to hang down her back. She wasn't wearing a veil, so I yanked off my niqab with relief. "My team has men," I warned her in case she wanted to veil.

"You and your team are welcome." I held up my hand to signal Strike Force forward, then walked under the sheet.

The women moved into a disciplined line in the space.

This had been someone's living room once. An oriental-patterned rug lay over a spotless tile floor.

My team came in one by one, saw the women, and moved to the other side of the room, where they lined up and stood at attention.

"I'm Lynx," I said in Arabic but pronouncing my name in English. I didn't know how to say Lynx in Arabic. "I bring you greetings of friendship." Shoot, was I supposed to protest being welcomed? That didn't feel like the right thing to do. I reached into my backpack and pulled out the box I brought of candy and dried fruit. I held it out with my right hand.

"This was too kind," Mushkila said.

"It's my honor." I held the box further out.

"I accept them with gratitude." She took the box then handed it over to the next woman in line, who took them and left the room. "I'm Sophia's friend and fellow resistor, Mushkila." She pointed at her chest, then went down the line of the other women's names.

The women wore loose camouflage pants that reminded me of the pants Hammer had worn in his video. They looked much cooler and more comfortable than the camouflage tactical pants I was wearing. The women had stuffed the bottoms of their hems into their combat boots. Their rifles were slung over their shoulders or propped against the wall close at hand.

Broad squares of cloth printed with bright flowers were tied around their heads or necks. I was surprised to have such vivid colors on a warrior. I thought it would make them an easier mark. But what did I know about combat? I wasn't going to second guess these warriors.

Wow, some of them looked young—mere babies.

One of them was wearing a T-shirt that had been hand-lettered, "War and religion were created by men. God is a woman."

Mushkila watched me read. "We want to create our own history." Her eyes traveled to my team.

"At ease," I said, not sure that was the right thing. They shifted to parade rest as I introduced each one. Before I got to Gator, Mushkila's phone rang.

She frowned and answered it. Her words were rapid Kurdish, and I had no idea what she was saying. Blaze leaned in, and the team drifted around to listen to him. "Two snipers from ISIS were shooting. She thinks they must have tracked our vehicles coming across the open road. She wanted to get to them and get them dispatched before they could report their findings to anyone. She's agreeing to something she's hearing. She's telling the person to come and speak to them. The name she said is Grey, like the color."

I smiled. Perfect. I had tried to find him through Margot, and that had been a dead end. But now he was coming to me.

When Mushkila hung up, she made a command, and her unit grabbed their guns up. "We can help," I said. "Just tell us what's needed."

"There's fresh tea in the pot. Make yourselves comfortable."

I watched as Mushkila, then each of the women dropped into a channel dug into the dirt. It allowed them to walk through the village ruins in a low crouch without exposing their heads.

"We'll be back, *Inshallah*," she called. *God willing.*

35

FOR SOME REASON, THE BLUE BEDSHEET HANGING ACROSS THE door to a room that opened to the sky gave the space a sense of security.

When I walked to the other side of it, I felt exposed, maybe a little vulnerable.

I thought, with Mushkila's unit gone, this might be my opportunity to contact Miriam and Doc. I wanted a plan before we got down to the nitty-gritty of our mission to find the possible Kaylie. I also needed to get in touch with Sophia.

Iraq was seven hours ahead of Washington D.C. and nine hours ahead of Wyoming.

It was strange to think that it was only seven-thirty at home. I'd wait a bit before I reached out to Sophia.

Searching for a quiet corner to have that conversation with Doc, I crawled through an opening. It looked like people had hacked through the walls so they could move freely from one building to another without being exposed in the street. Perhaps it was a means of escape as the bombs exploded their homes.

It wasn't yet sunrise in Wyoming. I called anyway.

Doc seemed already caffeinated when she answered her phone.

"I've met up with my team. I thought I'd give Gator and Striker a quick overview. I think it would be good if we can get Miriam together on a conference call, to go ahead and get that part of the intervention checked off our list. If our luck holds, we're going to be ramping up for a mission here soon."

"Fine. I'll call Miriam and get a secure conference call set up. I'll text you the code to get in. Do you think twenty minutes will be enough time to get Striker and Gator briefed?"

"There's not a lot to tell. Indigo was a madman and stitched me to Angel won't take twenty minutes."

"Not a lot in terms of words that need to be said. Absorbing it, though."

"Gator already has a clue on some level. You said he was in your space during our conversation back at the airport. Striker's going to have a harder time with this."

"If I get the call set up, and you need more time, signal, and we'll hold. Easier for us in the comfort of our homes than with you in the rubble."

"Probably true."

I signaled Striker and Gator that I needed to chat with them. They followed me through the hole to the private space where I'd left my bag. We sat on chunks of wall, and then I began, "So, are you ready for me to blow your minds?"

"This is our etheric medical team meeting." Doc took charge. "We're talking over an encrypted system, and no recordings are being made, so let's feel comfortable discussing what is a most unusual topic."

Striker looked over at me. Even though I'd explained this to him, he was having trouble wrapping his mind around it.

Weren't we all?

"When we come together again, I'll be functioning as the psychic surgeon," Doc said. "Miriam will, in effect, function as a surgical nurse. Miriam, in the ether, you'll be monitoring Lexi. Gator, your job is to guard the etheric space. Miriam, you've taught him the technique?"

"I didn't have to. That one comes naturally to him," she said.

Striker was holding my hand so tight I had no circulation. After I told Gator and Striker about what I had read in General Elliot's files, what Herman had transcribed, and what Doc had found, he grabbed hold of me with an iron grip.

I'd put up with it for as long as I could.

"Right," Doc said. "I'll tell you what, let's set the color of the energy around us to a soft pink. I can feel the space getting too charged. Calm is best. And while we're at it, let's also take a moment to ground and be present in our bodies."

I closed my eyes and went through the grounding rituals I'd used throughout my life—my Kitchen Grandmother Biji, who taught me yoga, Mrs. Wang, who taught me Buddhist rituals, Spyder, then Miriam. And before them, my parents. Meditation, and connection to my higher self, had been a lifelong practice that had served me well. The practice protected me from Indigo being able to lace my thoughts with malevolent seeds to twist me into his pawn.

Angel wasn't a meditator, but I had never met anyone who lived so solidly grounded before. He, like Striker, and the other men on Strike Force, were formidable by nature, living from a place that my Kitchen Grandmother Biji would call their lower chakras, where their focus was survival. They needed to stay solidly in their bodies to get their jobs done.

None of this *woo-woo* stuff for them.

Though, it was interesting that all the elite warriors I've been close to have acknowledged to me a certain sixth sense when it came to survival. Gator, Deep, they all had stories of near misses when they felt a tickle on the back of their necks that made them duck, a sponginess in the air that kept them from putting their foot on a tripwire. I'd have to talk to Doc about that later. Right now, I needed to let my monkey mind calm.

Center...

Once my breath came steadily, and without effort, I filled my aura with pink light as Doc told us to do. As soon as that energy started to swirl, I felt the affinity with the others—a connection.

I opened my eyes.

"Good," Doc said. "Much better. Back to our briefing. I'm the surgeon, Miriam focuses on Lexi's well-being, Gator guards the etheric space from anyone or anything that wants to take advantage of Lexi's vulnerable state. And Striker, you'll guard the physical space from outside the tent. That way, we know no one will interrupt. And frankly, your worry energy will be less intrusive." Doc chuckled. "Striker, you seem to be flummoxed by this set of circumstances. You're not alone. Stop squeezing Lexi's hand."

Striker loosened his grip and pulled me to the side to sit between his knees, then dropped a kiss on my cheek and whispered a sheepish, "Sorry."

"Two dogs are here in the ether, sniffing at me," Doc said.

I smiled. "Beetle and Bella, they're protective."

"I don't mind them being here. They're lying down now, just keeping a close eye. Fine then. Good girls." She crooned over my computer connection, then flipped her voice back to business-at-hand. "Once we're in trance, I want everyone to communicate in the ether only. While it's possible to speak in the mundane, it pulls us from behind the Veil and into our bodies. Unless it's an emergency, clairaudient or clairvoyant messaging only, please. The comms lines will stay open, though, just in case."

There was a murmur as everyone agreed.

Striker tensed. Communicating using the sixth sense meant he'd have no idea what was going on, but he wasn't selfish enough to insist that we talk so he could hear. Striker loved being out of his element and challenged by circumstances.

Except for the woo-woo stuff.

"Lexi, I did another check before I called in. I was a little confused. Let me clarify, Angel is dead?"

"He died in an explosion two years ago."

"I'm pulling those images and sensations back up. Angel feels so alive to me… I'm wondering what this could mean. It's…I honestly have never experienced this before. Indigo certainly did a piece of work on you two. I knew Allan Leverone, Indigo, for years. A kinder, more benevolent soul just cannot be found easily. But he was working day in and day out trying to improve our ability to function in the ether, and that created mental health issues like it did for everyone on the Galaxy project. After the program shut down, and what they did to him and his poor family—killing his wife and son, damaging his daughter's brain, Tabitha becoming obsessive as an effect. And Allan's guilt. He would have given her the moon if he could. It's understandable that when Tabitha locked her obsession on Striker…"

Doc was quiet for a moment.

I had a weird push-pull when it came to Indigo and Scarlet. I appreciated Indigo's early work and sacrifices. Then he did a one-eighty. I could certainly feel pity for Scarlet and her brain trauma from being poisoned. But she shot Striker in her certifiably crazy attempt to make him love her. When that didn't work, she sedated and kidnapped him. She could easily have killed him on the physical level. But her attack on the etheric level? That I had no pity for.

"Good Lexi, I see I stirred the pot for you. That makes things bubble up. You have such good control over energy, sometimes I have trouble seeing even with your permission."

Silence fell.

"The pictures I'm seeing tell me that Indigo had concluded that he would do this experiment on Lexi and Angel. I can see here he likened his actions to Nazi medical experimentation and that what he was doing would damage his soul. He fully expected that doing this to the two of them would stop him from being able to function in his soul's learning group and that this would be his last embodiment. Well, that's some heavy stuff. And, as I told Lexi over the phone, that's exactly what I saw happen to him."

I thought about what I'd said in my session with my psychiatrist, Avril Limb, *what you think will happen to you after you die is the construct of your reality in that near-death time period.* Doc was just offering me an affirmation.

Angel was still in Hell. Only maybe that was more Indigo's fault than Angel's. I was anxious to see what Doc could do to soothe his soul.

I tuned back into Doc as she was saying, "His goal was to see what happened next. To see if it would help Tabitha with Striker. Okay, you and Angel were in the same learning group. Everyone here was. We get that. Angel would die when it was his time to die in the manner he was supposed to die, per his agreements before he entered this learning experience. What I don't get is how he can be both alive and dead at the same time. He's dead?"

"Yes," Miriam and I said together.

"You know speculation in the ether is always a mistake," Doc said, "but I'm going to throw out a hypothesis—he's a ghost."

Huh. Okay, that's not one I'd imagined. I was being haunted?

"Let me fill that thought in a bit. Imagine if you would the illustration of the two bubbles that General Coleridge drew when he did Lexi's task for remote viewing. Now imagine two bubbles floating side by side, not touching. If one was popped, it would disperse in tiny particles into the air. Poof. Gone. But when you blow bubbles from a bubble wand, and there are twin bubbles, one attached to the other, and you pop it—"

"Then the one bubble absorbs the second," I said. "The two bubbles become one."

"Exactly. Exactly my thought."

I sighed, and Striker tucked me in closer to his chest.

"Disturbing," Miriam said.

"That's an understatement," Striker responded. "How would Indigo even think to try something like this?"

"It seems that what happened in Indigo's experiment on Lexi and Angel," Doc said, "was influenced by a surgery on his dog."

"Wait now. What? A dog?" Gator's hand wrapped his chin, and he had his teeth clamped down on his index finger. It looked like an old-fashioned picture of a guy biting a stick in the olden days before painkillers.

"Indigo wrote in his lab notes that the vet had suggested a gastropexy when he had his dog spayed."

"Spayed." It was a breath on the back of my neck; Striker was putting together the idea of Indigo spaying a dog and then doing surgery on me. I didn't think Indigo would have touched my reproductive organs. But if you asked me last week if I had my dead husband's soul stitched to me like when Wendy Darling sewed Peter Pan's wayward shadow to his foot, I'd have said that was preposterous.

Ridiculous.

Crazy.

"A gastropexy prevents bloat. Bloat happens when the stomach flips over and traps gas, making the dog die of sepsis." She stalled. "Indigo died of sepsis. Isn't that an interesting twist to the story?"

Not really, since I knew the sepsis was merely the vehicle for Indigo's death. It was Spyder McGraw who made sure Indigo didn't survive to be treated and released back into the world.

"Gastropexy," Doc continued, "is easiest to perform on female dogs as they're being spayed because they already have an invasive surgery. The vet also makes small incisions and tacks the stomach to the abdominal lining. This stops the stomach from twisting. It's what gave Indigo the idea for how to surgically attach Lexi to Angel, their souls, not their bodies. He sewed their souls together."

"What?" Miriam gasped.

"Indigo cut a small incision in Lexi's soul and sewed her to Angel," Doc said clearly.

There was complete silence.

"I'm going to give you all a moment to adjust to this idea," Doc said.

"Lexi, that makes sense, don't you think?" Miriam said. "If Indigo sewed you and Angel together, rather than moving on to his own afterlife, perhaps he became one with yours, and that's why you feel him with you all the time. Why Doc and I pick up on his vibration when we look at you with clairvoyance?"

"It would also explain why Angel felt like he was in Hell," I agreed.

"In general, Lexi, when you're hearing things with clairaudience," Doc asked, "do you hear specific information, or do you hear some interpretation?"

"Usually, children's rhymes, to be honest. Then I have to interpret them." I scrubbed my thumb into my thigh, wrestling with these ideas. "I'm, wow, really struggling with this idea even though it's been days that I've been wiping steam from this mirror. It's still not clear, is it? Right now, my mind is stuck on how innocent Angel is in all this. He was doing his life. We weren't even supposed to have been married in the first place. Our relationship, our connection is some terrible science experiment."

Silence.

"Then, Indigo happened. And even though Angel must have died when it was his time to die, for the last two years, his soul could have been tethered to this plane through me, against his will." Saying the concept out loud didn't help me to adjust to it. Didn't make it any less fantastical. Or claustrophobic.

"It's a hypothesis," Doc said.

36

"YOU HAVE A PLAN, DOC?" MIRIAM ASKED.

"I've called some healers I work with. I've done some studying on separating conjoined twins. I can try to do psychic surgery. I've got experience under my belt doing energetic surgery. I'm going to be honest. I've never attempted anything like this before. All my resources agree that what Indigo did was a huge violation of natural law. No one has worked with something like this before. I can't foresee an outcome. It's a choice that Lexi's going to have to make. This is going to impact her no matter what decisions she makes."

"And Angel," I put in.

"Exactly," Doc said.

"When you do the psychic surgery, he'll be able to go on to rest in peace?" I asked, noticing I used "when" not "if." Some part of me had already come to a conclusion. To be honest, I couldn't go on living this way, so anything was better, right? I crossed my fingers for a burst of good juju.

Doc didn't answer right away. Then offered, "One would hope."

"Okay, let's do this," I said.

"Lexi, you need to weigh this some more," Miriam said gently. "Doc said she's never tried anything like this before. She doesn't have any idea what the outcome will be. Everyone needs to understand that. We don't know if you can survive it."

"On a body level or a soul level?" I asked.

"Either," Doc said. "Miriam's right. You need to weigh this. You may just want to let it be."

"I *can't* live this way," I said emphatically. "Angel's calling me to him. I can barely function. I certainly can't enjoy and participate in life. I *have* to do this. I really have no other choice."

"Gator," Doc said. "I can see you both agree and hate this. So do we all."

Striker drew me even further back against him as if he could use his body to buffer me from this. "Whatever you decide, Chica, I'll agree with you."

Striker. God, what if I didn't make it through? What if my soul was shredded, and I wasn't the same person that he loved?

"Lexi, we're going to stay positive," Miriam said.

"There's another thing I need to ask you about," Doc said.

Striker and I both tensed. More?

"What I can see about you and your psychic experience is that you have always been gifted with clairvoyance, clairsentience, and clairaudience. I get that you can sometimes smell things, and sometimes you can prognosticate. You have a very thin veil and get almost as much information from your essential senses as from your corporeal senses. And this increased and behaved, if you will, as you gained control through your study with Miriam."

"That's right," I said.

"Miriam, I can see your signature techniques here. Very nice."

"Where are you going with this?" Miriam asked.

"When I did an etheric exam," Doc said, "I see the attachment scar. Off to the side, there's a tiny gash. It reminds me of a victim of a knife attack. The first strike is rarely a penetrating blow. It's much more superficial. If I were guessing, Indigo started and hesitated. Decided and proceeded. We've talked about this, Lexi. With his initial incision, it seems he left you open. When you tried to get real-time information about someone who was desperate for survival, their spirit sensed help was near, and like a drowning person, they grabbed on to you. The thing about drowning people is that they lose their minds and often try to drown the person who is trying to save them by climbing on top of them."

Gator shifted around in his seat. This nearly played out between us last summer. But that connection had saved his life.

"And in like fashion," Doc said, "I can imagine that their spirit used this tiny opening to climb into your bubble for safety. Once you were one with them, you would experience what their bodies experienced. Does this line up with your corporeal experience?"

"Yes," Miriam and Gator said together.

"That makes perfect sense," Miriam said. "Lexi and I had been training together for a good while. Lexi was very apt and made quick progress. Where I can pick up information from the past, Lexi was best in present time. It looked like we were going to be great partners. I had zero issues taking a crime victim's photo to Lexi on the night a detective banged on my kitchen door and said he was afraid a young girl was about to be brutally killed. I could see the abduction taking place up until the witness snapped the photo on her cell phone. We went lights and sirens to Lexi's apartment. I handed her the photo, and before I could even ask, she was gone. It was the most horrific, terrifying thing that I've ever witnessed. There was Lexi in her pajamas with a book in hand. The next moment, she was physically flying through the air and hitting the wall. Blood. Bruises. Screams. It was a torment. I remember in that moment thinking if I touched her or interfered that I would rip her further. And now that makes sense. If I caught on the gash, I could have ripped her wide open. It could have destroyed her soul."

"It makes sense to me, too," I said. "I was in the safe house after I was attacked by Travis Wilson. Striker's sister and niece were in danger. Striker, you'll remember this. You brought me Lynda and Cammy's photos. As soon as I put them in my hands, I flew from my body. But I had been protected." *Thank goodness, I was protected.* "I'm trying to reinterpret that scene in light of this new information. I was surrounded by and lifted by drumbeats. Striker had saved a village of women in Africa. I remember telling Striker, 'These women perform rituals daily and have cast a prayer of protection over you and yours. This ritual is what calls me through the Veil. Striker, your service to these women is being repaid.' I thought they meant that I was able to take care of Cammy and Lynda, and that might have been part of it. But no. I really think they were there in the ether protecting me."

"Tell me about that protection," Doc said.

"That night, their shaman spoke not just through me but for me, moving my lips and tongue. 'Listen to me and heed every word.' She spoke in first person. The voice was hers. I had zero control in that moment."

"Good," Doc said, "and what did she have you say?"

"I hold the fates of your loved ones. Their survival depends on your right action. Obey, or they will suffer, as will I. If you touch me, the rip you would create is a fate worse than death to me. Do not touch! Swear it!" I repeated it easily from memory.

"Yes, exactly," Miriam said. "That's what I felt when I dashed forward to grab the photo. And then you were in a recovery period. You slept for days."

"It must have been something that the shaman knew about," I said, once again in awe of her capacity in the ether. "That must have been something that was expected. My next instructions from Grandmother Sibyl had been 'Do you understand? No matter what you see or hear, you will not touch me. Striker—you will have to leave at some point, and you may come back. Jack, you must not go. And until I can walk out of here on my own two feet, I am not to leave this house."

"She must have seen this before. Do you have contact with this shaman?"

"Only in the ether. She came again to help me when I was held hostage in a jail. She told me I had to be brave and hunt with my big knife."

"What does that mean?" Gator asked.

"She wanted me to leave my body to get information. She said you all couldn't find me, and the only way I'd survive is if I were brave enough to escape on my own. She told me to run when Maria was coming to cut off my fingers to send them to you."

"And you've never met her?" Doc asked. "When we're done with this conference call, I'd like you to send me pictures clairvoyantly. It may be that she'd allow me to connect with her and ask her for guidance."

"I can do that, Doc. To answer your question, no, I've never met her. I don't even know her name. I call her Grandmother Sibyl just to call her something. She helps me because she says I belong to Striker, and she's Striker's protector just as he saved her people."

"Wait. She did this while you were still married to Angel?" Doc asked.

"Well, yes, come to think of it. She came to protect me and help Striker in the safe house. That was October. Angel died in November, then I was kidnapped in January."

"She said you *belonged* to Striker," Doc repeated.

"She said, 'These women perform rituals daily and have cast a prayer of protection over you and yours.' And other like things that refer to Striker and me as a couple." I didn't understand why there was this distinction.

"That means that she saw what I saw. In this lifetime, your bond was supposed to be with Striker. Angel was not supposed to have married you. And she must have understood that that bond would be fulfilled."

"Lexi, you had a terrible crush on Striker when you were a teen," Miriam said. "But you said he didn't know who you were. If I remember correctly, you still had that crush up until the day you met Angel. I remember saying to you, you're going to give me whiplash with how quickly you changed the intensity of your affection. We had that talk the day after Angel stepped into the scene."

"He was sewn in. But I hadn't recognized him yet."

"That's messed up," Gator muttered.

I sent him a smile. "I concur."

"But this all brings me back to my question, should I repair the tear?" Doc asked.

"Yes," Mariam and Gator chorused again.

"Lexi?" Doc pushed.

"I don't know."

"Lexi, say yes," Gator demanded.

"I don't know about that. If anything good came out of this terrible experiment, it's that I gained the capacity to meld with someone else. I saved Striker's sister twice, his niece, Cammy. I saved you, Gator, and D-day. You would both be dead were it not for this rip. The Strike Force team when Indigo had you all down in the cave with the gas and had shot Striker and Jack. I didn't get you out, but I got you help in time to save your lives. If Indigo hadn't left the tear, I wouldn't have a team. Blaze would be the only one alive. All I know is that I hate to go behind the Veil to become one with someone in dire straits. But it's a price I've been willing to pay. Not always. After all, I made promises. But still… No. That's not something I think I want to give up."

"That's one aspect, Lexi," Miriam said. "But I think you need to consider the repair. This opening can let other things in too."

"She's right, just like with any cut into a body system," Doc said.

"Look, there's every possibility that I'm not going to survive the operation to separate Angel and me." I instantly regretted throwing that thought out into the open.

Gator's and Striker's bodies recoiled like they'd taken a physical blow.

"Maybe we just see if I'm around, then I can meditate on this, talk to General Coleridge and Herman Trudy, Miriam and you, Doc. Gather some information, weigh it with Striker and Gator. If I made new soul agreements after this happened to me, and now I'm tasked with keeping people safe and alive, then if I, willy-nilly, remove that ability, it could upset the whole time-space continuum. I don't want to make a rash decision."

"What do you need to hear, Chica, that would make you decide to close this wound?"

"I think one step then another. Anything I decide now is clouded by Angel's soul. Can we start there? Please?"

37

STRIKER, GATOR, AND I MADE OUR WAY BACK BEHIND THE BLUE sheet to find the rest of our team.

Jack looked up from his tablet. "What's happening?" Jack was six feet five and built like a comic strip superhero. It came in handy for intimidation. It made stealth tough. He was Striker's number two. I wasn't surprised when he jumped to his feet, looking like he was ready to grab his rifle and run into the fray. The three of us must look shell-shocked. It's how I felt, anyway.

"Anything from Mushkila's unit?" Striker asked.

"Nothing," he said, collapsing the space between us in three strides.

Striker turned to me. "Our next move is to do some outreach, Lynx. I want you to start with Sophia and see if she was able to gather any intel on the slave auction. Then check in with Prescott. We want to make sure he's looped in on everything we do. Professional courtesy, but also we may need more resources than what we've got."

"I'll do that now."

As I turned to go back to the caved-in room we'd just come

from, I heard Jack ask, "Are you going to tell me what's going on?"

"I need you and Gator to go relieve overwatch. Make sure you have plenty of water with you."

What could Striker tell Jack? Everything. We should tell the team everything. And I would. Later. Before the surgery. I stumbled over a bent metal drawer and reached out to grab a piece of rebar to catch my balance before I realized it stabbed through what must have been a human hand. I threw my arms wide and managed to stay upright.

Back on the patch of ground still warm from my body heat, I sat down with the computer, calling Prescott on a line that couldn't be sniffed. No need to let the enemy know we were coming for them.

"Lynx, good that you caught me. We're heading to the airport."

"Where are you flying?"

"Turkey. Zoe programmed her system to let her know if any of the matches pinged in the system. It looks like the eldest daughter went through a humanitarian clinic at a refugee center. They now require a health assessment before children are moved out of the camp. I'm going up with the analyzer."

"There's no possibility it's another of Kaylie's children? A fourth?"

"Same three names. Same date of birth. According to Zoe, the next five entries in the system all had shared biomarkers, creating a familial cluster. Zoe thinks by age and gender. These are the girl's aunt and cousins."

"Will that be a problem?"

"I don't know. I'm going to test her with the machine to make sure I'm photographing the right child, then I'll ask for instructions. This one will certainly be harder than moving the boy back to the US without her mother present."

"When will her son be introduced to Kaylie's family?" I asked.

"I haven't heard. That's going to be complicated. Chances are, this is a child of rape and enslavement. Certainly not this kid's fault. I just don't know how the family will react. I'm not sure how I would react under these circumstances. We all think we'll rise to the occasion, and then we don't."

"Or do."

"Let's just say that I know this family, and they can be rather rigid about their associations."

"Kaylie's the outlier?"

"Black sheep."

"Still, we shouldn't assume how Kaylie will feel about these children. No judgment there. We don't know her circumstances. We've never walked in her shoes."

Prescott was quiet.

"So Turkey, the analyzer, vial of blood, then…"

"We register her with the Red Cross, we ask that she not leave the camp while Iniquus processes the results, meanwhile my team gets ready to look for the baby."

"I'd get diapers and baby food together while I was in Turkey, just in case you can swoop in and get her. The last the infant was seen was in Northern Iraq, right?"

"Yes, it'll be more of a grab and run than a diplomatic finesse. Have you heard from Sophia? I'm curious about the idea of the permaculture spaces. My gut says that's how we're going to find the baby."

"I'm calling her as soon as we hang up. I'll have her forward any images and their coordinates. Let me ask about the CIA's involvement in this. Are they working with you?"

"We're in communication. They know we're operating in the area. Why?"

"They need to get the ball rolling if there's any hope of getting a special operations team in to support us."

"Honestly? Unless you had confirmation of Kaylie's identity, that's unlikely. And even with confirmation, that's unlikely. I wouldn't depend on them to go to bat for her."

"Copy."

After I wished Prescott good luck, I tapped end, then typed in Sophia's phone number. It was 9:42 p.m. here, so 2:42 in D.C.

Sophia popped up on my screen on the third ring with Chance dangling from her hip and food smeared across her shirt. "Give me ten minutes," she said.

I laughed at the normalcy of that scene and clicked end.

Pressing my head back against the wall, I let my mind wander toward Angel. "I need some calm. I need to get through this assignment. I know you're in Hell. I'm so sorry. I am too, really. I think I found a way to free us both. Get us back in line with who and what and where we're supposed to be. You deserve Valhalla, not Hell. You deserve to be honored and not tethered to me and dragged along. I am so, so sorry." I let the tears come but pushed down on the raw sounds that quivered in my chest. I didn't want Striker or my team to come looking for me. Alone felt good. As much as I could be alone under my circumstances.

I jumped when the computer rang. After wiping my nose on my sleeve, I lifted the hem of my T-shirt to swipe at my eyes, then pressed enter.

Sophia thrust her face toward the screen. "Are you okay?"

"There's lots of debris in the wind. I should have brought goggles."

She nodded. "Let me get to this quickly, the boys are in destruction mode, and I need you to have this information."

"Ready."

"The end of the auction is Wednesday at midnight your time. They plan to begin distribution Thursday morning at nine. That's your window. I told Brian about this, and he took the information to Nutsbe to see if he couldn't identify the woman's picture amongst those that are up for auction."

"Thank you."

"There are about two hundred women. The resource who was able to find the Darkweb site believes that those who are not sold will be killed since they don't have the supplies to keep them alive."

"They wouldn't just let the women go or give them away?"

"They have a minimum bid. If they let the slaves go for too little or nothing, as a humanitarian gesture, then the slaves lose market value. It's a matter of balancing supply and demand. They talk about the women like they're livestock in terms of their cost to profit ratio. You've met Mushkila? Are you at her camp yet?"

"We shook hands, then she needed to go on a mission. We haven't really spoken yet."

"I need you to pass this along to her. There are two hundred and eight women and children being held. Provisions need to be part of any rescue equation. I told you that Mushkila is helping you because you're not going after the one possible American but all of the women."

"I…yes." Strike Force was tasked with one. What would we possibly do with the other two hundred and seven in a hot zone?

"Normally, slave distribution starts at the break of day to get everyone sorted before the heat. The city gates are opened after the first light. Distribution is scheduled to start three hours later."

"How do they do that? The distribution?"

"They put numbers on the slaves and line them up in order.

The man brings his receipt or receipts for his payment, finds his slave, then checks out. It goes pretty quickly."

"*God.*"

"Looking at satellite images, the auction site is near the south gate. Each gate has a major road and a market space. Following the southern road, by my calculations, the site that Mushkila has identified is three hours away by truck. The two pieces of information line up. That road has to be traveled by light of day because it's in disrepair, too bad to risk night driving."

I understood the axel breaking terrain, having come up one of those roads to find Mushkila. "You have all that for me?"

"I was working on it before Chance decided to become a Monet with his lunch. I need to get it in a file. I'll send the data and images to you and Nutsbe and the notes I took from my colleague, as well as my own thoughts based on what I know in the area. For example, those women are probably headed for hard labor. There's archaeologic tel in the area that has seen some recent action."

"You sound like you could use a bit of good news," I said. "I just got off the phone with Prescott. They found one of the children they were looking for, and they have a good line on the second one in Turkey."

Sophia scooped Chance into her lap and hugged him so hard that his little hand came up under her chin and pushed, "No, mama!"

She loosened her grip but put her nose down to his hair and inhaled, tears spilling past her tightly closed lashes. "Good," she said, then set the squirming Chance back down and watched him run away. "Which child is still missing?"

"The eleven-month-old. She's the one in the hot zone."

"All right." She swiped at her eyes and sniffed hard. Replacing the sympathy she'd just expressed with an iron will.

"Okay. I found something. Two somethings that might help. Looking at the GPS coordinates where the baby was indexed and then following your suggestion about looking for permaculture footprints, I have two locations. One is older than the other. They are the youngest of such indicators in a field of ten that my software has located so far in the circumference I drew based on all three children's GPS locations."

"That's what Prescott said he needed."

"I'll forward that to you too."

"Can you send the slave market data right now? I think I hear Mushkila's unit coming back in."

38

By the time I made my way back through the series of holes to the section of hallway that now made the façade of the building, the blue sheet had been tied out of the way. The women washed their faces and hands. Smiling at each other, their voices chittered with excitement. They must have been successful.

I followed them into the space. The air was already beginning to cool as the heat radiated off the dirt quickly, now that the sun was going down. Striker asked in Arabic if we, the men, could prepare a dinner for the women.

The women caught each other's eyes and giggled. Mushkila focused on me. I couldn't remember anything in the Iraqi handbook that addressed a guest preparing a meal. "You would honor us if you would please accept. They're simple MREs."

She hesitated for a moment, a quick glance at her unit, and I could see hungry eyes and a few swipes of tongues over cracked lips. I remembered that Sophia had told me to bring Chapstick with sunscreen as gifts. As I was gassing up my car on my way through Virginia to the airport, I'd gone in and bought the entire box sitting by the register. They were at the bottom of my backpack; I had enough to hand around. Before Mushkila could protest, I added, "Please, I insist."

She nodded.

When I moved toward my pack to find the lip balm, Jack asked if they required their meal to be Halal.

Mushkila said, "Food is food."

Food was food. I'd be grateful for it. Stress sucked at my reserves, and my stomach was growling. Jack was mixing the lemon-lime packets into cups of water. I picked them up and distributed the drinks and the balm around.

We ate.

The change in temperature was drastic now that the sun was down. The women lit a fire. Then, making a ribbon by joining hands, they danced and sang.

Mushkila made her way over to sit beside me. "You are here looking for an American woman."

"We are. Our mutual friend Sophia thought you might be able to help us."

"Do you see that light?" She pointed at the bouncing movement in the distance.

"Car?"

"An American friend. He's ten more minutes away. Then we can talk, yes?"

I flexed my back. "John Grey?" I asked using the English pronunciation of his name.

She patted my knee and went to where her fighters were calling her to dance with them.

I lay back, pillowing my head on my hands, looking up at the great expanse of sky. The moon was sliver thin. We would be sleeping here tonight.

I sensed a concerted effort on Striker's part to keep himself distracted, doing busy things like making tonight's dinner. He was down at the cars with the others, gathering our sleeping bags and kits for tonight.

Overwatch had come in to eat.

Jack and Axel were taking their turn in the sniper's nest. I'd ask Striker to replace Jack for a while so he could be in on the briefing when I talked to Mushkila about Kaylie and the slave auction.

GREY CAREFULLY STEPPED over the debris as he made his way to the campfire. I'd watched him clairvoyantly through Gator when Gator was accepting a mission last July. Gator had wigged out when he had a whole video playing in his mind's eye for the first time about people and circumstances he didn't recognize. As he flailed, Gator caught hold of me in the ether, and I watched it, too. I guessed it was that wayward incision that allowed us to do that. At this moment, I was thankful that I knew some back story on Grey. His name had been floating in my brain for days when it had no reason to. And I wasn't surprised at all that this was Mushkila's CIA contact. I felt like the universe was lining things up the way they were supposed to be. I'd wait to let things unfold naturally.

I felt a zap of electricity and turned my head toward Gator. When our gaze locked, he tipped his head toward Grey and mouthed "interesting."

I nodded.

"Right, down to business. Your team is here," he said to Striker.

Striker shook his head. "Lynx commands this mission," he said.

Grey had a pop of surprise and tamped it down, then turned to me. He was speaking in Arabic so Mushkila could understand. "My apologies," he said. "Your team is here to find an American woman who went missing in Nigeria seven years ago, Dr. Kaylie Street. The NSA believes they might have an image of her as she moved toward an encampment with a group of women and a few men. Do you have further information that might verify that she's with this group?"

"You're familiar with an initiative by medical groups to spread good health in the area? A hearts and minds project to reach out to every man, woman, and child?"

"You're aware of this?" His demeanor changed. I could see him reassessing his first impression of me. "Is that how you tracked Kaylie here?"

"We tracked three children. Does the name Bakar Wajdi Fayad sound familiar?" Nutsbe had just texted me that the third child's name included her personal name, a father name, a grandfather name, and less-commonly her great-grandfather's name. So this would have been the only child of the three who had a name that would tell us who the father was. And, as it turned out, Bakar Wajdi Fayad was a big name in the area.

Grey's eyes dilated; this news excited him. "He's the main slave trafficker in this area."

"I met a man with seven wives." This was him. This was the man I had made the hazardous journey to confront; I *knew* it.

"Bakar Wajdi Fayad provides labor for the poppy fields and archaeological digs, and sex slaves for the ISIS fighters."

I tipped my head to the side. "Does the CIA believe it would be good to take him down?"

"Of course, but that's not going to happen. He holes up over the border in Syria. He sneaks into Iraq, does his deals, and heads right back into his hole to hide. We don't know what he looks like."

"Information about his movements, his contacts, those might be important pieces, wouldn't they? And someone who could identify his image?"

"You're saying he fathered a baby with Kaylie Street?"

"We believe so."

"Believe."

"If you could talk to Kaylie, her knowledge would be a boon." I paused to observe Grey. Nope, that didn't do the trick. "If she was his slave, and even if she was his willing wife, it's very possible that she saw and heard things that would be helpful in not only disrupting the slave trade but the effects of the slave trade—lower fighter morale, lower fighter recruitment, fewer slaves for labor thus affecting their money flow. And not just the money flow, but the people with whom he would have done business."

Grey whistled between his teeth. "Are you kidding me right now? This would be gold."

"Golden enough that you can get us help going after her?"

"Here in Syria? You're a hundred percent positive you know where she is?"

"We have a guess."

"Not good enough. There's no way I'm going to get that green-lighted. Let's get you all the data we can. I can help you plan. I can probably even get your equipment. I just can't get you boots or gunslingers."

He stood and strode into the distance with his satellite phone in his hand.

My own phone buzzed. It was Prescott. I walked away with my finger in my ear so I could focus.

"Hey," he said. "We had some Marines in the area of Kaylie's third child. The baby's in the wind. The village where they had done the medical intake was flattened three days after the medical."

"All right. We're meeting with Grey from the CIA now. Sophia sent me pictures of what looked like it might be the start of a new permaculture footprint. I wouldn't get too excited. It could be that someone who learned Kaylie's system and is implementing it. I'm thinking of Sophia's tomato story."

"I got the images from Sophia, too. Unless Zoe has another location hit on one of the family members from the dad's side, I don't know where to go from here. We're going to gather some more information, and I'll keep you abreast. How's it going with Kaylie?"

"We should know by tomorrow night if it's her or not." I turned my head to see Deep standing up, waving me in. "They're flagging me over. Any last thoughts you want me to share with Grey?"

"Not with Grey, but with you. Stay safe."

"Roger that," I said as I moved back to the circle.

"Lynx, you're looking for a woman in a place where women are invisible. It's already astonishing that we've found two of her children. If you and your team can find Kaylie, it'll be a miracle."

"We'll pray for a miracle then."

39

IT WAS WELL OVER AN HOUR BEFORE GREY CAME BACK TO THE circle. Mushkila's unit had gone off to their sleeping mats.

Strike Force and Mushkila herself had waited for Grey's return.

"Our intelligence says that Sophia found the right spot," he said without preamble.

"We have to go in tomorrow night after dark. My team and Mushkila's, we'll need every advantage. Striker, Jack, and I had the computer booted up and spent time imagining different scenarios."

I gestured Grey over to see the screen.

"That's it. Our satellites have movement in the area." He used his finger to point out the area, and I zoomed in. "We project from the number who were on the trail that there are about two hundred women who survived the ISIS attack," he said, shifting his weight and putting the soles of his feet on the ground, wrapping his knees with his arms and holding a wrist with his opposite hand. I looked around, and everyone was sitting this way.

I had pulled a sleeping bag over my lap and was sitting cross-legged with the computer resting on my thighs.

"We believe they're in this building here. There's no movement in or out of this building in the last twenty-four hours. But we're familiar with it. We know that ISIS has warehoused women here before. There are ten trucks lined up here." He pointed behind the women's barracks. "If we can get to them, we could use the trucks to transport the women out of the conflict area."

"That would solve a lot of problems," Mushkila said. "They'll probably be too weak to walk."

"We'd be hard-pressed to get in there without giving them a big ol' heads up that we were moving in," Gator said.

Grey nodded. "I've been working the phones. I was able to get your air transport."

"Eleven per bird if they're Black Hawks," Jack said. "We'd need three to get Strike Force and Mushkila's unit in."

"You're going to have to winnow that down. I can only get you two birds. They're drop and go. Once you're in position, it'll be up to you to get back out."

Mushkila nodded. "I can leave some of my fighters back."

"The two helicopters drop you on this side of the mountain." Grey reached over. "Here."

"Okay," I said.

"The rise in elevation would mask any noise. If they fly dark, no one would ever know you were there. Eyes in the sky would tell us if you have anyone patrolling the area."

Strike Force nodded. They all had what I called their "combat faces" in place. Focused. Processing. Visualizing. They'd be looking for holes in the plans from their vast collective experience and training.

I wondered if they were being quiet, so I looked like I was in charge. That wasn't a good idea. "If you have thoughts or questions, I want everyone sharing."

"Here's the thing," Grey said. "You're going to have to go in fast and hard, take out communications, so they don't have back up heading your way. You'll have to kill or incapacitate every single one of ISIS fighters. I've seen women in this situation. They are going to be weak, ill, and traumatized. The faster you get in, the faster you get out, the further you get away, the better your chances. Remember, I got approval for the helicopters because we're getting as many women out as possible. It's the morale blow we're after. I get that your job is to find Dr. Street, but you're getting an assist for a bigger picture."

I didn't see any other way, so I said, "Okay then, let's all get some rest, and tomorrow we'll fine-tune our strategy."

THE WOMEN from Mushkila's unit had never been on a helicopter before. Neither had I. Strike Force had outfitted them with night vision goggles. They already wore camouflage pants and boots. Striker insisted that they wear the heavy bulletproof vests even though we didn't have any that were woman-sized, even for me.

We made do.

In the Blackhawk, they held hands like a family saying grace over the Thanksgiving turkey as we sat behind our Army pilots, getting ready for takeoff.

As we climbed into the air, they gasped and clung tighter. After about ten minutes, they relaxed, and I even caught a few smiles.

The pilots flew low and without lights, using their night vision and the helicopter readouts to keep us safe.

I tried not to think about it.

Just as planned, the Blackhawks set down on the side of a hill, two kilometers from the compound. We'd hike in.

I guessed my gear was only about fifty pounds. Much of what I carried in my pack was first aid. Things that might be needed to save one of the women's lives that we found in the camp. Things that I might need to save one of our teams' lives.

I tried not to think about that either. I tried not to think anything at all.

The pilot had called into the TOC, the tactical operations center, where Grey and his team were monitoring the situation. I knew that the CIA had a whiteboard up where each step of our mission was listed and the time that the piece needed to be completed. The goal was to stick with the plan and keep the mission on track. I could imagine Grey pulling off the top of the marker and putting an X in the box next to "Insertion."

The next step was getting from point A to point B.

Maybe I'd underestimated the effect of being wrapped in an extra twenty pounds of armor while carrying fifty pounds as I hiked through the desert night.

I looked around, and no one seemed fazed by the packs they carried. Strike Force was weighed down with the equipment—ladders, crowbars, bolt cutters, and blast strips. They came ready for any eventuality.

Or most eventualities.

The fathomable ones.

They do this. This is what they do. Everyone here was battle-hardened and battle-ready, except me. I knew they were trying not to call too much attention to that fact. And I didn't want them to think they needed to circle the wagons to keep me safe.

It wasn't that I didn't have skills.

It was just that I'd never applied my skills in this type of event before.

"Striker." He used his call name to announce who was speaking over the comms. "We're in position."

"TOC. Good copy. If you see anything that we didn't plan for, you let us know STAT. You hear?"

"Copy."

Blaze and Axel were on overwatch. They moved up into the hills and set up their sniper rifles.

We laid on our stomachs, watching through binoculars. The first step was up to them.

"Blaze. I'm in place, and I've located two of the three perimeter guards. I'll paint him with my laser."

"Striker. Got him," Striker said. "Do you see that, Axel?"

"Axel. Roger. I have the third one in my scope, and there's a guy at the door where we think the fighters are sleeping. That's all I see."

"Striker. Copy."

"TOC. That's the count. Four heat signatures outside of the buildings."

The women's faces, glowing green in my night vision, were set with ferocity. While Strike Force was calculated, methodical, and unemotional, these women were controlled, but they seethed with anger. Those men were enslaving their women. This was personal.

I thought back to Melody's nightmares of the lions ripping flesh from her sister and devouring her. That wild hunger was what I felt in these women as they champed at the bit.

One by one, I watched Strike Force turn their heads toward the women, feel their power, and turn back to the task at hand. I wondered what they were thinking right then.

"Striker. Snipers, I'm in control." Striker paused with his binoculars up. "Three. Two. One. Execute. Execute. Execute."

Four suppressed pops from a distance. Four bodies down. We

waited to see if anyone heard that and were coming out. It was easier and safer for us to attack from a distance, but too, we didn't want anyone calling in reinforcements.

"Striker. Forward." By the time we got to this point, Mushkila didn't seem to question why Striker was yelling orders and not me. Surely, her warrior's eye noticed I was out of my element, and the men were a cohesive fighting machine.

I clomped and slid down the hill and over the open land, ready to throw myself on the ground and wait for orders should someone from their side start shooting. That was the plan for Mushkila's unit as well as for me.

Not a sexist thing. Again, Mushkila didn't argue the point. She must have also realized that these weren't your every-day kind of mercenary units; these were elite soldiers. They needed us down so they could maneuver. No one wanted a teammate to die from friendly fire.

Now that we were within the perimeter, we ran forward to the positions we'd been assigned. I was to head right to the women's barracks and report on the locking system and door. Whew. Now I knew that I needed to practice my morning jogs with a bullet-resistant vest on and build up my pack weight. Fifty pounds hadn't felt like much until I tried to maneuver in it. And a vest that included boob space would be awesome.

I knew that from the safety of the TOC, Grey had us up on the computer system, watching real-time with drone imagery. Green blobs against black. Each of us had a decal on the top of our hat that made us identifiable as being team Kaylie. The fibers in our body armor lit us up on the night vision, so we wouldn't target each other.

On other screens, Grey's team was monitoring each of us from our helmet cameras. They could see what we saw. They were able to keep track of who's camera view they managed by the automatic picture that came up in the corner of our camera feed, including our names and GPS locations.

"We own the night," I whispered under my breath. "We own it. We own this mission. It's our outcome."

I'll admit it, I was shocked that I was this calm. I had expected the adrenaline to be racing through my veins like it had when I had escaped from the Honduran prison and flown the plane through the storm trying to reach American soil.

By the time I ran past Strike Force, the men were stacked up outside of what we thought was the fighters' barracks.

"Striker. Breacher up."

Blaze slapped the blast strip into place to enter the men's quarters.

I flattened against the wall outside of where we thought the women were held. A low murmur of moans came from inside the thin-walled building.

Through my comms, I heard. "Striker. I have control. Breach in Three. Two. One."

I crouched and waited for the blast, knowing things were about to get crazy.

BOOM! The concussion followed.

I rounded to the front to check my door. Depending on what we needed, someone would run up. We hoped bolt cutters would do the job.

The women's wailing rose up and swirled the air, raising gooseflesh over my body. The last time they'd heard blasts was probably as the RPGs landed on their fellow evacuees. Death, mayhem, and capture had followed. I'd allow myself to sympathize later. Now, we needed to get them on the trucks and get them the heck out here.

The door didn't seem to be bolted. There was a crack where it was open.

That didn't seem right.

"Lynx. Striker, the door's ajar."

"Striker. Stay put. I'm sending Gator up to be first man in."

Seconds later, Gator moved up. Standing to the side, he stomped the door open.

The women's wails turned to screams.

Gator rounded in, got a visual, and moved back outside to guard the door. "Gator. Team Mushkila up," he said in Arabic with a Cajun twang.

That was me, too.

My fellow teammates glowed acidic green as they moved from cover to cover, leapfrogging forward then moving in wedge formation. Someone had trained them well. They were professional about their duties.

We arrived at the door, and everyone stacked up behind me. Gator gave the nod, and over the comms, I heard him say. "Gator. Female building is open. Mushkila's team entering."

"TOC. Good copy."

We raced in quickly, moving from bed to bed. The women lay in rag piles on the dirt floor. Mushkila's soldiers grabbed the women's blankets and jerked them off. "Sisters, we are here to help," they yelled. They were using different languages. That had been the plan, so that should the women come from different regions, they could understand and hear a female voice. My role was to call in English for Dr. Street. To use that name so she'd know I was there for her from a professional search. She needed to be with Strike Force. And it had been agreed that the best time to find her was when the women were all in one place.

The stench from the room was putrid. It reminded me of the time I spent in the Honduran prison. My memories were lighting my nerve endings, and I needed to clear the images so I could stay focused on this task.

The barracks was like a warehouse. On either side of a narrow corridor were bunk beds about the width of a double mattress, but they were merely wooden platforms. Two or three women rested on each platform. They were stacked three high and ran at least fifteen deep. I did a quick calculation. Grey and Sophia were right. There must be two hundred women in here.

On my command, we pulled up our night vision goggles and Three. Two. One. We clicked on our headlamps.

Women. Children.

They were in terrible shape.

The women squished their eyelids tight, throwing their arms over their eyes to protect them from the sudden brightness of our high-lumen lights.

The smell. The open wounds. They were dressed in rags. Their greasy hair strands fell in their faces.

We made our way through the barracks. Amongst the fear screams, one rose up higher, pitched with terror and pain.

We were calling to them, "You're safe. You're safe!"

At first, they cowered into balls, then some ran into the night. This was what we didn't want to happen.

Shots had been ringing out, and we didn't want the women to be caught in the crossfire or held as a shield. Gator used the length of his rife to push them back in place. It was good that he wasn't pointing the barrel at them.

He closed the door and stood inside, bodily blocking their exit.

The screams lifted higher, then I saw it—the man, the glint of a bright edge, a drip of blood.

"Blade," I yelled into my comms.

I threw the other women to the side, forcing my way forward, trying to grab at the man's hand. It plunged again. He was protected from me by the lip of the bunk. I grabbed at his turban.

Blood was on the cloth below him.

I yanked his head back, kicking my boot into the back of his knee. Standing on his leg, I forced him down. I reached around and grabbed his beard to drag his face into the light of one of my teammates.

It was bedlam.

The screams and the frantic movement. The dark and the sudden strobe of bright lights that destroyed my ability to see. The weight and bulk of my equipment that kept me from maneuvering.

Mushkila grabbed his barefoot and dragged him around.

I scrambled toward the injured woman.

I heard Mushkila behind me demanding. "Does anyone know this man? What is this man's name?"

And I knew before I got my light on her face that the woman who was under attack was Kaylie Street.

In Arabic, I heard. "That's Bakar Wajdi Fayad."

I whipped off my pack and grabbed my kit to stop the bleed. Praying under my breath that she'd survive. "Dr. Street. United States. We're here to rescue you. Stay with me, Kaylie. Keep your eyes open."

Beside her, a one-year-old baby was hysterical.

40

WE DROVE THE TRUCKS OVER THE OPEN TERRAIN TO THE BORDER. We were nearly out of gas by the time we reached the Army outpost. The soldiers brought food and water to the women. They gassed the trucks and took over the driving, taking the women to a humanitarian camp, leaving our unit and the Army outpost behind.

Mushkila's team and Strike Force would have bunk space at the outpost once we cleaned up.

Kaylie and her baby were in the infirmary. Her wounds had been superficial. Thank God. She was being well cared for by a female doctor. She had answered all three of our questions accurately.

"What grade school did you go to?"

"What was the name of your childhood cat?"

"What dorm did you live in at university?"

Her question for us. "I have three children. This one and two others. Please, can you help me find them? *Please*?"

I got Prescott on the phone to let him know what was

happening, then handed it to Kaylie so she could hear a familiar voice tell her about her other children.

Her medications took effect, and I pulled the phone from her ear with Prescott still crooning, "I'm coming, Kaylie. I'll be there soon. I'm coming."

"Prescott, it's Lynx. She's asleep."

"*God.*" His voice caught.

THREE MAJOR SUCCESSES—THE release of the women, finding Kaylee Street and her child, now Strike Force was waiting for Grey to arrive. We had bagged an important prize. Bakar Wajdi Fayad.

A good night's work.

The sun was just starting to shift the night sky. Mushkila's unit had started a fire and had waited for their adrenaline to settle. Adrenaline dropping out of the system made the body exhausted. They went off to sleep.

The first thing Grey did was inspect our prisoner, confirmed his identity, then sat down with us, a cup of steaming coffee in hand.

After so much noise, smells, and craziness, this quiet around the fire seemed like a good thing.

Mushkila was talking to me about what life had been like before ISIS. She said that losing a husband to war was a terrible thing.

I pulled out my cell phone, ineffective here for calls. I was reliant on the SAT phone. But it had my pictures. I scrolled to pull up my wedding picture with Angel. "My husband," I said. "This was our last picture together. He died in an IED explosion two years ago."

She had stilled beside me; her brain was working hard. I reached out and flipped to a picture of a close up of grinning Angel.

Her muscles tightened and a frown formed on her face.

"You knew him, didn't you?" I asked gently. I had no idea under what circumstances she might have met Angel. They could be very bad circumstances—triggering circumstances. It would be nice, though, to hear a story about him.

She took my phone from my hand and moved closer to the fire. She tipped it toward Grey and said something, then they both looked my way. They obviously knew something about him, and that something I watched them silently agree not to tell me.

That wasn't okay.

I walked over and sat next to Grey, accepting my phone back from Mushkila.

We sat in silence, but Mushkila grew more uncomfortable as the minutes ticked by. Finally, she stood, tipped her head back to drink the last of her tea, and said she was going to get some sleep.

Once we were alone, I sniffed and looked into the fire. "I know you. You're looking better. Last time I saw you, you were running over the rocks with one sock on."

He shifted around so we were face to face.

"It was a harrowing escape, being pulled out of that jail cell. She's a hell of a pilot, D-Day."

His mind worked on the puzzle; that jailbreak was highly classified. He worked in a non-permissive zone. Somebody had to have talked.

"The little girl, the one with the too-big dress and the red bandana holding back her black curls? She wasn't the one who gave away your position. The ISIS fighters had warned the fighters of your direction via radio. They didn't see the Little Bird, only the Blackhawk. But your pilot was about to set down anyway. D-Day didn't have enough fuel to get much farther. She lost too much fuel from the hole in her tank. The place in the tank the shooter focused on while Delta Force Echo pulled you across the ladder."

"I thought you worked with Iniquus." His words were measured.

"Yes."

"That was a secret op."

"It still is."

He didn't reply. He rubbed this information back and forth to see if he couldn't get a spark of understanding.

"You won't figure it out because I won't explain it to you. Just like you've decided that you won't explain to me your connection with my husband." I paused while he absorbed the idea. "Of course, you're obviously not the only one with the information that I want. I'll get it, one way or another, before I leave Iraq."

His focus was on the fire. His brain was on fast forward.

I reiterated, "I'm not going home until I know. I won't give up until I know. You have to weigh that into your decision making. It might be that we could sit here at the fire, and you could tell me a little story. It could well be that you'd find it less of a problem if it were you who were quietly telling me what I want to know rather than my poking and prodding, perhaps putting something at risk. It might even be, should I not find what I'm looking for, that I could bring up my experience with some of my reporter friends here, and they could help me sniff around. Because something is very wrong with the picture of my husband's death."

Grey picked up a stick and poked at the fire, making the sparks erupt in a fountain.

"The funeral was held in Puerto Rico. They told me that Angel's remains were unrecognizable, and so it was a closed coffin." I covered my eyes as the breeze blew smoke in my face, and I shifted to the side. "I was down there not even a week ago and had the coffin exhumed."

Grey nodded, acknowledging that he heard me.

"There was a tooth in a little box. There was a piece of boot with his dog tag. There was a portion of his other dog tag."

"I'm sorry for your loss." His body language read as guilty.

I wondered if they hadn't been working an op, and Grey was the CIA officer who had given bad intel. Maybe he thought he put the team in the wrong place at the wrong time. But that didn't make any sense at all. Mushkila was Syrian. Her husband died after Angel did. She became a warrior after her husband died. She recognized Angel and took his photo with a warning look over to Grey.

He tipped his head back to take in the great bowl of the galaxy. The stars were so numerous that it was hard to find the constellations.

"Seriously? You're not going to just tell me?"

Nothing.

"Let me tell you a little bit about me. I wasn't on the op that helped save you. I wasn't connected to your rescue in any concrete way. I dreamed about it. I saw it in my mind's eye. I can tell you more. I can tell you that you had gone without food or water for so long that when the Deltas pulled you out of the window, you thought you were hallucinating. You had assumed that the next time you left that cell that you would be tortured until you spilled all your secrets, and then you'd die. You wondered how long you could hold out against the torture. You wondered if those few hours you might buy your assets would help them and their families escape or not. You wondered, was it worth it? And you had tried to devise a plan to suicide, but your brain kept tripping up. You couldn't get a solid leg to stand on. A strong enough thought process. Dehydration can do that to a brain."

He scrubbed his hands over his face, then laced his fingers, resting his elbows on his splayed knees. His gaze still on the fire.

"I've been dreaming about Angel all week. Not dreaming. Nightmaring. Not nightmaring. Hallucinating about his going to Hell." I swiped a finger toward my ear. "I keep hearing Angel in my head calling to me. 'Help me. I'm in Hell. I'm burning.' The sound of his plea brought me here. I'm not going home without answers."

"If you tell my story to anyone, many people could die."

"I understand that's what you're caught on. I'd like you to move past that. I'm not threatening you or your assets' lives or covers. I'm here about Angel. Unless, of course, these two things overlap. And then I'll find out why they overlap, one way or another."

"'Help me. I'm in Hell. I'm burning' is in the present tense?" he asked the fire.

Of course, I realized this too. It was Angel in Hell screaming at me. I hoped Grey wasn't pointing out to me that this made no sense, and then I'd have to decide how much more to tell him. I thought in terms of psychic information, I'd probably said all I felt comfortable saying. "Present tense," I said.

"And you think he's in physical danger and want to get him help."

I...*what*? "Yes."

"This will be delicate."

"I get that." Actually...*what*?

"I'll have to come up with a plan. It risks a lot. But listening to you, hearing you, I think I have the picture, and…okay, yes." He slapped his hands on his thighs. "I'll have to do something immediately." He stood, stepped over the fire, and strode away.

I chased after him. "You're leaving?"

"I need to talk to some people. I'll be back."

"When? Where?"

"Here. As soon as I can. No more than twenty-four hours. When did this start?"

I rolled my eyes up in my head, trying to remember. "I think ten days or so ago."

"Jezus." He walked away with long strides.

I stood there with my arms dangling, watching him go. *What just happened*?

I headed back to Strike Force. I wanted to tell them about this odd exchange and ask them what they thought. I thought that Grey was telling me that Angel was present tense. That he was alive.

I couldn't even wrap my mind around…everything.

I needed my family. I needed Striker.

41

"I HAVE SOMETHING TO TELL YOU," I TOLD MY TEAM BEFORE launching into what I had discovered in the last few days about Indigo and his experiment, Doc and her research, and now Grey at the campfire. "Then he said, 'I'll have to do something immediately,' and left."

"Wait. Whoa. What does that mean exactly?" Gator asked his hands on his hips, a scowl on his face.

"It sounds like—shit, I hate to say this out loud—Angel isn't dead?" Blaze said.

I breathed a stream of air between my lips. "I wanted your take on it. It sounded that way to me. But I'm off my game when it comes to all this stuff. Beyond the nightmares, the physical issues have been pretty intense."

"Tell me more about the physical issues," Jack said.

Striker turned his back to me. I think he just didn't want me to see his face. I couldn't imagine being in his position, engaged to a married woman who was…well, soul attachments aside, this put yet another twist in our relationship. *How much could one man handle?*

"The closest way to describe it is that I've felt physically terrible. I kept taking my temperature, but it's always perfectly normal. I went to the Iniquus clinic, and they did a blood check. My white cells are where they belong. Everything came out just fine. But I've felt feverish, sweaty, no appetite, light, and sound sensitive, exercise averse, exhausted beyond belief. I felt like I was in and out of consciousness. And then there was the pain. Excruciating pain like my eyeballs were catching on fire. When I was called in to be on the Kaylie Street case, I knew I was hitting my wall, something needed to change. And this must have been it. I was told through a *knowing* and through the Galaxy viewers directives to go looking for Trouble. Here I am. I guess now I wait and see what Grey comes back with."

I rubbed my palms together. "He's on the other side of the Veil. The Veil is shimmering."

"For a long time?" Gator asked.

"Since this energy ramped up. Grey asked how long, and I'm guessing ten days."

"You didn't try to go and look, did you? Even with Miriam there to support you?" Jack asked.

"You promised your team you would only go to *save* yourself or a loved one. And I get this is a loved one, but he's supposedly a dead loved one. I'm sorry to be blunt," Gator said. "Where exactly would you go?"

"The only explanation I could come up with to understand this to myself was that in the afterlife, Angel had gone to Hell. He's been asking me to save him from Hell. I didn't go behind the Veil, no. I was too scared. You all remember the time I was saving that young woman. The time when you could see what happened when I traveled behind the Veil to get information from a victim."

Heads nodded solemnly.

"There was an added risk of staying with her because she wore the vial with the cyanide in it. She was instructed to take the poison should she be discovered by authorities, and if she didn't, they would kill her baby."

"Striker was some kinda pissed at you that you stayed behind the Veil and put yourself at that kind of risk. If she'd a swallowed that poison, you weren't sure that you wouldn't die right alongside her."

I snuck a peek Striker's way.

Striker bent over, his hands on his knees, his eyes on the ground.

"I cain't say that I blame Striker." Gator shot a glance Striker's way. "Of course, like you said, you don't know the consequences for joining up with someone in the ether and them dying."

"Yeah, I was all out of brave when it came to Angel. I could see the shimmer. I knew I could go through the Veil. I was just afraid that I'd join him in Hell, and I wouldn't be able to find my way back to my body."

"Do you see the shimmer now?" Jack asked.

Striker stood and turned my way. His face was bright red. His tone was even. "Chica, you promised Dr. Greer that you wouldn't reach out to Angel. You decided to think about the cut in your soul. That's harrowing enough. I'm not pressing you on this. It's your decision what you do with yourself. But on the Angel front, you made an agreement. If this guy Grey has information, if Angel is alive, we need to hear him out. Honestly, how could that be? The military has its flaws, makes its mistakes, but I can't see this being one of them. If there were any question, they would have told you he was Missing in Action, presumed dead. They wouldn't have conferred Gold Star status on you."

"Never say never, right?"

He crouched down in front of me. “Tell me the last exchange again, Chica.”

“Grey said, ‘And you think he’s in physical danger and want to get him help.’ I responded, yes. Then he said, ‘This will be delicate.’”

“*This* will be delicate,” Blaze said.

Jack’s brow was drawn tight with concentration. He rubbed his fingers into his sternum. “Hard to interpret that.”

“I said, ‘I get that.’ Which, to be honest, I didn’t get at all.” I reached out and put my hand on Striker’s shoulder.

He reached for me and pulled me into his arms, like a protective covering and an anchor to hold me in place.

“I hoped that Grey thought I knew what he was talking about, so he’d feed me more information. Before he got in his vehicle, the last thing he said to me was he’d to come up with a plan. He said, ‘It risks a lot. But listening to you, hearing you, I think I have the picture, and…okay, yes. I’ll have to do something immediately.” I looked from one of my teammates to the next. “How would you interpret that?”

Blaze shrugged his shoulders. “Sounds like he’s spooling up a mission. I can’t imagine what that would look like.”

Deep spit on the ground. “Angel’s been alive all this time?”

“You know better than to jump to conclusions,” Gator said. “Lynx, I can see the waves of anger coming off your skin like a heat mirage.”

“Emotions more than anger. Confusion for sure. I can’t imagine Angel doing that to me. Add to that, we’re freaking stitched together by a mad scientist, and, in my mind, it makes this scenario absurd.” Hopefully, Grey would come back soon and explain what was happening. I turned in Striker’s arms. Pressing my face forward until we were nose to nose, I whispered, “I love you. No doubts. Right?”

"None."

I nodded, then turned to snuggle back by his side, appreciating both the physical and emotional warmth he provided. "If Angel's alive, wow, is everything complicated."

"That, Chica, is putting it about as mildly as it can be put. One step and then another. No one could have foreseen this trajectory. Not how the demise of the Galaxy project would play hell on everyone's lives, not how Indigo would decide to experiment on you and Angel. It's chaotic right now. And in the midst of the battle, the thing you have to do is stick to your mission, accomplish your goals, and deal with the next step after the dust settles. We're still here on the mission."

"The mission's over. Kaylie's safe."

"No, ma'am," Gator said. "General Elliot gave us orders to follow you to the ends of the Earth and make sure *you* made it home again."

42

The phone call from Doc and Miriam made us all jump.

"We're ready. How about you?" Doc said.

My team blanched. It was the craziest thing to see—just all of a sudden, white as ghosts.

My hands were shaking pretty hard. "Ready as I'll ever be."

"You've got a crowd," Doc said.

"My family's here."

"Nice. Okay. Give everyone a kiss, and let's get this done. The area you're in is not a great one for hanky pankying around."

Jack leaned over and whispered in my ear, "You trust her?"

"Who else could I trust with this? She worked for Galaxy at General Elliot's request. She's just no-nonsense."

He bent and gave me a tight hug. They each did. Except Striker.

Man, oh man, the torture in his eyes.

"I love you. I'm going to marry you. Trust me."

"Yes, with every fiber of my being." He stared hard into my eyes as he clenched his teeth.

Jack slapped a hand across Striker's shoulder and moved him out of the tent.

"Looks like they're sitting all the way around the tent like they circled the wagons," Doc said.

"Yes, ma'am," I said.

Gator sat on the bunk, looking positively green now.

"We need to move this forward. Your Grandmother Sibyl is in the ether. Lay yourself down now. Grandmother Sibyl has actually seen this before. And she knew you had this attachment. But she believed that you had made that connection voluntarily. When Miriam and I did a meditation to try to connect with her, she was sitting on a flat rock out in the grass. Alongside her were round huts and women working. Her hair is in a braided bun, with shells. And she is beautiful and toothless and wise. I'm telling you this for affirmation."

"Yes, that's her. Hello Grandmother." A sob escaped my lungs. "I'm joyous you're here."

"Come." I heard in my head. "Come lay your head in my lap as you've done before. I didn't know that this was done to you against your will. I thought you welcomed this man to be part of your journey. It seemed to me you welcomed his presence."

"I was confused, Grandmother. I didn't know he was attached to me like this. I thought I simply held him with love in my heart."

"This was an evil thing that was done to both of you. And we will set it right."

She had what looked like a cigarette. She breathed in the smoke and blew it across my face. The drumbeat started, and it pulled me away from consciousness. Away, away, away…

"GET STRIKER IN HERE," Miriam said from far away.

"Striker." Gator sounded rattled. Gator didn't do rattled. Where was I?

There was a bang. And silence.

"Call her back." I heard Grandmother Sibyl say.

Doc repeated the command.

"Call her back from where? What's happening?"

"She slipped past me. I reached for her but—" Gator. I only heard him this anguished when he was in a trance, grieving his lost love.

I looked around at nothingness. No sound. No light. Nothing. I was nothing. The voices had been far, far away. Somewhere else.

Here was nothing.

"I love you, Lexi. I need you. Come back to me, Chica. Come home. Come back to my arms. Come back to me." Solid. He was so solid. Like a boulder. Like a mountain. "Come here. Come to me."

That was closer. I want that voice. I wanted that connection. That was the connection I was supposed to have.

"Lexi, come home to me. Come home."

I was almost there. I looked around to where Angel had always been in my dreams and…nothingness. Nothing.

I sat up gasping like I'd been underwater for far too long. Striker wrapped his arms around me and squeezed me hard, realized it was too hard, and released me.

Smoothing my hair from my eyes, he cupped his hands around my face. "Chica?" He looked deep into my eyes.

I nodded. Not quite ready for words.

"Chica, do you know who I am? What's my name?"

"Gavin Rheas."

"What do you call me?"

"Striker."

"Who am I?"

"The love of my life. My soulmate. And now, my one and only."

He laughed. Threw back his head and laughed. I could feel it rolling through my body as he pressed me into him. And then he sobbed into my hair. He pulled himself together enough to ask, "How did it go?"

"She's fine. The surgery is done. Grandmother Sibyl was here," Doc said. "She has an amazing technique. I think I may go over to find her and see if she won't teach me a thing or two."

I closed my eyes and sent love and light to Grandmother Sibyl.

"You're welcome, my child." I heard in my head.

"How does it feel?" Gator asked.

"Odd, to be truthful. Like I've misplaced part of me."

"You're not to go looking for him in the ether," Doc said. "You took an oath."

"And I'll hold to that promise, Doc. But I was talking to Grey. Then you were on the computer pressing to hurry. I'm *whew!* a little overwhelmed. How did Angel do?"

"He was relieved on one level but frightened on another. I'm going to ask you again. Is Angel dead?"

"Apparently not," I said.

"What?" Miriam all but yelled. "What in the actual heck!"

"Why was Angel frightened?" I asked.

"Your connection was his only hope. He says he's in Hell."

"Tell me where that is!"

43

Grey came to find me at the tent just as I was getting dressed. I tied my boots into place, and we walked away together.

After several minutes he said, "Thank you for helping to save me." He didn't raise his eyes, his focus trained to the path in front of us. "I'm very sorry for your loss."

"All I lost was time, apparently," I said softly. "And sanity."

Slowly, he brought his gaze up.

"I don't know how this black ops crap works," I said. "But I'd like you to be candid with me about this much, is it better to save your operator's life, or is it more important to protect a mission by allowing them to die?"

In my mind, I had a lot of emotions to sort through. It was going to take time. Ha! Here was a set of circumstances that I'd never share with Avril Limb, even if she had a high security clearance. Nope, this I'd have to work out with those who went on this journey with me. For now, as an emotion came up, I just let it drift on by. Emotions had no place when lives were on the line. *Later*, I promised myself. I'll vent all of this, the fear and anger, the betrayal, the victimization. All of it. But now? I had to save my husband from Hell.

He pushed his hands into his pockets. Whether it was from the early morning cold, or he wanted to hide something, I couldn't tell. So I pushed. "There was speculation on the mission to save you. I wasn't privy to the orders. I don't know what was authorized. I do know what was discussed. Everyone has their limits. Under torture, everyone will say whatever it is that they think will make the pain stop. I've been in torturous situations before, and I've begged for death before. I'm not talking about this from a place of theory."

I watched his blink rate increase with his stress levels. That was my job, to crank him up just like Doc had back when she wanted to see my emotions about Indigo.

"The Delta operators were there to pull you out of the prison," I said. "The Night Stalkers there to fly you to safety. They did that. But they also anticipated failing, especially after the Blackhawk took the RPG hit. The Little Bird took off with you. But there was discussion about what to do with you if they failed at any of the points—from contact until mission accomplished. The feeling was that everyone would prefer to take a bullet in the head from a friend. The impression I got was that if someone there thought they were going to fail, and they had a shot, they'd do that. Kill you. Out of a sense of camaraderie. We're all in this battle together."

"To answer your question, it depends on the operation and if losing the one operator would put others in danger. We have to weigh out the repercussions on everyone. Of course, where we can save a life, we try."

"Are you in communications with Angel?"

His body jerked involuntarily.

"Angel needs a rescue mission to get him out."

"Angel told me to expect this."

"His situation?"

"You. When I recruited him, Angel said he'd do it, but someday his wife was going to show up here in the Middle East and track him down, no matter how dead we made him look." He checked his watch.

"There were actual bodies in coffins. Even if you gave me the empty box, other wives were actual widows. I'd appreciate knowing the story."

"Angel's team was negotiating with a tribal leader. In order to get information, we had to save his daughter from the people who were holding her. She was caught and enslaved. The Rangers got her out."

I thought about what Miriam had said about the woman sitting next to Angel in the truck, a stop, a go, a blast. "They got out of the truck," I whispered. "Angel and the daughter."

"Angel has a great facility with languages. He picks them up with ease. He can mimic anyone and knows how to adjust his body language and tone to manipulate and fool people. He suggested that he go and speak as a businessman and say he could get the daughter back."

"He was playing a role when he told the father he'd get the daughter back in exchange for some information. Okay. Then what?"

"Angel was allowed to negotiate on their behalf. Up until the point when the truck drove away, the woman was blindfolded and didn't know she was with the Rangers. When they took her home, Angel couldn't very well pull up in their Army vehicles, so Angel decided to get out and walk the ten kilometers. He wore no comms, so if they searched him, he would seem legitimate. He was going to do recon and make his way to a predetermined rallying point with the information we needed about where ISIS was holding an American soldier."

"Oh."

"He walked off, turning his head just in time to see the vehicles and all of his buddies blow up."

That must have been what happened when I woke up that night, two years ago. I was in shock. He was in shock.

"He had been five minutes from death, and he survived. I think that's why he let me recruit him. He was living on borrowed time. He wanted to put it to good use. That sounded terrible. I'm sorry. After being in the camp and seeing the women who were enslaved, he wanted to put this extra time he was given toward saving as many women as he possibly could. He knew he could easily be killed. But each day was a gift he was given to do more."

"You hadn't recruited him yet, right? He saw the explosion and continued on his mission?"

"He had no comms. The truck hadn't reported that they dropped him. They probably were waiting for a good tune to be over before they turned it down to do the communication. I don't know. I went to the point where I was supposed to meet him because I had a gut feeling he would be there. I decided to recruit him. It was several weeks later. You had already been told and had already buried him. He is so good at what he does. He has saved so many lives."

I thought back to what Margot had told me about going black ops. At the time, I had been thinking about the possibility of that being the reason for Kaylie going missing. I guessed my subconscious was also wondering because some part of me knew and had always known that Angel wasn't dead. "The Army went along with this. They knew."

"They were told at the upper levels. They know."

"And he agreed because…"

"In the CIA, he can stay in the field. In the Army, he has requirements that would make him rotate out. It takes time to build relationships. His work is important. He fights to shut down the slave trade. You know. You saw. Kaylie Street has been their victim. Thousands of girls have been their victims. ISIS used the girls, and these were just girls barely into puberty. They used them to raise money and to incentivize the fighters."

I nodded. "I came to save his life. After that, he can stay dead." It sounded cold. I was just numb. My emotions were frozen somewhere inside. "I'm certainly not going to interfere with that. He's right. As pissed as I am that no one could come and knock on my door and just tell me how things stood, I would never be so selfish as to force Angel to do something other than what his convictions told him to do."

"You're handling this very well."

"I most *certainly* am *not*. I'm not handling this at all. And I'm not going to try to handle it until I've done what I came to do. Save my dead husband's life."

44

In the time that Grey had been gone from the camp, he'd tapped on the shoulder of his informants and located Angel at a compound along the Iran Iraqi border.

A Taliban leader thought Angel might not be who he said he was. They didn't suspect him of being American. They suspected him of being a slave poacher. They were trying to extract a confession.

Angel was deniable. And State had decided to deny his existence.

Angel had been developing relationships in Iran, and that was a bad look for America in our present impasse over the diplomatic handling of nuclear capability.

No special ops teams would engage.

"Fine, I'll get him out myself," I'd said. I guessed they had been spectacularly impressed that I'd discovered not only that my husband wasn't dead, but I'd found my way here to Iraq and confronted the right guy, John Grey, that they thought that was probably something I'd attempt.

And I would.

Grey and his buddies were going rogue for this operation, but he figured that, like Angel, he was living on borrowed time after his escape from his torture prison experience.

Strategies were quickly basted into place. It was going to be tricky. This compound had an underground jail.

Grey's informant lived inside. The scenario went that Grey was going to visit with his wives. Three of us, me and his two CIA buds—who were small enough to get away with the ruse—would dress in burkas. We'd move into the compound and straight up to the informant's apartment.

Snipers would be positioned.

A helicopter would be at the ready.

Operation "**Get Angel The Hell Out Of There**" was in play.

We were waiting in the truck. Disguised. Under my Burka, I wore my tactical vest and plates. I also wore a bag that replicated a fake pregnant stomach. It would make me untouchable by the other men at a glance. And too, it was a wonderful way to bring in medical supplies.

I would probably feel like I was a kid dressed up like a ghost for trick-or-treating if this wasn't life or death.

I'd sat back for the planning stages.

We were supported by Nutsbe back in the Panther Force war room.

Deep launched a pocket drone from the East hilltop.

"Nutsbe. I have control of the drone," Nutsbe said.

Through the binoculars, I watched it tracking a grid over the space.

Grey called his informant to come to get us. The man drove his truck out to "pick up his friend and his friend's three wives." The man spoke Kurdish, and I was glad that no one would speak to me or wonder why I didn't reply. Under this burka, I was, in essence, hiding in plain sight.

"Blaze. There are men in each of the watchtowers," Blaze said. "I'll take north and east."

"Deep. Roger that," Deep answered. "I'll cover south and west. If the shots are pretty, they'll drop straight down and be hidden. After dark, no one will notice."

By "pretty," Deep was saying that they needed to try to hit the brain stem.

"Nutsbe. I have three men in the courtyard with rifles."

We had the schematics out. The informant leaned over the hood of his car and was explaining where everything was.

I pulled Striker aside. "I say, since I changed out my Indigo burka for the black, that I shadow walk my pregnant belly around and find him."

Grey leaned back. "And if you're caught?"

"First, I'm never caught. Second, I'm pregnant. I think I could do a pretty good rendition of a fierce contraction."

Grey translated that, and his informant, Assad, threw back his head and laughed, smacking Grey in the chest, pointing at me and making some comment that brought a grin to Grey's stony face.

"So here's the deal," Grey said, turning to us. "We go in. We search for Angel, where Assad says he'll be. We pull Angel out. If we get caught, we go down guns blazing. Put a last bullet in your front pocket for yourself. You don't want to get captured."

"That was sunny," Gator said.

Gator was in the armored vehicle that could plow through the gate if need be to pick us up, along with Jack and Striker manning the big guns.

They hadn't uttered one word about me being incapable or unprepared for this mission. I was one of the team.

Now, I just had to not let them down.

Or Angel.

This wasn't a contracted mission. They were here on General Elliot's orders.

I wondered for a moment why Strike Force was so gung-ho about going after Angel, a man they'd never met. Then I remembered that Doc had said we were all part of the same warrior clan. We'd fought side by side over our lifetimes.

I believed that.

Here we were powering forward.

The pick-up truck moved through the arch, where massive wooden doors stood open. They would close after sunset. We'd have to convince the guard to open it back up. We figured that getting me home to my mother for the birth of my fake baby would convince him.

Hiding Angel on the floorboards, we hoped to drive Angel back through the gates. But I'd learned that druthers meant nothing on missions. Things going sideways was the norm.

45

We were inside. I was sedately walking between Jones and Smith, Grey's CIA buds. We all had our fingers running along the trigger guards on our 45s under the voluminous cloth of the burkas. Smith and Jones trailed silently behind Grey and Assad as they joked, and they moved inside.

We continued the subterfuge as we headed to Assad's apartment. They told me not to turn my head and look around, to face forward, and act like I was a gosling following Grey, the mama duck, to the pond.

I could see very little through my burka screen anyway, especially with the ambient light dimming.

Buds in my ears, Nutsbe came over the comms. "Nutsbe. You have incoming—two pickup trucks. I'm counting fourteen heads. They have rifles, and they're churning gravel. Twenty minutes."

The door to the apartment shut. "I wonder what that's about," Jones said, ripping off his burka and taking a position by the windows.

"This is fine. It's probably some of the Taliban who are

coming for a meeting with our elders. You were planning to stay in here until dark anyway. They'll be gone by then." Jones was translating the conversation between Grey and Assad over the comms so everyone could hear the information.

"This happens often, Assad?"

"Frequently, yes."

"So not unusual. No one's concerned about your coming in with my wives and me?"

"Not at all. Everything's fine."

I watched his body language, and I believed him.

The men sat outside in the courtyard in a circle. Food was served. They said their evening prayers. The sun set.

I was sitting with my back to the wall, my feet on the floor with bent knees, and my burka flipped up in the front, resting on my combat helmet with my night vision. I really preferred not to do stealth in the dark with night vision and a burka, to be honest. I had never practiced it and had no idea how this was going to go.

We rested there an overlong time; I was antsy. It came as a relief to hear Striker over the comms. "Striker. Go time, Lynx."

I flipped my burka down then decided this was insane. I pulled out my KA-BAR

and cut out the mesh panel.

Jones and Smith would come with me to the back stairs. We walked as a huddle of three wives. Since the door at the top was the only way in or out, they'd guard the top entrance.

Once we got to the stairs, I was on my own.

"Lynx. Moving," I said.

"Striker. Take your time Lynx, slow and steady wins the race."

"Copy."

I took in a breath, calmed my system, and projected out the

grays of the shadows around me. The light was dim. I didn't appreciate all of these extra cloth. I two-fisted my pistol, front end heavy with a suppressor. I wondered if I shot the gun through the fabric, would my burka catch fire?

Curious minds want to know, I said to myself.

Down, down, down.

"Nutsbe, do you copy?"

"Nutsbe. Your breaking up, Lynx."

Down, down, down.

"Nutsbe, do you copy?"

…

"Nutsbe?"

Yup, we thought this might happen. I was on my own with no way to communicate with my team.

Footsteps echoed off the tiled hallway. I stilled. Slowing my pulse, slowing my breathing. A man in long robes came closer, an electric lantern in his hand. I lowered my lashes to look from the waist down, so this person would feel no eyes. I wish he'd leave. Instead, there was a rattle of keys, the screech of a door.

I chanced a glance to see if he had gone in somewhere. There was a slap of hand against flesh.

I moved further down the corridor past the open door. The room was dimly lit with the lantern on the floor, casting eerie shadows.

He stood wide-legged in his leather sandals. There was someone in front of him tied to a chair. I couldn't tell if this was Angel or not.

The man reached out his hand and grabbed the man's hair and lifted his face. His mouth was bloody and laughing. "What's so funny, you little shit." The man spat out in Arabic.

"What's so funny is that you're about to die," Angel slurred.

The man threw his head back, laughing. And when he did, I

dragged my KA-BAR across his carotid. Blood spurt from the wound. Just in case he could still cry out, I reached up and wrapped my hand around his mouth and nose.

My brain kicked in. How did I get my knife in my hand? How did I cut him? I looked around and saw the burka lying on the floor and had no idea how my body had moved through the steps.

"You came." Angel breathed out.

"Of course, I came." My hands were shaking so hard that I wasn't sure I'd be able to cut his bindings away without slicing off his hands while I did it.

I started with his ankles tied to either leg of the chair.

I moved to the ropes on his hands. I didn't trust myself. I couldn't even pick the knots. My fingers weren't cooperating. I bent down and grabbed the rope in my teeth and yanked my head back, making progress.

Footsteps were banging down the stairs.

I moved in front of Angel and took a knee, resting my elbows against my ribcage to steady myself, ready to pull the trigger on anyone who rounded the doorway.

I pulled up when I saw burkas and heard Jones's voice. "Don't shoot."

"You didn't answer your comms," Smith said, moving behind Angel and finishing the job I had started.

"There's no signal down here."

"They've got trouble brewing. Glad she found you, man. You're not out of the soup yet."

I looked back at Angel when he didn't answer. He looked zoned out of it like he had no idea what was going on around him. His mouth and eyes were open. I was grateful for the wheeze in his breath that told me he hadn't just up and died.

"What are the instructions?" I asked.

"No idea, we just came down to get you. There's a fight brewing out front. Right now, it's a lot of yelling. Come on, Angel, don't give up, man. Stay with us. We're getting you out of here."

Angel made a valiant attempt to bring his head upright and to close his mouth.

"No time to waste. Leave these damned burkas off. I'll carry him," Smith said. "Jones take point. Lynx cover my six, and—Three. Two. One."

I grabbed the burkas and shoved them into my pack, and made a quick scan to make sure that we left nothing behind with the body. I hoped this didn't burn the asset.

I'd let Grey figure that out later.

Angel choked on his moans as Smith dragged him over his shoulders, fireman-style. I rounded my pack onto my back. With my knife stuck back in its sheath, I reached up and dragged my night vision goggles into place, then reached forward to do the same for Smith.

"We ready then?" Jones asked. "On me."

I pulled my gun and wrapped it in one hand, laying my other hand on Angel's back to steady him.

Off we moved back down the hallway toward the stairs.

General Coleridge was right. This was where he'd seen Angel, down. The task drawing looked very similar to the structure we were in. He'd drawn downward arrows. And yes, there was a helicopter out there. We just had to get to it.

I focused on Angel, dangling from Smith's shoulders, and wanted desperately to get him some first aid.

Jones was over the comms. "Nustbe, do you copy?"

Static.

We climbed, and now I could hear gunfire.

"Nutsbe, do you copy?"

"Nutsbe. I copy Lima Charlie." Loud and clear. "Sitrep."

"Bravo. One tango down. We have the package. I repeat, we have the package with injuries."

"Nutsbe. The Taliban are firing their weapons into the air. Grey is reporting a lot of commotion. The situation is unclear and unstable."

"Copy."

"Striker. How bad are the injuries? Life-threatening?"

"Possible. We're not in a position to assess."

"Striker. Bravo team hold."

We hovered at the top of the stairs.

"Striker. Bravo team move to the southwest corner by the guard tower. The door on the western side. Transport will meet you there."

"Copy," Jones said.

Smith bent at the knees, and as he powerlifted, he moved Angel up to a better position on his neck.

"Striker. Alpha team is proceeding to secondary exfil location. Delta standby,"

"Blaze, copy."

"Deep, copy."

"Grey, join up with your Bravo team."

"Grey, Copy."

"Striker. Extraction helicopter inbound."

And all of our ducks were in a row.

Now to leave the Taliban to their fight up front as we slink out the back gate and get out of here alive.

46

I SAT ON THE BED, BARELY RECOGNIZING ANGEL. HIS BEARD AND hair were shoulder length. His face was battered. He'd lost another two teeth.

He was such a brave man. I appreciated the sacrifices he made to help others. And I understood, at a rudimentary level, I was never supposed to be part of his equation. I was never supposed to be in the picture.

Through circumstances outside of our control, we had forged a relationship that wasn't part of our life's plan.

He'd gone his way. I'd gone mine.

But if he knew I was coming, it meant our connection hadn't been any easier for him than me.

When he woke up, he didn't say anything to me. Just held my hand. Tears dripped now and again.

I knew these feelings of being saved after all hope was lost. I'd lived them.

Quiet was good. A chance to recalibrate.

Angel had been captured eleven days ago. From the burn

marks left on his body, they had been using electrical shock to get him to tell where he'd taken the stolen slaves.

He'd resisted all that time.

He'd called to me all that time. He just didn't know he was doing it.

"I owe you an apology." His voice was hoarse. "You can't imagine the guilt I've carried for the last two years."

I could, though. I knew. "Grey told me what happened. How about you tell me from your point of view why you thought that making everyone mourn your death was best. If you had just told us your plan, let us know you were out there being a hero, do you think I wouldn't let you go?"

"Lexi, you were nineteen when we got married, a virgin because I got drunk and passed out on our wedding night. We'd known each other for three weeks. I thought you'd say yes, go do your thing, save those people. But then there you would be. I knew you wouldn't cheat on me or move on, and so I trapped you into a terrible relationship. That life wouldn't be fair. If you thought I was dead. You could move on. You moved on, right? Striker?"

"Yes. I'm engaged to be married. Can you imagine the place you put me in? A bigamist?"

"I didn't think I'd live this long, to be honest. I'm surprised to be here today."

I bit my lip.

"Working where I work, fighting against who I fight. ISIS is pure evil, and they have done terrible things to the Muslim peoples."

"Yes. I agree."

"They have networks all over the world. If they found out who I was and that you were my wife, or Abuela Rosa was like a mother to me, they could use you against me. Horribly. What I went through was nothing compared to what they would do to you in front of me if they caught you. That you came here and risked, that is…horror is the only word my brain is feeding me right now. When I agreed to work black ops, I said I had to do it as a dead man. But I couldn't shake the feeling that you were always with me. Always *right* there. I even told Grey that someday you were going to show up looking for me."

With a deep breath in and a long sigh out.

I patted his hand. "I didn't move on. I couldn't move on. I tried. But that part is not your fault. I understand that you're doing with your life what your purpose has always been. I get that. I laud you. I want this for you."

He closed his eyes, and the tears dripped from behind his lashes.

"When you're done with your work here, I think we'll be friends. I'd like that. Now that I see you again, I know that I'll always love you. But I am not *in* love with you. I don't think of you as my husband. Family, yes, always."

He opened his eyes.

"I am going to allow Grey and the CIA to work this out. I want a divorce as quickly as possible. I want that divorce decree to be sealed to protect everyone. I want your permission to whisper to Abuela Rosa what is happening. She is suffering, and I can't allow you to do that to her."

His face turned red.

"She'll understand. She'll be proud. But she can't suffer this way. You fill her dreams."

"Are you happy? Are you okay?"

"I'm working on it."

STRIKER WAS WAITING for me outside the hospital room.

He wrapped his arm around me, and we walked down the long corridor. "Did you get everything worked out?"

"He agreed to divorce."

"How did you feel? Did the operation work?"

I offered him a tired smile. "I felt friendship and absolutely nothing else. No shimmer. No irrational bond. Just a member of my Abuela Rosa's family." We took a few steps. "Kaylie?" I asked.

"Prescott's with her. When she's released from the hospital, they're going to go get her daughter in Turkey. Her sister, Melody, has Kaylie's son in Virginia. The DNA sample came back as a positive match. But anyone who sees him says it's obvious." He kissed my head then reached to push the door open.

We stepped out under a sky filled with stars.

I stopped to look up at the glory of it. Closing my eyes, I breathed in deeply and exhaled. Yes, I felt different. A little off balance. A little strange. But good. Solid. Calm. When I opened my eyes, I found Striker staring at me with that assessing look of his.

I offered him a smile. "Let's go back to the camp. I'm planning to get a good night's sleep for the first time in years." I slid into his arms. "And wake up in the morning able to love you with my whole heart and no distractions." I reached my hands to his shoulders. "Just think how wonderful this is going to be."

Striker snatched me by the waist and twirled me around.

"Miraculous," he said, sliding me down his body until his lips found mine.

The kiss was slow and delicious.

Being here alive, in love, and whole was just that, *miraculous*.

This is not the end . . .

I hope you enjoyed this next step in Lexi and Striker's story.

Hyper Lynx is the next book in the Lynx Series.

Follow along with the World of Iniquus as men and women of courage and valor fight for the ones they love and the greater good.

If you want to know more about Dr. Zoe Kealoha and BIOMIST, read WASP

If you want to learn more about Dr. Sophia Abadi and her work with satellites to save Syrian antiquities, read RELIC

If you want to know more about John Grey and his rescue from prison, read InstiGATOR.

If you want to learn more about the work, Zoe did in France and why Thorn put a guy to sleep in the men's bathroom, read THORN

If you want to read more about Lynx's knowing, "Jack be nimble. Jack Be Quick. Jack JUMP" that had him leaping from a third story building, read JACK Be Quick.

If you want to learn about the funeral that made Striker worry about Lynx's safety read, YOURS.

OR, you can read the world in chronological order. Listed on the next page. Enjoy!

Readers, I hope you enjoyed getting to know Lexi and her Iniquus team. If you had fun reading Gulf Lynx, I'd appreciate it if you'd help others enjoy it too.

Recommend it: Just a few words to your friends, your book groups, and your social networks would be wonderful.

Review it: Please tell your fellow readers what you liked about my book by reviewing Gulf Lynx. If you do write a review, please send me a note Hello@FionaQuinnBooks.com so I can thank you with a personal e-mail. Or stop by my website www.FionaQuinnBooks.com to keep up with my news and chat through my contact form.

Turn the page to see the Iniquus World in Chronological Order.

THE WORLD of INIQUUS

Chronological Order

Ubicumque, Quoties. Quidquid

Weakest Lynx (Lynx Series)

Missing Lynx (Lynx Series)

Chain Lynx (Lynx Series)

Cuff Lynx (Lynx Series)

WASP (Uncommon Enemies)

In Too DEEP (Strike Force)

Relic (Uncommon Enemies)

Mine (Kate Hamilton Mystery)

Jack Be Quick (Strike Force

Deadlock (Uncommon Enemies)

Instigator (Strike Force)

Yours (Kate Hamilton Mystery)

Gulf Lynx (Lynx Series)

Open Secret (FBI Joint Task Force)

Thorn (Uncommon Enemies)
Ours (Kate Hamilton Mysteries
Cold Red (FBI Joint Task Force)
Even Odds (FBI Joint Task Force)
Survival Instinct - Cerberus Tactical K9
Protective Instinct - Cerberus Tactical K9
Defender's Instinct - Cerberus Tactical K9
Danger Signs - Delta Force Echo
Hyper Lynx - Lynx Series
Danger Zone - Delta Force Echo
Danger Close - Delta Force Echo
Cerberus Tactical K9 Team Bravo
Marriage Lynx - Lynx Series

FOR MORE INFORMATION VISIT
WWW.FIONAQUINNBOOKS.COM

ACKNOWLEDGMENTS

My great appreciation ~

To my editor - **Kathleen Payne**

To my cover artist - **Melody Simmons**

To my publicist - **Margaret Daly**

To my real-world friend Allan Leverone who lent me his name to do what evil I should wish.

To my Beta Force - who are always honest and kind at the same time. Especially E. Hordon, M. Carlon, J. Scaparotti.

To my Street Force - who support me and my writing with such enthusiasm. If you're interested in joining this group, please send me an email. **FionaQuinnBooks@outlook.com**

Thank you to the real-world military and FBI who serve to protect us.

To all of the wonderful professionals whom I called on to get the details right. Please note: this is a work of fiction, and while I always try my best to get all of the details correct, there are times when it serves the story to go slightly to the left or right of perfection. Please understand that any mistakes or discrepancies are my authorial decision making alone and sit squarely on my shoulders.

Thank you to my family.

I send my love to my husband and my great appreciation. T, you are one of my life's greatest miracles.

And of course - thank YOU for reading my stories. I'm smiling joyfully as I type this. I so appreciate you!

ABOUT THE AUTHOR

Fiona Quinn is a six-time USA Today bestselling author, a Kindle Scout winner, and an Amazon All-Star.

Quinn writes action-adventure in her Iniquus World of books, including Lynx, Strike Force, Uncommon Enemies, Kate Hamilton Mysteries, FBI Joint Task Force, Cerberus Tactical K9, and Delta Force Echo series.

She writes urban fantasy as Fiona Angelica Quinn for her Elemental Witches Series.

And, just for fun, she writes the Badge Bunny Booze Mystery Collection with her dear friend, Tina Glasneck.

Quinn is rooted in the Old Dominion, where she lives with her husband. There, she pops chocolates, devours books, and taps continuously on her laptop.

Visit www.FionaQuinnBooks.com

COPYRIGHT

Gulf Lynx is a work of fiction. Names, characters, places, and incidents either are the product of the author's imagination or are used fictitiously, and any resemblance to actual persons, living or dead, business establishments, events, or locales is entirely coincidental.

ISBN: 978-1-946661-35-7
Chesterfield, VA
Library of Congress Control Number: 2021910708

Cover Design by Melody Simmons from eBookindlecovers
Fonts used with permission from Microsoft

CPSIA information can be obtained
at www.ICGtesting.com
Printed in the USA
BVHW080311151221
624011BV00004B/87